W9-AVB-712

MISADVENTURE

A NOVEL

by

MILLARD KAUFMAN

McSWEENEY'S BOOKS
SAN FRANCISCO

www.mcsweeneys.net

McSweeney's and colophon are registered trademarks
of McSweeney's, a privately held company with
wildly fluctuating resources.

ISBN-13: 978-1-934781-54-8

To Lorraine Paley Kaufman with love and gratitude,
for her warmth and wisdom shared day and night, in every season

MISADVENTURE

ONE

She lay enshrouded in mist, wedged between two rocks. A dead body with the sea below and, above, the brow of the cliff.

The fall had already transformed her; she looked vacant and unremarkable, utterly unlike her vivid, discontented self. Her death felt lunatic in its incongruity.

Wave after mutilating wave curled and crashed. I felt by turns compassion and relief. All my imponderables were in the past; even had I weighed every conceivable pro and con and what-if and then-what, it wouldn't have mattered now.

Far out beyond the kelp bed, a solitary boat tossed on the water. Among its running gear, inevitably, would be a pair of binoculars. Were they trained on me? Had its radio already patched into the marine police at Santa Monica?

What else had I overlooked?

With unsure steps, I climbed up the tumble of rocks, over the edge of the precipice, across the sprawling desolation of that rose garden where I had first set eyes on her, when her beauty was an astonishment. So far in the past that it seemed another country, another age—all of six weeks, on a day not unlike this... with the wind biting into the car, hanging a curtain of sand across the dying sun, sand crawling across the road like a procession of sidewinders.

I was driving back from Ventura, musing about that not-too-distant day when this whole decaying coast, according to the gospel of global warming, will slip, without bubbles or regrets, beneath the unimpeded sea. Odd thoughts, certainly, for a real-estate agent operating along the southern tip of the San Andreas Fault.

The phone balanced beside me began to rasp. Beat as I was down to my socks, I didn't answer. It had been a bad week; a week of chasing leads that went unprofitably nowhere. And it had ended badly in Ventura, where I had appraised twelve acres of a tangled, unsalable nursery for a tree farmer.

The rasping continued. Such dedicated persistence, on a Friday evening, could only signal Gayle's desperate need for a new jar of that health-food mayonnaise she doesn't seem able to live without. I could have ignored that, too, but then I'd face a prickly weekend of cross-examination—why hadn't I answered? Whose house was I in, anyway? How come it took so long?

We were on a collision course, Gayle and I. Our days of desultory togetherness were about to expire, but as they languished and sputtered to an end I wanted to evade as much commotion as possible. For once in my life. So I reached for the phone.

"Hey, Jack," Jerry Fleet yelled through the speaker—I could have heard him without it. "We just got a call—Senior wants you to stop off at Four Pines Point. You know where that is? Above the Ventura line? We've gotta knock off an appraisal on a beach house…"

"Can't it wait until Monday?"

"Not this one—the lady's on her way to meet you. She's all tied up next week, she says."

"Shit," I said. "What's her name?"

"Norton. Mrs. George Norton."

"Rich?"

"Yeah," Jerry said. "She's got to be loaded. That kind of address ain't no pigsty."

My tree farmer. I felt a twinge in my gut. "Jerry, about Mr. Dickens…"

"Who?"

"The old guy in Ventura."

"Anything we can turn a buck on?"

"Not really. But—"

"Then forget it."

"His wife needs surgery. He's got—"

"You want to flag down a buyer? In Ventura? Christ, if the place was worth anything he would've had a man up there handle it."

"It's worth something."

"Mortgage?"

"Yeah. With a second."

"Jack, this guy your grandfather or something?"

"Not that I'm aware, no."

"Jack, Fleet and Fleet is real estate, not Sandy Claus. We're not a tax-exempt foundation dedicated to..."

"Yeah. Yeah. I guess so."

"You guess so. You guess so. I swear I can't figure you. You tryna convince yourself you're captain of the good-guys club? Lemme tell you—you're not. You gotta get down off the ledge, Jack."

I pictured taking Jerry with me from a high sill. "I'm not—"

"The Boy Scout ledge, I mean—you've gotta get off it or you're never gonna make it in real estate. You'd prolly be happier doing—I swear I don't know what."

Silence while he searched for a job I might master. Finally, "Lemme put it this way," he said. "When I was a boy, next door was this kid my age and a swimming pool. The kid spent all the time in the pool with his hands cupped—"

"His hands what?"

"—saving bees from drowning. A fucking Sunday School wanko. And that's what you should be doing, if there's any such job."

"What's that address again?"

He repeated it. "She said you can't miss it. Anything else?"

"Yeah," I said. "What's he up to now?"

"Who? The kid in the pool? What're you talking about?"

"Your old man. Whenever Senior hollers on you I get one of your scholarly lectures on salesmanship."

"Jack, I'm tryna to help you..."

"You can help me by snapping out of your shit, Jerry. I don't appreciate the pointers, if you didn't know that."

More silence, then: "We got this call from the Malibu lady. I wanted to meet with her—I could of charmed her tits off—you know me."

"I sure do."

"But Senior says hell no. He wants you should do it. And he wants me to call you about it."

"Yeah. That was hard to take, I bet."

"Believe you me. I swear life is one big endless obstacle course. Everywhere you turn. Even my own father obstacles me. Know what I mean?"

"Yeah, Jerry. I do. But I got to get off the phone."

He hung up before I did.

The house dominated a promontory; you could see as far as you could point. About eight acres, six hundred running feet of beach frontage, with an Olympic-size swimming pool coated with slime and dead leaves. Another acre was devoted to the cultivation of roses. Roses on a rock-bound cliff.

I rambled around, waiting for her to show, sucking on a tin paper clip, my confectionery of choice since I quit smoking fourteen months ago. There would be one hell of a commission on this stone pile, if I got a little lucky. It was the kind of house we seldom handled, the kind that Tod Hunt, our legendary better, would make an extravaganza out of. Pick up the prospective client in his Rolls. Offer him a thick Cuban cigar. Serve a chilled white wine of a comet year.

I had often toyed with the notion of getting a job with Hunt; what kept me at F & F, busting my hump for the Old Man and Jerry, was their craphound operation in Mexico. They had a rat-infested office in Mexico City, costing next to nothing but supplying Senior and Jerry with a cover for write-off vacations. What the Mexico office needed was somebody down there with clout, I told Senior. I wanted to be that somebody. I was compelled by something more than two weeks of poolside tequila: let's start with a profound lack of cross-examination. The Old Man, however, thought the office should be run by locals.

I'd tried to talk him out of that belief a number of times, employing an improvisatory mix of self-promotion and xenophobia. Senior would sigh and reach for his gold toothpick—he was a man full of exquisite little self-tortures, all of them inflicted by that toothpick. His wife had given it to him before she passed. In moments of stress, it probed between his teeth, beneath his fingernails, into his long ears, which hung on each side of his marshy head like wax question marks. In private, he probably stuck that toothpick up his ass.

"You can't sell from an empty wagon," I'd persist. I didn't quite know how that quaint adage applied, but it went unchallenged.

"What's to sell?" he'd say, and he was right, until recently. Now, though, with the mortgage crisis in Southern California refusing to go away and fore-closures gutting the margins on our bread-and-butter properties, there was value to be had beyond the border. And foreigners were still suspicious of the local brokers—I could do a lot on the ground.

Of course, there was no health-food mayonnaise in Mexico. Those rat-infested offices would make for a clean break with Gayle: no collision, and diminimus commotion. And that could be defined as progress.

I hadn't been able to nail Senior to the floor about it, but he was never sufficiently emphatic in his demurrals for me to accept them as irrevers-ible. So I stuck around, rattling his cage every week or so. Each interview ended with him probing with his toothpick, smiling like a nervous animal, vacantly repeating, "We'll see, we'll see…"

There was something else, though—something was going on in the shop, some kind of shake-up. A heavy, secretive air of excitement hung over the place. The salesmen conjectured about it in undertones as they huddled around the coffee machine, pathetically eager to trade dry crusts of rumors, cringing whenever Senior or Jerry walked by. They were scared shitless, but I figured come fire, flood, or famine, I could only benefit from it.

A car approached, silently. Not even a dish antenna could have picked up the purr of that Rolls in the gusting wind. The smoked-glass windows were raised, reducing the woman at the wheel to no more than a gauzy shadow. I noticed the vanity license plate, a four-letter genitive: HERS.

The door opened. I saw a long, slim leg, breathtakingly perfect in a tennis shoe, and, above it, the tight tennis skirt, fringed teasingly, curling upward on her thighs. A white shirt mostly unbuttoned, a hank of yellow hair and a cheek peeking out from under a kerchief bright as a butterfly.

She stepped out, slipping off her dark glasses, shaking the butterfly scarf free. Her hair tumbled down to her shoulders. A long horizontal scar, the color of watered wine, cut across a cheekbone.

I couldn't pull my eyes from her. Under the heat of my look I swear she blushed; maybe she thought I was staring at the mark on her face. Turning, she leaned back into the Rolls and reached out, stretching as I watched the vibrant thrust of her ass.

She straightened up, clutching a camel's-hair coat, and squirmed into it, veiling her loveliness in modesty. The car door closed with a rich metallic click.

"Hello," she said shyly. Her white teeth glistened as her lips parted in a timid smile. Her proximity bewitched me into dumbness.

Mrs. Norton had a face, scar be damned. It was a volatile one, though: one swift moment it held a stained-glass tranquility—the eyes displaying a sad vulnerable blankness, the nose small and straight as a nun's, the lips firm and finely chiseled like those of an emblematic statue of Virtue, perhaps. And then, with a modest change of light or shadow, a tilt of her head, a fractional lift of her chin, the slightest parting of those molded lips, as if by magic that face was plunged into wantonness.

She tried again: "You're...?"

"Jack Hopkins. From Fleet and Fleet."

She gave me her chaste hand and a moment later gently reclaimed it; I had held it too long. Walking toward the house, through some atmospheric feat of refraction she seemed to become fused with the bronze and scarlet radiance of the dying sun. She assumed I would follow, and of course she was right. We entered the foyer and she stopped, pulling a curtain. She stood in the light and shivered.

"Cold in here," I said supportively.

"It's the chill factor," she said in a Texas accent so thick that her tongue might have been coated with the wild honey of the Panhandle. It was at once singsong and unmelodic and so soft that had the house not been as silent as an icy grave I wouldn't have heard her.

"Which, at a time like this," she added, "has nothing to do with temperature."

I didn't know what she was talking about; I thought I'd better not ask. And yet...

"What do you mean?" I asked. She glanced at me not as though my question was gauche, but with a kind of delicate tolerance, as if she didn't want to embarrass me by acknowledging how slow I sounded.

"Nothing, really," she murmured. "It's just, this place holds memories, and now we're getting rid of it..."

"It's a great house," I said, pulling out my measuring tape to change the subject. It took sixty-four feet just to record the length of the living room. I made a few quick notes and calculations on my clipboard.

"And a nice beach," I added, walking over to the window. I was not totally unfamiliar with it, in fact. Gayle and I had scuba'd off this coast a couple of times in the past year.

"Yes," she said, "that's what I'll miss most—the beach and the kelp bed. Although the kelp isn't the way it once was." She blinked rapidly; I thought she was going to cry. I stared out at the kelp. It looked sickly, full of woe.

"The seals and the grey whales," she went on in that hushed low voice, "in their, you know, migrations, they come closer to shore here than anywhere from Alaska to Mexico."

I felt I should say something. "That a fact?"

"They come here and die. They get tangled up."

"In the seaweed? The kelp?"

"The problem is plastics thrown off boats. The current, the tide deposits these little plastic bits in the kelp and the baby whales and all think it's food, and it like clogs them up when they eat it and they die."

For a moment she brooded silently. Then, "It's really sad," she said. "That's one reason I want to get rid of this place."

I tried to think about whales, to show a shared interest and keep the dialogue flowing, but all I could remember, and imperfectly, was one of those mildly pedantic nature programs on cable TV with close shots of belugas fucking.

So instead I moved toward the dining room, thinking that even as she bewitched, she confused. How could a girl who under that camel's-hair tarpaulin looked like a *Playboy* centerfold be so laden with limpid modesty, scarlet blushes, shy whispers, and the proclivities of a startled fawn? Against that lovely body her innocence seemed outrageous.

"Like a drink?" she asked.

"No, thanks," I said. "I'm on the wagon."

"What wagon? Does it get you where you're going? Does it...?" She stopped short. Ripping the tab off a can, she sloshed coke into a tumbler. "I don't drink," she said. "Booze, I mean. Not even socially." She wrinkled her elegant nose. "I don't like the taste. Although," she held the glass up to the light, "I'd purely love to find a wagon to climb on."

I moved into the master bedroom, trailing my trusty tape.

"How long are you going to be?" she asked from the doorway. "What's it worth on today's market?"

"Not long. Another fifteen minutes, maybe."

"Not that I'm in a hurry." She smiled, and her cheek dimpled.

I could have told her then and there what the place would bring, a ballpark figure, but I wanted to wangle as much time as I could with her. And I wanted to see her again, and soon.

"Let me give it some thought," I told her. "I'll draw up a comp and get back to you."

"No," she said, "I'll call you. You see, I—" She bowed her head as if she were expecting a reprimand. "—Mr. Norton doesn't know I'm thinking about a divorce. If he did," she said, "he'd kill me."

"Serious as that?"

"Of course not," she said, trying to smile. "I'm always exaggerating. Were you hitting it hard? The booze?"

"Not really." Which was the truth. Despite the fact that I won't be twenty-nine until next December, that I scuba dive and, until I gave it up, played a fairly fast game of singles, I was beginning to add a circumferential notch about the beltline. I couldn't do much about the slight bald spot on my head except part my hair to cover it (which I refused to do), but I could stop drinking.

"I just quit," I told her. "Cold turkey."

"I don't mean to pry," she said. "My friends say I don't give a damn about anybody. But I do—I like to know what's going on, you know? How other people live. What are they up to, what goes on in their heads, what they do for kicks, are they having any fun..."

"Are you?"

"Me? Having fun? No, not really."

I nodded sympathetically. "A divorce can be rough, even under the best of circumstances. No matter how civilized both parties try to act, no matter how much they agree on a separation..."

"Tell me about it."

"...there's the investment of time. When things fall apart, it's bound to be rough."

"You think so? How many times have you been divorced?"

"Never. I've never even been engaged."

"It's really very simple," she said. "I hate his guts."

I glanced at her, finding an edgy consolation in the fact that her vehemence was not directed at me.

"It'll pass," I said evenly. "It's just a question of time before you snap out of it."

"Snap out of what?"

"This... not having any fun."

"That's got nothing to do with it."

"Would you like to have dinner tonight?"

"Thank you, but I can't."

"Got another date?"

"You're sweet. What?"

"Got another date?"

"God, no. There's nobody to date—I don't have any friends who aren't friends of my husband. If he thought I was seeing anybody, he'd..."

"We could go to some quiet place."

She shook her head. "As it is, he'd like to cut me off without a cent. And he damn well could."

I almost said "A prenup?" before I caught myself. I didn't want to talk about her husband.

She sat on the bed, crossing her perfect legs. The bed bounced, her coat flew open, the front of her skirt flew up. I glimpsed a lovely Mound of Venus under her tight panties.

"It would be different if I had a profession or something," she said. "But, Jesus Minnie, I can't even work a computer."

"I know a little place just this side of Oxnard..."

"No," she said. "I'm not hungry. I don't feel like talking. It would just be my luck to bump into somebody."

She finished the Coke, leaning against the headboard, uncrossing her legs, crossing them again at the ankles. I worked the tape around the room, finding it difficult to read the digits. Her mattress was oval and enormous and spread with a dark fur. The lighting was low and indirect and kind of ingenious: you couldn't see the fixtures, not even in the reflection of the mirror that covered the ceiling. I looked up at the glass and my eyes locked with hers. A finger was in her mouth, the little white teeth gnawing at a cuticle. She looked away, tracing a pattern on the misted glass in her hand. I wanted to go to her.

What the hell, I thought. "We don't have to have dinner," I said. "But I want to sleep with you."

Seconds of silence ticked off for what seemed like a month. Finally, in a whisper, "Okay," she said.

TWO

There I was, tossed on a rising, falling sea of tanned, firm, fragrant flesh—I moaned, I could hear myself moaning in delight, and then a sharp prickly pain in my left leg dragged me out of that hot, wet, palpitating dream into cold, sweaty wakefulness. I reached for my calf; Gayle's foot was on it.

We all have our small eccentricities—little tics with the talent to disturb those closest to us. One of Gayle's is curling her toes around the hair on my legs and pulling.

"You were sleeping on your back," she said.

I made a furry noise deep in my throat and turned over, away from her.

"I'm sorry I woke you," she said. "You were groaning."

"It's not the waking that bugs me," I told her. "It's the way you do it. Why can't you shake me, gently, or... or... oh, shit," I said. "I'm tired."

"Where were you today?" she asked. "Why are you so tired?"

"Because it's the middle of the night."

"You spend the whole day on that tree farm in Ventura?"

"Yeah," I said emphatically, and then I said, "No." Gayle has an oppressive habit of calling Jerry Fleet every now and then. Without being aware of it, he manages to fill her in on my every move. Or maybe he knows what he's doing—he informs as payment to her for allowing him to get semi-obscene on the phone. Jokingly, of course.

"No," I said again. "I did an appraisal on a beach house."

"Whose?"

"Some guy. He's loaded."

"You meet him?"

"No. His wife."

"She young?"

"Yeah."

"Pretty?" In the darkness she was staring at me accusingly, a severe inquisitor with a wintry face.

"Kind of."

"How come it took so long?"

"It got complicated."

"I'll bet it did."

Gayle thinks of herself as a free spirit undemolished, an emancipated woman. Marriage, she was prone to say over a drink, was a hollow rite and not an essential of love. But I got the feeling, although I never told her this, that she'd be more relaxed in our relationship if we were securely, or even insecurely, married. She'd be more alert, have more energy. Her heartburn would dissolve; she'd lose that rigid slouch of a walk, the one that made her look as if she were always afraid that the earth was about to collapse under her. Her hair would shine. Maybe she'd even stop munching on plaster, which she did from time to time—an odd snack, it seemed to me, for a health junkie.

"The appraisal got complicated, I mean. Will you, for Christ sakes, let me get some sleep?"

"I tried to reach you. I wanted you to bring home some yogurt."

"Would you feel better if I got up and went out and bought some?"

"You're sadistic."

"*You're* sadistic—waking me in the middle of the night, pulling the hairs on my leg."

"You're a bastard, you know that?"

I pulled the blanket up over my ears. But I couldn't sleep. I thought about Mrs. Norton's long legs holding me in parentheses. She'd gone from Alice Sweetass to Zelda Succubus in a split second—a hell of a quantum leap. Which, I wondered, was the imposter?

When we'd finally untangled ourselves on that oval bed, she'd lit a cigarette, exhaled a long, elegant stream of smoke, and said "Thanks."

"My pleasure."

"No," she said, "you don't understand. What I mean—let me put it this way—for more than a year now, eight months at least, my husband hasn't fucked me." Her vocabulary too had sprouted, nurtured by her new enriched and liberated persona.

I said, "Relax, honey. Your troubles are over."

She smiled, kind of wanly. "Not quite," she said. "I have a wealth of troubles."

"What about him?"

"Him?"

"Your husband. Has he been sleeping around?"

"I don't know. I think he's had maybe three or four affairs. In ten years of marriage, you can hardly consider that cheating."

"Then...?"

"There's this girl, eighteen, nineteen years old... She was a maid in the house. He was screwing her, I think. Jesus Minnie, he's fifty-eight. Old enough to be her granddaddy."

"How old are you?"

"None of your goddam business. Twenty-eight."

So. She had been married for ten years, spliced at eighteen to a man thirty years her senior. And now he was sniffing around another bambina.

"That must have been unsettling—having the girl in the house."

"I fired her."

She snuffed out her cigarette in the silver and ceramic ashtray next to the bed. "I've been so damned horny," she said, in that curious unmusical singsong. She looked up at the ceiling mirror and ran her hand lightly across the flat of my belly. "This morning, on my way to the club, I drove past a truck fixing the road, you know, spreading asphalt or something. There was this big black studdybuck stripped to the waist, with a body like what's-his-name? The fighter? He... I swear I wanted to stop the car and have him ram his big black dick twenty inches into me..."

I considered suggesting that we go back to talking about the kelp. "When can I see you again?" I said instead.

"I don't know. After the divorce."

"That's a long way down the road," I said. "I'm no good at waiting games." I didn't like this way of talking through the mirror, either, bouncing dialogue off it as if it were a satellite. I turned on my side, staring at her. "And I don't think you're any better at them. Nothing ever comes to those who wait."

"I need a little time..."

I waited for her to go on...

"Jack... Jacky...?"

"Yeah?"

"What are you thinking?"

"I'm not thinking anything. I'm trying to sleep."

"He doesn't even know I want a divorce. I wish to Christ he'd get hit by lightning or something. That way it would be so much simpler."

"And you'd have it all."

"Not all—I'm no pig."

"Who else is there?"

Instead of answering she rummaged for another gold-tipped cigarette. I took her lighter and gave her a flame once she'd found one.

"Don't go anywhere," I said. "I'll be right back."

In the bathroom I took a long, enjoyable leak. The heavy brass handles of the sink were shaped like roses. I spun them both until the splash of the water drowned out the click of the medicine chest as I eased it open. Back in the bedroom, she was already lighting a fresh smoke.

"You were saying...?" I climbed back in the kip.

"Nothing," she said. "I mean, I swear I..." she blew a vaporous swirl up to the mirror. It hovered over us, a smoggy little cloud.

"What, Mrs. Norton?"

"Nothing."

"Tell me."

"You want to know what I really thought about screwing that big old studdybuck? Why the thought occurred?"

"Why?"

"Because I thought, I thought then I could get him to drive his asphalt truck right the hell over my husband. Flatten the sonofabitch." She blew out another cloud. "What do you think of that?" she asked.

"I think you're very pissed off at him. Mrs. Norton."

"Well, congratulations, you have discovered the obvious. But," she added, "you lack other skills."

"Such as…?"

"First of all: the fucking was pretty good. It's like we fit together— sometimes that happens, I've been told, but it's never happened to me. Ne-ver-the-less," she stretched each syllable to the breaking point, "you're a dope, once the fucking's over. Socially you're a basket case."

"What do you mean, Mrs. Norton?"

"I mean…" Now she seemed amused. "It's kind of—I don't know— obscene? I mean, here we are, topless, bottomless, and the whole place smelling like come and you call me 'Mrs. Norton'?"

"You never told me your…"

"Darlene," she said.

"I don't believe you," I said. "Unless you're leasing your medicine chest to Mrs. Tod B. Hunt. Her name's on everything in there—pyribenzamine, fiorinal, donnatal, and all the other candy."

She jackknifed to a sitting position. Her eyes went orange, like a mad pinball machine. She looked around for a heavy ashtray or a blunt object, anything, I thought, to put a dent in me. Then she relaxed, stretching, raking her shiny helmet of hair back from her shoulders.

"You're pretty sneaky," she said, throwing a long leg out of bed. "But I've got to go. I have to be home in case I get lucky and Tod shows up for dinner." She reached for her bra. "Do you know him?" she asked. "Being in the same business…?"

The same business. Which was like saying U.S. Steel and the village blacksmith were in the same business.

"You hear me or am I talking to myself?"

"No," I said. "We've never met."

But I did know a bit about him. Hunt ran the most prestigious operation from Beverly to the sea. He seemed to be in the news as much as he was in his office. He magnetized cameras: Tod Hunt at the wheel of his tri-dex drophead Duesenberg SJ. Tod Hunt parting the seas off Acapulco in the *Quel Tapage*, his hydrofoil speedboat. Tod Hunt on Golden Fleece, his magnificent Arabian, girded for the polo wars in Palm Springs.

In one respect it may be said that he was truly unique: unlike all those painfully grinning poseurs who populated the same pages of the same journals, he seemed totally indifferent to the cameras focused on him. It was perhaps this quality as much as any that inspired envy; those whose envy was verbal said the horse was named for its owner's agency operation.

I suppose I envied him too, partly because I would have enjoyed being envied, a hankering induced by the indisputable fact that nobody envied us. We—Fleet & Fleet—were also-rans in the race that Hunt dominated—chickenshit gleaners after Hunt reaped and prospered.

"Well," she said, "if by any chance you ever do—"

"No reason I should."

"—I want you to make up your own mind about him. I won't say anything, except that he's... unbalanced."

I imagined him astride his mount in mid-gallop, effortlessly swinging to one side and striking me with a mallet. "Where's home?" I asked her.

"Home?"

"You said you were going home."

"You can't call me there. Sometimes Tod works at home. He's good at putting two and two together, and he's got a temper. Once in Palm Springs he damn near killed me."

"What for?"

"For nothing. So minor I can't remember. He hit me in the face with a leaded riding crop, his weapon of choice." Gingerly she touched the memory of a violated cheekbone. "You never know when he'll explode. It's like out of nowhere being chased by a chainsaw." She blinked rapidly, turning away, rubbing a knuckle in a leaky eye. It was an adorably childish gesture. "I'm embarrassed," she said, "telling you all my woes. It's just I've got no one to talk to."

"Isn't there some place you can go until the divorce? Some place he can't get at you?"

"Oh, sure," she said. "Outer Mongolia. The headwaters of one of those muddy rivers on TV."

"That sounds safer than just waiting around for him to unload on you."

"It's safe enough for the moment. Old Tod's working on some kind of super-colossal deal. He doesn't have time to notice me." She leaned her forehead against my chin. "I'll keep you posted," she said. "Okay? Can I call you at the office? I'll say..." She took a phone book from the lower ledge of the bed table, riffled through it, scanned a random page. "I'll say I'm Mr. Katz's secretary."

"And suppose I have to call you back?"

"Sorry, Mr. Katz cannot be reached—he's about to leave the office."

"You'll call back?"

"Of course I'll call back," she whispered. "I swear."

"Yeah," Jerry was saying, "I know it's undeveloped land—but it's got a large future. You got to remember, and I shit thee not, land's the only thing on God's green earth that'll never blow away."

It was after seven. The office was empty except for us, and I was furious with him.

"Jerry," I said grimly, "I got to talk to you."

"Sure," he said. "Want to have a drink in the local hell on the corner?"

"I don't drink."

"Sure, I forgot."

"Sit down."

He sat down, uncomfortably, on the edge of my desk. "Jerry," I said, "you've got to stop spilling your guts to Gayle on the horn."

"Me?" He looked hurt.

"Spilling *my* guts to Gayle. I don't give a shit what you tell her about you, but—"

"What did I do?"

All he had done was—I'll start from the beginning. It's more soothing that way.

A week had passed since I'd met Darlene Hunt, and every day, every ten minutes, I thought of her. I'd been practically crouched on the edge of my desk, snatching the horn every time it rang. Then I'd decided fuck her and gone out on a job and not once did she cross my mind, and of course that was the day she phoned.

"A Mr. Katz called you," Jerry told me when I got back.

"Oh?"

"Who's Mr. Katz?"

"Some guy I met at a party," I said. "He owns some property south of Brentwood and I thought we might handle it for him."

"What kind of property?"

"Couple of duplexes. I haven't seen them."

"That kind of shit's hard to move."

"What'd Katz say?"

"Said he'd call back."

Next day I was out in the field again. When I got home Gayle was wait-ing for me with a tightness around her mouth. She followed me stiffly down the hall and into the bathroom, her eyes flinty, like some shaggy beast's in the zoo.

"Have a good time at the party?" she asked.

"What party?"

"Mr. Katz's party."

"Oh, him," I said. "It wasn't exactly a party."

"You told Jerry Fleet it was a party."

"An office party—he doesn't listen. I met this Katz last Christmas."

"And he just called back? Five months later?"

"I gave him my card. It wouldn't have surprised me if he'd never called."

"I don't believe you." Her lower lip quivered.

"Oh really? How about we worry about this subject five minutes from now? I'd like to wash up and take a leak."

She slammed out of the loo.

"Jesus, I'm sorry. All I said was—"

"I know what you said, Jer—I'm still bruised by it."

He said, "Now J for just-a-minute..."

"I mean, if you got to tell her about parties, describe a few you've been to. Or just talk dirty, for all I—"

The phone rang. He stared at me while it rang again, and a third time. Then he grabbed at it without uncurling his fist, sending the whole thing crashing off my desk onto the floor.

"Fleet and Fleet," he barked, when he'd recaptured it. He listened for a second and then pushed it to me.

Mr. Katz's secretary coolly asked how I was. Mr. Katz, she said, would like to see me in an hour.

"Where would Mr. Katz like to...? Okay." I hung up.

"That was Katz," I said.

"Yeah," he said with a chickenshit smirk. "I know."

"Do me a favor, okay? Call Gayle and tell her—"

"Call her yourself."

"Come on, Jerry. For Christ sakes…"

"What'll I tell her?"

"The truth—I got to see this Katz. I'll be home as soon as I can. Okay?"

"Okay," he said through ruffled feathers. Which wouldn't be ruffled long. I already detected a gleam in his eyes. Any excuse to call Gayle, he'd take it.

THREE

She was there when I pulled up in the compact. She came out the door, a corona of light behind her, etching her mink in a kind of phosphorescence.

"Let's get a little air," she said. "It's still stuffy in there."

We walked to the edge of the cliff.

"You'd never think flowers could grow in all those rocks," she said. "Johnny-jump-ups, trilliums, lady slippers, lambs' tongues, shooting stars... I looked them up in a book."

"Interesting," I said, freezing my ass off. I wanted to go inside and climb into that oval bed. Her white face appeared, disappeared, reappeared in the ectoplasmic mist.

"Do you like seals?"

"I've never thought much about it."

"I love them," she said. "They shed tears, you know. They like music. They're the souls of the drowned."

"That a fact?"

"According to Irish folklore. I don't know if it's a fact," she frowned, "but I do find it remarkable."

"Let's go in the house," I said.

We got as far as the door. Without a word or a sign, without the blink of a blurred and ruttish eye we came together. I plunged into her before we hit the rug. She gasped. We slithered across the room like two dogs on ice. Her face gleamed with sweat, her lips were waxy. We slammed into the rough stones of the fireplace and she screamed. Another shrill, alien voice joined hers, strange until I recognized it as my own. Then a few more hoots and hollers and total collapse, a boneless cave-in of exhaustion and repletion and sweet quiet breathing.

A log fire burned. A pot of coffee percolated on the bar. I sat basking in the blaze, holding her big toe.

"Isn't this a great little place?" she asked.

"Some little," I said. "You could float the *Queen Mary* in here."

"I'm all mellowed out," she said. "I can never relax with Tod. With Tod, uptight is a way of life. But with you..." Her flat singsong voice went soft. "Until you came along, I thought the whole fucking *fucking* business was grossly overrated. Lordy," she said, "what I've been missing."

The fire popped and cackled. The wind wailed. The surf pounded the rocks.

"What are we going to do?" she asked.

"Isn't there such a thing as a quick divorce?"

"Not one that Tod would grant."

"So I'll just have to make do with being your studdybuck for a while?"

"No," she said, "I don't want that."

"What do you want?"

"Oh, I don't know. A little action."

"That's what I'm talking about."

"Not that kind of action." Her eyes narrowed. Her little jaw was set like a cool, persistent kitten with a mouse on its mind. "I want a piece, a big, fat piece, of just one unit. Maybe two."

"A unit?"

"That's Texas talk—oil talk—for a hundred mil."

"That's what he's worth? Community property?"

She nodded primly. "He was worth no more than five million when I married him. The rest of it should be half mine. Why are you staring at my scar?"

"Sorry. I didn't realize."

"Maybe you weren't. Maybe I'm just self-conscious about it." She paused. "I've been flirting with all kinds of notions."

"You could have it fixed, you know. Spiff it up like new."

"Not about that. And I don't want it spiffed up, anyway. Not now. That scar should be worth an additional ten, fifteen million in court." She frowned, pursed her lower lip until it swelled, bee-stung. She twitched a nipple of a breast between thumb and forefinger. That I found disturbing, or maybe provocative, all the more so because she seemed oblivious to its effect on me.

"That ten to fifteen," she said, "was what I wanted to put aside for you."

The fire was hot on my face, on the back of my hands.

"Why?" I asked.

"Why?" she repeated. "In return for a favor." She frowned again and cradled her breast. "I think I'd like a real drink." She said. "Throw some scotch in my coke, please."

I crossed the room to the bar. I poured scotch into her glass.

"You're not joining me?" she asked.

I thought about it. Then I poured myself a large trembling cup of coffee, lashed it with bourbon, and, succumbing completely, lit a cigarette from her pack on the low table. I sucked in the smoke and tasted nicotine for the first time in more than a year. My head spun. I kept puffing while I carried our drinks back toward her across that long arena of a room.

"All you have to do," she said when I'd set it all down, "is burn him. There you go. I've spelled it out for you."

Her overture didn't shock me. I'd seen plenty of whack-outs when I was a kid. Once, I remember, before finishing him off entirely, some neighborhood psycho sliced off his victim's penis. I'd never heard such screaming, and I was a block away.

The year I turned twelve my father died playing poker. He and a riotous flake name of Dodgie Burns accused each other of cheating in a friendly game of No Limit. The game became considerably less friendly when Burns, who like the other gamblers was to have left his weapon at the door, stuck a knife between my father's ribs. Dad died within the hour.

According to the unwritten but inflexible code of barriocracy, if somebody snuffs a kinsman, even a second cousin twice removed, you're expected to do something forceful about it. A week later on a dark street I dented Dodgie's skull with a baseball bat, a deed which the fuzz indifferently investigated. I think they approved of the venture. It tidied up the neighborhood somewhat. Dodgie didn't die. He hauled the hell out of town and, according to a sidebar in the LA *Times* about a year later, was shot to death in Miami Beach trying to hijack a speedboat.

And now, fifteen years down the line, this girl offers me ten million to commit murder and I'm off on a tangent down Memory Lane. Her voice cut into my reflections. "What are you thinking?" she asked. "What's your input?"

My input was that what vetoed any thought of complicity in her unspecific plan was the ditsiness of Darlene herself. I didn't trust her; I certainly wouldn't share with her any kind of wild-ass escapade as potentially explosive as a killing. Her immediate, enthusiastic target was Tod Hunt. Tomorrow, if things took a sticky turn, it could be me, at which point it would not matter how much money I had or had not cleared. Not that the money made any difference in my thinking anyway. Or that much of a difference.

"You lose the power of speech?" she said.

"I've got to think it over."

"What's to think over? Aren't you up to taking a chance?"

"Not just yet."

She contorted her face into a grotesque mask. "You're never going to do it," she said. "You've got the balls of a fucking eunuch."

"It's a bad idea," I said emphatically. Perhaps a bit too emphatically, because she snarled, "Don't give me that sanctimonious shit."

Slowly I got to my feet. Her voice chased me across the room. "If you say one word about… about what went on tonight, I got a friend who'll burn off your dick with a cattle prod."

"Sure you have," I told her, my face hot. "That's why you want me to waste your husband."

Her glass flew past my left ear and shattered like a shot against the bar. But she wasn't done yet. Her tinderbox brain was still seething, stalking the ultimate insult she could whip me with before I got out. Finally, "I got to tell you," she began, and I realized from the satisfaction in her voice that she thought she'd found it, "I got to tell you," she said again, "you are one lousy fuck."

I walked out. I could take her imprecations—but why had she offered me this lunatic proposal? What did she know? You like to think you can leave behind your violent tendencies before they start to leave a stink on you— I thought I had, at least. And now she had me thinking I was carrying some mark of Cain under my slacks.

She knew nothing, I told myself.

One thing I knew: she was in bad trouble with a heavy-handed spouse who smacked her around with a leaden whip. She needed a savior; I'd tried to play that role too many times already. But even after almost taking a tumbler to the chin from her, after coming close to smacking her around myself, the impulse to act the protector was still there, whetted by the scalding juices of lubricity. She was beautiful, and lost, a conjunction of irresistibles that inspired half-baked rescue fantasies and shortsighted chiv-alrous impulses.

And then there was the possibility, however dubious, of my pocketing... ten million? Fifteen million? Enough to go away, as I'd have to anyway, without waiting for Senior's okay. Did the money even exist? Was it really collectible? Was I really considering taking out some Croesus-rich brute I disliked without even meeting?

I shook my head violently. Hell with both of them.

Gayle was gone when I got home. I'd crept across the dark apartment and peeked into the bedroom, planning some kind of silent infiltration, but she was out. Christ, I thought, all that tippytoeing, that holding of whisky breath, for nothing. I stripped and scrambled into the sack.

She stumbled in a half-hour later.

"Where have you been?" I asked coldly.

"I was having dinner."

"Dinner? At two o-fucking-clock in the morning?"

"What about you? Where the hell you been?"

"That's different—that's business. And anyway," I lied, "I've been here for three hours."

She snorted derisively. She was pissed and having trouble with the fas-tener of her bra.

"Who were you with?" I asked, climbing out of bed.

"None of your beeswax," she said haughtily, groping for the hook, circling eccentrically, like a puppy chasing its tail. "That's for me to know and you to find out."

I couldn't have cared less who she was with. Or so I would have thought. But inexplicably, something inside me, stirred up by Darlene, was erupting like scalding bile. I went green-eyed, grabbing her wrist, yanking her close to me. She sniffed audibly, her eyes widened.

"You've been *smoking!*" she said, aghast, pulling away. Stumbling, she tripped on her own feet and fell. I caught her and the ball of my hand grazed her cheek.

"You hit me!" she cried.

"I did not," I said, grabbing for her again. "And don't change the subject. Who were you with?" I repeated, stalking her around the ring. It occurred to me that I had more to confess than she, but self-awareness failed to abate my rage.

"Nobody!" she screamed. And between sobs she said, "Jerry Fleet."

"What did you do?"

"Nothing."

"You expect me to believe he spent most of the night with you just whispering sweet filthies in your ear?"

"You can believe any damn thing you want." She snatched up a pillow, ripped the blanket off the bed, and strode out the door.

I didn't follow. I took a breath, wishing I'd picked up some cigarettes. After a minute I went to the couch, looking down at her in the darkness. "I'm sorry," I said.

She shrugged. Her breath caught convulsively. I eased myself to the tentative edge of the couch. She lay with her hands clasped in her lap, over the coverlet, like a corpse on a bier. I took those hands in mine. One was cold, the other hot and wet with tears. "I'm sorry," I said again.

"You don't give a damn about me." Her voice was a whispered monotone.

"Of course I do. If I didn't, I wouldn't have—"

"I don't mean tonight. Tonight," her voice broke tiredly, "you shamed me."

"Goddammit, I didn't hit you."

"Don't yell at me. What I mean, you haven't given a damn for months." I bent over, burying my head in her shoulder.

"You don't even make love to me the way you used to."

Jesus. I didn't want to sleep with her. I was already overextended. I climbed on the couch. It was a tight fit.

"You don't even talk like you used to. Why do you pretend to be so… unvarnished?"

"I talk what I am. Every profession has its own… whattayacallit? Specialist vocabulary."

"I'm talking about the way you talk to me. The way you act toward me."

"Can't we for shit's sake discuss this some other time?"

"There you go again. Your language is—"

"Okay," I said. "Okay. I'll try to change."

A long silence. Then she said softly, "I think you cuss because you're angry all the time. I think it's because you hate your work. And you hate yourself."

I didn't answer.

"You used to try writing screenplays," she went on.

"Everybody in this town tries to write screenplays. I wasn't any good at it."

"Maybe you didn't give it enough time. Maybe you could have learned."

I could hear her breathing, feel her warm breath against the hollow of my shoulder. Something wholly unexpected happened. The slumbering dwarf between my legs stirred.

"Let's go to bed," I suggested.

"No," she said, "Let's… it's been a long while since we did it on the couch…"

FOUR

I got to the office in the middle of the morning; of course Senior and Jerry were in before me, although there was little to do. The bottom had fallen out of the market. Foreclosures were rampant, but we didn't even have anybody to evict.

Gray-faced, Senior sat growling at his desk in the center of the disreputable shed, causing my colleagues—both of them—to sham a rabid busyness, bustling with phone and papers, flattening themselves over idle work, cringing whenever Senior snapped his sullen eyes on them to bark instructions and criticism and importunate demands from his revolving chair. His son prowled about, meanwhile, detailing his lackluster exploits to anybody he managed to sneak up on. A frayed bolo curved like a noose at his neck.

Jerry's topics of choice could be counted on one hand. He enjoyed badmouthing his daddy above almost all else—Old Sitting Bullshit, he called him, resentful of all the turbulent indignities Senior had hurled his way. The story he told repeatedly concerned Senior's attempt to sell his wife's (Jerry's mother's) false teeth when she died.

Further and foremost, though, Jerry devoted our talks to schemes. His favorites he fed me like delicacies, such was his fondness for them. The fact that he hadn't a clue about how they could possibly be realized in no way impeded his fixations.

Today, arriving at my desk just after I did, he began with his determination to develop a substitute for gasoline.

"Ethanol?" I asked, having about as much knowledge as he did about combustibles. "That what you're talking about?"

"Ethanol," he said scathingly, "is a scam, a political gimmick for farmers who've filled hick states with bins of corn they otherwise couldn't give away. "Want to try again?"

"Chicken fat? I read somewhere—"

"Chicken fat!" he repeated scornfully. "You want the whole country smelling like a fucking barnyard? You got one more shot."

"I don't know."

"Kelp!" he whispered triumphantly.

"Kelp?" I repeated. "Seaweed?"

"Seaweed," he said emphatically. "It's safe and sane, it don't stink, and we got a whole ocean full of it. Stuff grows in clusters so thick and deep you could hide a herd of elephants in one." Without even a pausette he segued into his next enthusiasm: the invention of a delectably healthy cigarette. He was certain its production was just around the corner, if the right chemist took it on. I realized I already felt like a smoker again. Before he could say anything else about his fake cigarettes I excused myself and went in search of a real one.

When I got back to my desk, empty-handed, Jerry was still sitting on it. "Christ sakes," he said, "you took off like lightning with a bug up its ass. Senior wants to see us, you know."

"What's he want?"

Jerry shrugged. "Maybe we ought to find out."

Suddenly where I was and who I worked for snapped back into focus. I was in the deep shit, I realized. "What's this Katz business and why didn't you tell me about it?" Senior would ask. "Nothing," I would say, "it fell to pieces, a short circuit." And he would think I was copping a plea, that I blew the deal. And then he'd check it out himself and find out the whole shkla was a crock and... And what about the Hunt property, the "Norton" property as it was known to Jerry? Suppose Senior wanted to know...? I was sweating now, and a sour smell assailed me, the smell of decay, myself decaying. Fucking Jerry, couldn't he keep his mouth shut about anything?

He led me into the musty room where records were stored, then dragged in three folding chairs and closed the door. Senior was already there, tooth-pick held between two fingers, twirling it in the light, admiring the glitter. In his other hand was a cell phone. "Yessir," he was saying into the mouth-piece with the exaggerated sincerity of a bad actor, "if I can't make a deal on your building, Mr. Swann, I'll eat a cockroach. Right. Right."

He hung up. He smiled at me, his eyes half-hooded in ecstasy, like a can-nibal sniffing a steaming pot. A police siren wailed insanely not too far away. Senior continued to twirl his glinting toothpick until it was quiet again. "You prolly never noticed," he began, "that we've been diddling around this past month with something hot. A regular assburner. Well, it's beginning to shape up, and it's time you knew about it."

Jerry belched resonantly. His father looked at him half in anger, half in scorn. "Why the fuck," Senior said, "do you have to eat Limburger cheese for breakfast? I can smell your goddam breath all the way over here."

"Sorry, sir."

"Shit." He took his toothpick and worked it lovingly under the nail of his pinky. "F and F," he said when his dudgeon had simmered down, "has been tendered an offer to merge with Hunt Realty." His voice held the triumph of a little boy who has finally been asked to play with the big guys—in this case the biggest of them all. Who happened to be Darlene's husband, who beat her face with a riding crop. How would that complicate my life?

"You going to do it?" I asked dubiously.

"Are we going to do it?" Senior repeated. "Does a bear shit in his tutu?" He eyed me darkly, disappointed in my lack of enthusiasm. What he wanted, I suppose, was for me to kiss the toothpick, his sacred symbol of office, to mumble reverently, "Senior, you've done it again!" as though he were pulling off the financial coup of the century.

"Congratulations, Senior," I mumbled reverently. "You've done it again."

"Yeah," he agreed, beaming.

"Thing is, what's Hunt want out of it?"

"He wants half our tamale pie," Senior said. "He thinks there's a big future in Mexican property." He stuck the toothpick daintily in his ear. "That's where you come," he said. "You're going to head the Mexico City office, to make damn sure Hunt's people don't steal our ass off."

I said nothing. Any other week, I would've been jumping for joy, but suddenly being under Hunt's thumb didn't sound so comfortable.

Senior continued to glare at me, perplexed. "Don't that grab you?" he asked. "You'll get a raise and a piece of the action. But," he added grudgingly, "don't depend on it—first things first. But even before that," he looked at his watch, "in a half an hour, we got to take a meet with Hunt." He got to his feet. "I told him you were our designated hitter to run the shop in Mexico, and he wants to look on you," he said. "If he likes what he sees, I guess we can firm up a deal.

"And oh," he added, as I was grabbing my jacket, his big gray teeth bared in a wolfish grin. "This came for you. Love letter?" He flipped me a creamy envelope marked *personal*.

I went to the can and tore it open. It lacked both a salutation and a signature, but the message was clear:

If you'd like to re-hash what we recently hashed over maybe this time from a different point of view, leave me a message at the Card Room of the Palisades Country Club.

I flushed it down the toilet. Darlene.

One minute with Tod Hunt told me his wife was a mythmaker. How she got the scar on her face I didn't know, but I know he didn't put it there.

He was a lean, unspectacularly handsome man, fifty-eight Darlene had said, with a face that held a quiet and impressive majesterialty. Eyes like denim, the bluest eyes I had ever seen, gave total attention to whatever Senior and Jerry had to say, which was for the most part, in their insecurity before him, unclear and at times loutish. They couldn't help it.

He wore a gray flannel suit and a striped shirt. The stripes were not blue, which would have been too much, too theatrical with those eyes, but a kind of greenish-gray, with a dark silk tie. His mane of dark hair was streaked with white that ran to silver. The curvature of his lips fell just short of delicate. His voice was softly urbane. He never used his hands to punctuate what he had to say. The overall effect was electrical; he seemed to shoot off elegant sparks.

Even his office surprised me. I expected glass and chrome with fluorescent lighting, something modern and functional, like a premier realtor's office should be. Instead it was dark and intimate. Wood-paneled walls. A beat-up desk gleaming in the lamplight. A fireplace of rough stone under a walnut mantel. It was a lair.

Hunt's business was different from F & F's. We did whatever we could latch on to, while he specialized in a relatively few rarified houses, each of them priced somewhere between five and a hundred million. Of course, with that kind of clientele you could turn a fairly luxurious buck on a six percent commission. Senior estimated that the Hunt office had averaged about ninety million in sales for each of the last five fiscal years.

"Would you like a little white wine?" Hunt asked in his cool, soft voice.

"Why the hell not?" Senior answered with ferocious good humor.

"Bet your ass," boomed his only, foul-faced son.

"Thank you, sir," I said cautiously.

He poured from a bottle with a smudged label that read PINOT CHARDONNAY.

I settled back, holding hands with the chilled white wine while Hunt, Senior, and Jerry put a burnish on the merger. I studied Hunt, from the top of his head to the gold snaffles of his loafers. He controlled the meet, no question about it, carrying his own spotlight. He was long on charm; more than any man I'd ever met, he had dominion. Am I repeating myself? I was carried away, if that's an excuse.

He could also be still. Most men can't, you know. Have you ever noticed people at a ballpark, standing for the national anthem? They shift their weight, as if one leg were painfully shorter than the other, pick their nose, scratch their nuts.

But with all his brains, his ability, his charm, he had some difficulty making contact with Senior and Jerry. Hunt would explain an element of the deal, or ask a question, and they would look at him blankly or say something inexpedient or exchange a bleak glance and have another shot of wine. Hunt would get to his feet, move around the room, and repeat the point, slowly, with infinite care, as if he were handling crystal.

Sitting or standing, this gray-maned eleganto was impassive. When Senior finally got to the point about Mexican holdings and rates and payrolls, Hunt almost seemed to be savoring some acute pleasure or passion he had lately embarked upon, or was about to pursue. Or maybe it was my imagination.

"Perhaps, if I may...?" I volunteered modestly.

On the drive to Hunt's office, while Senior and Jerry indulged themselves in great expectations, as if they were already the inheritors of Hunt's domain, I sat alone in the back of the car, arming myself with wariness, fueling the high-octane intensity of my aversion for the man. And here I sat, half an hour later, enjoying his hospitality, beguiled by his magic, yielding to his magnetism. I wanted to please him, to snare his approval, to show off; mostly I wanted him for a father.

In Palma Aldea, the housing project in east LA where the old man and I had lived, I'd always envied the kids who didn't know who their fathers were—I would rather not have had a father than the one I had. He was a world-class wash-out, a fuck-up with a perpetually flat wallet, which was why he plunged into poker each Sunday—his unreliable attempt to fatten his cash flow. It worked slightly more often than not; he'd manage to rack up a few dollars, which he then hopefully wagered and lost every Monday morning on the lottery.

He was always in a state of flummox, usually in a money mess, occasionally in a tangle with a woman. He was seldom successful with the lookers he chased because he lacked the throw-around money that most pretty women required.

What had my mother required? What was she capable of condoning? I never knew. We didn't even have a snapshot of her. Whenever I asked my father about her, he always managed to sidle and stumble and trip on his one endearing (Freudian slip. I meant to say enduring) memory: that my mother died in childbirth—mine. The inference, of course, was that I killed her. After a while I stopped asking questions altogether.

Senior was rasping his rheumy throat and twirling his toothpick as if it were a magic wand to guide me back to the present. He was nodding now, eager for me to step in and untangle his knots, as I had volunteered to do about five seconds ago. So I explained the Mexican operation as I had to Senior so many times before—not in terms of how it was run, but how it *should* have been run, blending my quiet enthusiasm with knowledgeability and a third factor which I stressed because it was obvious to me, even if it escaped the dismal intelligence of Senior and Jerry: why Hunt wanted that conduit to Mexico. We were in the middle of an inflationary depression that, along with the current pandemic of foreclosures, would possibly be with us for years. The wily *conquistador* of Brentwood was switching his operation south, where *palacios* and vast acreage could still be picked up for comparatively short dough.

I finished my dissertation. "*¿Hay preguntas?*" I asked.

"I beg your pardon?"

"Any questions?" I translated.

"Yes," Hunt said, "quite a few."

"Sorry," I said, "I thought you spoke Spanish."

He turned to Senior. "I know you gentlemen are busy," he said. "Perhaps I could have Hopkins here for a few days?" It wasn't a question; it was a command.

"Of course," Senior said, pretending he was granting a request.

We got to our feet. We shook hands.

"Tomorrow at nine?" Hunt said to me.

"Yessir," I replied, snapping my eyeballs. I recognized an order when I heard one.

How Tod Hunt had developed his gem-like skills he never confided to me. When I tried to get him to talk about himself, he'd shake his head and reach for the white wine.

"You'll have to pardon me," he said once, "but I hate retrospecting."

Retrospecting. He used words like that, a fancy, curveball way of talking, but it never made me feel uncomfortable. I sat back in a big chair, looking around the room with a little sigh of contentment. My attitude toward that room had changed in the past four days. It was conducive to quiet talk, quiet well-being.

"You've got one hell of a track record," I told him.

"Only in real estate," he said, "which is a rather limited arena. And I'm tired of it. I'd like a shot at a more significant target."

"Such as?"

He smiled and shook his head as if there was much he could tell but saw no reason to. The silence sprawled limitlessly. It was as if he had vanished. I cleared my throat and reached for the wine.

"Sorry," he said, refilling my glass.

In that lovely dark room we would lift our glasses and drink our wine and all the while, roaring in my head like a wild river, was the obscene aware-ness: *His wife wants to kill him.* What, I asked myself, should I do about it?

"How's it going with Tod Hunt?" Senior asked me a few days later. I'd slipped back to Fleet & Fleet in between appointments with our better to make sure Jerry hadn't been stealing my mail.

"Fine," I told him.

"You've been spending more time with him than you have with us."

"There's a lot to iron out. I've told you—"

"What the hell's he want? I mean *really* want?"

"Just what he says—some high-visibility locations in Mexico, which we've got."

"What do you think of him?"

"Well, for openers, he's a broad-gauge thinker."

"He's glued together real nice," Senior said peevishly. "He could charm the warts off a fucking hog."

"He's a stiff shirt," Jerry said.

"You think we should pounce?" Senior asked.

"I think that would blow it. I think we should look and listen."

"I think he's giving us the finger," Jerry said. "Right up the shaft."

"How long's it going to take?" Senior asked. "I mean, either take him home with you, boy, or stop patting him on the ass."

"He'll pounce, in his own good time."

"Try to goose him a little."

I didn't answer.

"I know you're trying, Jack," Senior said. "I know you want that job in Mexico. And Christ, I want to get my hands on some of his properties here. They're ambrosia."

"You will," I said. "But don't rush me."

"Okay, *okay*, but…"

Senior always had to have the last word; still he realized I was taking no shit from him.

He smoothed down his thinning hair, snarled by the winds of change howling through the office. "Put a lock on it, will you?" he said. I felt exhilarated.

*　　*　　*

"The French mathematician, François Viète," Tod Hunt said, "ushered us all into the modern era in 1576."

"What did he do?" I asked.

"Like to guess?"

I thought for a moment. "He produced a map of the world?"

Tod shook his head.

"He discovered carbon paper?"

Tod smiled. "Good try," he said, "but no cigar." This sort of catechism was his way of taking my temperature. I was pleased because he was pleased with my guess.

"He invented the decimal point," Tod said. We were in his office sipping our Chardonnay.

"Did you ever go to real-estate school?" he asked.

"No."

"Good. They produce a kind of trained incapacity, as Thorstein Veblen said of the English public school system." He poured himself a couple of fingers of wine. "Most realtors are licensed delinquents. Scum."

That word annoyed me. The snobbism. The disdainful twist of the mouth. He was the kind of man who accepted one self-made law for himself and another for the rest of humanity.

"That's a pretty broad generalization," I said. "You're hip-shooting."

"Don't be a bore," he snapped. "I wasn't talking about you."

"How would you talk about me?"

"Only in the most glowing terms," he said, bemused and, I thought, faintly derisive.

"And how would you describe yourself?"

"Only in the most glowing terms," he repeated, in that same self-derogating voice. He thought for a moment. "Me...?" He stabbed gently at his chest with a thumb. "I'm a Narodnik."

"What?"

"The Narodniki were Russian intellectuals who went out in the fields and worked with peasants."

"Most people work in one kind of boiler room or another."

"I couldn't do that," he said stiffly, and I thought *he* was becoming annoyed. But then he grinned. "I can't even sell small houses—I could never see myself huckstering those barren, baleful stencils."

There was a gentle knock on the door. At Tod's bidding, his personal secretary entered, a middle-aged madonna in severe English tweeds. Her hair, blue-black as stove polish, was lacquered in a tight bun at the nape of her neck. Once she might have been beautiful. She handed him some papers.

"Thank you, Ms. Velasquez," he said, and told her we were not to be disturbed for an hour.

"What about that phone call?" she asked in a hushed voice.

He said, "Make the appointment." She nodded and closed the door solemnly behind her, as if it were the portal of a shrine. He ran his eyes over the papers. "How," he asked me, "would you characterize the Fleets, *père et fils?*"

I hesitated.

"Would you say that they present an impeccable silhouette?"

Instead of answering, "How do you see them?" I asked.

"Senior," he said matter-of-factly, "is a routine-besotted mutt. Jerry..." he shook his head, "is the runt of the litter. If Senior saw Jerry as he really is, he'd drown him."

The phone rang. Tod depressed one of the buttons on the key shelf of the base. "Yes, Ms. Velasquez? Thank you." He cradled the arm. He looked at me.

Finally he said, "What do you want to do in Mexico City? It's not exactly a town roaring with temptation..."

"It's a job that I think I could handle."

He snorted. "Why don't you stick around here and be my all-purpose shock-absorber?"

I'd waited three years for Mexico, and every time it seemed to get a little nearer, another obstacle sprang up—and now the biggest obstacle of all: an opportunity. It was hard not to think that I'd been banging my head against the wall at F & F for long enough. Not to mention that taking Tod's money through honest work sounded a fair bit better than skimming it off his dead body.

"I continue to see a growth opportunity, and you at the center of our... operations in Mexico, down the road," Tod reassured. "I appreciate your hesitation to—"

"Absorb shocks," I said. "What, more or less specifically," I asked, "does a shock-absorber do?"

"For openers, Ms. Velasquez has arranged an appointment for you tonight." Sonofabitch. He had assumed, he had known damned well he had me hooked, making the "appointment" before he had so much as mentioned it. "I'd like you to represent me to..." he cleared his throat, "...to Miss Carmen Ochoa and her family. They'll be expecting you at eight."

He rearranged a few papers on his desk. "Miss Ochoa and her family, with the exception of a brother, speak no English. While Ms. Velasquez speaks Spanish, there are certain matters I'd rather not entrust to her."

He got up, moving with authoritative grace around the room.

"Miss Ochoa," he said, "used to work for me, or rather my wife—she was a maid in the house. My wife suspected there was a little something between us and fired her. She—Miss Ochoa—is an obedient treasure." He paused, then, "To tell you the God's truth," he went on, "I never laid a hand on her, although once, in a car, I tried." He frowned. "I struck out," he said, and then he asked, as if the ridges in his forehead gave him pain, "Do you shock easily?"

"I don't think so."

"Miss Ochoa," he said dryly, "is fourteen."

For a moment it was so quiet you could have heard an ant pissing on cotton.

"What would you like me to do?" I asked.

Gayle drifts to and fro in a rocking chair, reading the *TV Guide*. Abstractedly she reaches inside her wrapper and scratches a naked shoulder. The wrapper is pink and frayed at the cuffs. She must have bought it at a garage sale.

I sit with a copy of *Sports Illustrated* in my lap and no idea what I've been reading for the past twenty minutes. What Hunt told me about Carmen Ochoa had wiped me out. Not the fact that she was fourteen, but what Hunt wanted from me... I glanced at my watch. I had another hour before my meet with the family. I should have told Hunt he had me pegged all wrong. Told him to get another boy...

In a way it was a ticklish assignment, this wild hair of Hunt's, yet it was foolproof. Greed was the golden apple that no man, certainly no fourteen-year-old girl, could resist.

I got to my feet. "Got to go," I said.

"Go? Go where?"

"Out. Work. For Hunt."

"You didn't tell me."

"It never came up." I threw on my jacket and walked toward the door. The phone rang. Gayle answered it. "Hello!" she snarled, deflecting her anger from me to the plastic dumb innocence of the instrument, whose only transgression was tinkling at the wrong time.

"For you," Gayle said. "Mr. Katz."

It was the wrong time, all right. "Yes, Mr. Katz...?"

"Why the fuck don't you answer my letter!" Darlene's voice exploded in my ear. "Do I have to put a goddam bell around your neck to—"

"I've been tied up, Mr. Katz..." I said calmly.

"Bullshit!" She was getting wild again. "And don't give me that Mr. Crap Katz!" she screamed, violating the order of basic syntax.

"I'll call you tomorrow." Out of the corner of my eye I saw Gayle staring at me suspiciously. "Thank you, Mr. Katz."

"Listen, you turd..."

I hung up. I wanted her out of my life, now and forever, yet lodged in my mind was that face with the scar on it as she lay on the bed beside me, her hair flowing over one shoulder, her eerie, mesmeric Tex-speak.

"Who was that on the phone?" Gayle asked in a tight voice.

"Mr. Katz."

"I mean the girl."

"His secretary."

"She works this late? I don't believe you."

"I don't know how late she works." I exhaled sharply. "I'll be home soon."

"Don't hurry. I may not be here when you get back," she threatened. "I might go to a late movie."

FIVE

The Ochoas lived in a tilted house at the base of a steep hill, east of the free-way, south of Alvarado. From the top, downtown LA was a glittering forest. At the bottom the darkness closed in, its density only accentuated by a naked street lamp, flickering, throbbing, hissing in the night as if its nervous system was mangled by the rock that had shattered its globe.

I parked behind a crumbling pickup. Across the street was an empty lot where a huge black tank of a Chrysler writhed like a beached whale dying. The detonation of cracked plugs, sprung bearings, and ruptured cylinders was deafening.

A team of grave young mechanics bent over the tortured engine, oblivious to the spray of oil, while a pack of dogs in stately procession marched around the whale as if it were a maypole, pausing now and then to piss on the tires. The engine gasped, sputtered, and died. On a wavy fender a ghetto blaster made itself heard, pouring out mariachi syrup.

"Why," asked one of the mechanics, "does this magnificent beast of two hundred horsepowers have the sick?"

"It has the horsepowers of two hundred chickens," a colleague replied, snapping his fingers to the music.

I leaned into the open door of my compact, reaching for the two lush and fragrant bouquets reposing in the jump seat. I cradled the yellow roses in the crook of my arm, like a chorus girl doing a springtime number, and then a hand big as a watermelon came out of the darkness, pulled me backward, spun me around, and slammed me into the side of the car.

"You Hopkins?" he asked me. I'd seen bigger, thicker men, but never off a football field.

"That's right." I extended my hand. He ignored it.

"You fucking people insulted my sister," he said. "You dumped her without even a letter of reference." His face was putty-colored, all crags and queer contours, tight with the tensions of a man spoiling for a fight.

"Would you listen for a minute?"

He listened by smashing the heel of a hoof-like hand into my chest. "You get back in that heap and haul ass," he said. He rammed me again. I stepped back and he came on slowly, methodical and flat-footed. His eyes were narrowed and too steady, the puddled orbs of a doper.

How long did he expect me to stand there, clutching my flowers, his personal, impassive punching bag? He curled his twin watermelons into fists, measured me, ready now to jump them into my face. Christ, I thought, if he lands just one, I'll be in drydock for six weeks. If I fight back I could bust my hands on him. I'd have nothing but split knuckles to show for it.

The yellow roses as if of their own accord sprayed into those puddled eyes like a gallon of thorny mace. I lifted a leg and brought the knee emphatically into his nuts. I thought his eyes would come out of his head. His cheeks fluttered as though he were running hard. His mouth opened but he was too paralyzed to suck air. Then he crumpled and fell in the gutter, clutching himself.

A full two minutes passed before he focused his eyes on mine. "You ready to listen?" I asked, helping him to his feet. It was like raising a monolith.

Señor Ochoa answered the doorbell. Unlike his son, he took my hand when I offered it. His was the hand of a much larger man, gnarled and twisted by a lifetime of grunt labor, a hand that was a tool. His house was my house, he said, bowing.

I followed his chalk-white *guayabera* down the dim hallway. Napoleon followed, holding his insides together with a hand in a pocket, purged of all pugnacity, as if his greatest desire was to die in bed like a good little boy. We took our assigned places in the living room; I, the honored guest, in the overstuffed armchair bandaged in a serape to keep its guts from pouring out. The family—father, mother, son, and daughter—fanned out around me, all of us under the drooping Indian eye of a melancholy *Cristo* on the distempered gray wall. Another crucifix of some waxy black stone hung from Señora Ochoa's withered neck, and a third, a running sore in reds and blues, was tattooed on the son's massive forearm, over the smudged and emblazoned hosanna, *Olé Jesus*. On his other forearm was a naked lady with a tight little thicket of pubic hair.

Señor Ochoa broke out a jug of that bullying red wine found only in the corner *mercados* of Mexican neighborhoods. It was enough to give a gringo cavities, but I found it soothing, I knew it well; it was like a reunion. I had drunk that wine throughout my puppyhood, and sucked the bottom of the glass.

I suppose it was the wine that breached the floodgates of memory, most of it unpleasant. My barrio, mean and troubled, should have ever been darkly overcast, blanketed in fog, curtained by gloom, wrapped in a cold drizzle—appropriate atmospherics for what went down there. But we were perennially bathed in sunshine.

My boyhood was, I would have thought, had I ever attempted to examine it, normal and unspectacular. Backward, perhaps, because I didn't start drinking until I was twelve. I stole hubcaps and lifted nickels and dimes from little kids to pay for the tiger-pissy alcohol. I seldom used drugs but regularly sold them to young people from the beta-burb triangle—Beverly, Bel Air, Brentwood.

It was all a question of survival as I saw it. And life was even more difficult for my deracinated friends than it was for my father and me. They were impeded by English-speak, their irregular second language. They lived by a credo of duality, an identity of opposites. On the one hand they recognized the Pauline dictum that Money was the Root of all Evil, and on the other they weren't unaware of the Shavian counterpoint that the Lack of Money was the Root of all Evil.

Nor was I, a lookout at seven, a runner at ten, a dealer of snow and meth at fourteen.

All went well for three years, but then I got in a bind with the fuzz. Not for dealing pharmaceuticals, but for theft: like a true son of my father, I was unable to resist the slightest temptation.

The beer truck was loaded, the tailgate open, and nobody around. I lifted a six-pack and the driver, who was almost as big as the truck, came out of nowhere and ham-handed me to the authorities. For batting Dodgie's head in, I hadn't even been investigated by the prodigiously unconcerned cops. For ripping off the beer I must have been considered a major threat to capitalism. They unloaded on me.

The judge on my case had two bouncy chins and false teeth that fit badly. "Come with me," he said when he closed the hearing. I followed him into his chambers. He said, "Son, you're a good-looking kid. I could send you to a correctional facility for a couple or three years. You'd get ass-raped every night including Sundays and holidays, or you can enlist for a tour in the Marine Corps. Which do you prefer?"

I chose the Corps, although it was hardly a jaunt in MacArthur Park. Particular difficult was our platoon sergeant, who would break us out of the sack in the middle of the night to do endless push-ups until somebody passed out, or line us up under the cold starry sky and crash his fist into somebody's belly. "That's for nuthin'," he'd say. "Do somethin' and see what happens."

When I got out, I never, not even once, returned to the old neighborhood; it wasn't an environment that grabbed you in a nostalgic embrace. My honorable discharge accessed me to a community college up north. And then, like an iron bar from out of nowhere, came the nastiness with Bainbridge and MacDevitt...

A voice jolted me out of the past. "I'm sorry, I did not hear...?"

"It is nothing," Señor Ochoa said. "Would you like more wine?"

"Thank you." I held out my glass. "It is a good wine."

"It is a somewhat wine. But it has a strong expression." He sipped calmly on his tongue.

Did he have any indication of the rockslide I was about to unleash? Did his wife? She sat beside him, patient and courtly, with the exquisite good manners of the poor. She was one of those people who could sit there forever, sealed in silence, sniffing her roses or subduing one hand with another, and stirring every nine months or so to drop a baby. Now and then she glanced at her husband, at me shyly, back to him—it was always the look of people who ask questions eloquently but only with their eyes, who do not feel entitled to impatience.

Not like her son. Napoleon was one of those *machos* born looking for a party, a guy who found fucking all the sweeter if he had a good fight first. I had to be careful with this Carmen business or he'd try his fists on me again.

Carmen! His sister, the reason we were all gathered together under the lusterless gaze of that shaky-loined, limp-wristed Jesus on the wall. I didn't know what to make of her.

She looked younger than her fourteen years. Her movements were slow and meager, but she managed to infuse them with a kind of sultry detachment that was both disconcerting and hypnotic. She sat in a hollow of the couch, cupping a little claw of a hand over her crotch, the hand clamped between her tightly scissored legs. From time to time, staring at me blindly, dreamily, she ran her scarlet tongue across her mouth to caress a fever blister. She had a stuffed nose. To ease her breathing she sucked air, her lips parted in a rounded O to reveal a flash of bright metal. Gold teeth in one so young? Not at all. She wore braces, another gift, I was sure, from her admirer, along with the fashionable slacks and the sleeveless cashmere sweater.

Yet there was something about her, a sly, sluggish potential. It was that firm little ass, burrowing into the hollow of the couch, and her skin the color of pale honey, the moist shadows below her black almond eyes that held some secret, sexy promise I doubted even she was aware of. But she would be, and soon. She was destined to be pursued on planes, trains, and elevators, in public parks, down nighttime streets, in hotel lobbies, at taco stands. But not quite yet. Was Hunt the connoisseur, putting her in the deep freeze for a couple of years? While there was time, before the competition got too heavy, before the young lechers queued up, snorting and pawing the earth, groping, blundering, contaminating?

The time had come to plunge.

"I am here, as you know, at the behest of the Señor Tod Hunt, who has a great fondness for your daughter."

Ochoa nodded solemnly. Napoleon scowled. Carmen's eyes sounded mine, drowsily. Her hair shone like blue-black silk above the yellow roses in her lap. She parted her lips and her white teeth gleamed and the braces glittered and she sneezed violently. It was a beautiful thing to see, because her pert untethered breasts shot up in unison.

With some reluctance I turned from Carmen and zeroed back in on Ochoa. "The Señor Hunt would like to be to your daughter a benefactor." My smile, limpid with sincerity, spread to include the girl. Coolly she raised her arm, curving it around her face and head, like half an oval frame. It was her most strenuous activity of the evening.

"The Señor Hunt is aware of Carmen's ambition to become a nurse. He would like therefore to supply an English tutor, to help her through high school and on to UCLA, if that is her wish. He will further provide her with a dwelling of her own, where she may pursue her studies in peace and quiet. So that she may devote her full time to her education without it becoming necessary for her to take on some stupefying job below her intellectual capacity, he will provide her, additionally, with two hundred and fifty dollars a week."

That drowsy expression on Carmen's face hadn't changed while I ran down the proposed list of benefits. I was conscious of staring into her shadowed and tufted armpit. Now, I had never been electrified by an armpit before; all I know, I had this sudden, overwhelming desire to thrust my hand through the armhole of her sweater and take it from there.

"Moreover..." my voice broke in a strained yolky falsetto; I began again. "Moreover... to demonstrate his fidelity as Carmen's friend and protector, the Señor Hunt would like to reward all of you, and in so many ways that you will have to like one or two of them..." And here the courier smiled boyishly, charming (he hoped) his audience like so many swaying cobras. Ochoa did indeed seem enthralled, and slab-chested, glint-eyed Napoleon leaned forward. Now he knew my batshit had something to do with money, and it stirred his blood like the bugles of Chapultepec.

"If you, sir," I said to his father, "wish to become an American citizen, there are certain procedures familiar to the Señor Hunt which could assuage your efforts. He is also aware of your excellence as a builder in stone and brick. If perhaps you would like your own masonry business, the Señor Hunt will provide thirty-five thousand dollars toward the enterprise—the purchase of a truck and materials, a yard and so forth. Or if you prefer, you may return to Mexico with the money—whatever is your wish. And there will be an additional fifteen thousand dollars for Napoleon, to help him achieve whatever his goal in life might be."

Señor Ochoa gasped. Napoleon's pig-iron body shot forward to the edge of his chair. His arms were twitching in his excitement, Jesus and the naked lady doing a little dance. I thought I had worded Hunt's case quite well, particularly the bit about Napoleon's goal in life. What would it be, I wondered—a restructured, parrot-colored Cadillac? A bottomless lake of tequila? A three-year supply of hookers?

"It is no light matter," I went on smoothly, "to accept the guardianship of a young girl like Carmen, but it is a responsibility the Señor Hunt is prepared to accept. Not for a week, or a month, but…" I paused for emphasis "…for ten years. Ten years devoted to Carmen's development. After which, having matured into a woman of grace and education, she no longer will have the need for the Señor Hunt's guidance."

I finished my wine. Ochoa did not offer to refill it. He was far too immersed in his own reflections.

"The Señor Hunt would like your decision as soon as possible, in order that Carmen's education might commence forthwith. But of course you must have time to deliberate."

Silence. The fate of Carmen, of her family, of Hunt, would be decided under the faded eye of the Cristo in the next few moments. I glanced at Señor Ochoa, torn by the jagged horns of a father's dilemma. He sweated, he clenched his fists as if he were preparing to defend himself against the onslaught of temptation, and at the same time he licked his lips as if he were already tasting the rewards of non-resistance. I shifted my eyes to his wife, frozen in rock-like passivity. She was either unaware of the outrage Señor Hunt was attempting, or pretending to be.

"The Señor Hunt will do all those things?" Ochoa asked.

"He will, because he has said he will do them. He is an irrevocable man."

"How soon could the arrangements be made?" Napoleon asked hoarsely.

"Immediately. A place will be found for Carmen tomorrow. I will take her there and return here with the money."

"Then I think," Ochoa said, "I think there is no further need for deliberation." He turned smiling to his daughter. "A place of your own," he said. "An education." He beamed with the wonder of it all. "Can you be ready by tomorrow?"

"No," she said.

"When will you be ready?" I asked.

"Never," she said.

"'Never,' she said? She said, 'Never'?"

"That's what she said. She's not interested in a long-term lease."

Tod Hunt's tan went pallid and then slowly came to a boil. "You screwed it up," he said scornfully, his jaws locked, only his gray lips moving. "You cocked it up good."

"I don't believe so," I said, trying to ignore the sound counsel of a piercing inner voice. *Kick him in the nuts*, it screamed. *You don't have to take his shit.* "I think I handled—"

"You're a fuck-up." It was the first time I had ever heard him use an obscenity. "I should have known. Anyone who could spend three years in that snake pit of an office with those two clowns—"

"What do they have to do with it?"

"Maybe they should have," he choked. "Maybe I should have sent Jerry."

"All right!" My tongue was thick and I was shaking, and right then two other clowns flashed before me, the smell of dry rot and dusty books mingling with chalk and Lysol, and Bainbridge standing there in his gaudy threads like the leader of some moldy rockabilly combo, and MacDevitt in his gruelly double-knits—he thought they lent a scholarly air to his otherwise Neanderthal presence, but his students joked about the way (so they claimed) his undertaker dressed him—and Bainbridge getting to his feet, his flat eyes wide with fright as I came at him, and I thought, I'd better get out of here, away from Hunt before I... I exhaled deeply. "What do you want me to do?" My voice was cool and controlled now. "You want me to look for a rope and a tree?"

"Not a bad idea."

I had come to his office, where he had been waiting for me with a silver pot of caviar, little crustless sandwiches, deviled eggs, petits fours, coffee, booze. I was starved, but I swear if I had so much as reached for a chunk of cheese he would have hacked off my arm at the shoulder. So I refrained, and the juices of rage and hunger curdled in my stomach.

"There's one thing still worth considering," I said.

"Yes?" Icily.

When I'd left the Ochoas', Napoleon had seen me to the door, sighing with each desperate footstep. He followed me out into the street and leaned on the car. He lowered his head like an anguished bull and banged it again and again against the metal roof. The old heap groaned and shuddered on its springs. I took a good bouncing around in the driver's seat; I had trouble inserting the ignition key in its lock.

"Pull yourself together," I told him. "I just had the goddam wheels aligned."

He sighed once more and fell back into a settled melancholy.

"She got another guy?" I asked.

"I don't think so. It's something else, I think." Sadly, in his agitation, he rolled his eyes and kicked another tire, as if he were thinking about buying the compact off me. "That dumb fucking horse's ass sister of mine," he said in English, "she would change her mind, I think, if Hunt would maybe marry her a little." He held up his thumb and forefinger, easing them together until they were no more than an eighth of an inch apart. "Make with her just a waif of a marriage," he said plaintively, reverting to Spanish.

I don't think he realized the enormity of his wistful suggestion. Thickjawed, loutish Napoleon, wearing his God on one arm and a naked girl on the other, saw the issue clearly and unclogged. And if I could jockey the Señor Hunt into embracing the concept, I'd be smugly ensconced as his factotum, as he called it. Maybe I could modulate Darlene's blood-and-money obsessions at the same time, induce her to accept a sensible slice of a sensible divorce, latch onto a chunk of her settlement—I'd delight everybody, then ditch them all for an office in *Zona Rosa* and weekends floating down the canals of Xoximilco, masticating roast chickens and tortillas and sipping jugs of iced Dos Equis. There remained but one question: how deep was the Señor Hunt's lust for Carmen? Enough to marry her?

"Marry her?!" Hunt exploded. "You're out of your mind! You *and* her brother!"

"Now wait a minute. It's just an idea that—"

"It's a compound fracture of an idea. S-S-S-Stupid."

"Don't call me stupid!" Again I felt that uncontrollable urge to snap off a few of his teeth. I lunged to my feet, but in that splintered instant between the thought and the deed, I found myself switching my attack to the caviar. I shoveled a hunk of it onto a slab of toast and stuffed it into my mouth. "If you want the girl bad enough you might—"

"*No*," he cut in sharply. Then, with an astounded shake of his head, "The nerve of that spic bastard—thinking I'd marry his sister."

"Not exactly marry her." I swallowed another cone of caviar. "You could get one of those Mexican... approximations. In Tijuana."

"I got a wife, for shit's sake." He was pretty upset.

"I gathered you weren't too fond of her."

"Fond of her?" he laughed savagely. "Look—I'll let you in on a secret. I've got a list, composed over the years in the dead hours of the night. It's the passenger list on a spectral ship that's doomed to wander the seas of Antarctica forever—the SS *Olivia P. Shitstorm*. There were something like two hundred and seven names aboard at last count—I count them the way some insomniacs count sheep." He paused. I took a little sandwich and poured myself a cup of coffee. He waited, an aggrieved look on his face, until I had stopped chewing. "Mrs. Hunt made that list within a year of our marriage. She started at the bottom, to be sure, but she's risen steadily with the passage of time. Right now, she's at the very top, with small chance that any challenger might unseat her." He shook his head, refusing the plate of sandwiches I offered him. "So you've gathered correctly," he went on, "I'm not too fond of her."

"In that case..."

"One of the primary reasons I'm not too fond of her, she's a pig. In a divorce she'd take me to the cleaners."

"Could she? How far could she get?"

"First of all, she's pretty—that prejudices a judge in her favor. Second, she has the earning power of a Pismo clam. She's tried from time to time to get a job—Jesus, the things she'd come up with. Like once she wanted a concession on those idiot wooden horses hitched outside supermarkets, you know, for kids to ride—put a dime in a slot and it gives you a bounce for three minutes. I got it for her and, Christ, she never knew whether she was making money or losing it—she can't even count dimes. Then she came into the office for a month or so. She couldn't even answer the phone. She couldn't—shit, she couldn't sell diamonds to Elizabeth Taylor. So much for her earning power. And third, she'd never settle for less than a split, right down the middle, of community property, equity. So..."

"So why not let her have it? Hell, none of us lives forever. What precious little time we've got should..."

"I'd like to let her have it with a blackjack."

"You're cutting off your nose to spite your face."

"God," he said, reverting to a bored, theatrical voice, "I've never heard it so well put." He stared at the wall clock for a long time, elaborately checking it against the watch on his wrist.

I got up. "It's late," I said. "We can kick it around tomorrow."

"No," he said. "We'll not be seeing each other again."

I couldn't believe my ears.

"If you drop in at your office tomorrow," he said, "your severance check will be waiting."

I felt shipwrecked. Swindled out of my future. My idyllic Sundays in Xoximilco had evaporated because a fourteen-year-old kid refused to succumb to Tod Hunt's money. I wanted to say Hold it, wait a minute, take it easy, don't do this to me. But that would have been cringing and contemptible and it wouldn't have worked anyway. In the shock of the moment, the wine of affection turned to vinegar. All of a sudden I wanted to do him all the harm I could.

Obviously he felt the same way toward me. "It's time," he said, getting to his feet, "for you to find some other endeavor. Something where your delusions of adequacy will be less of a handicap." He moved stiffly to the fireplace. "Matter of fact I've booked a room for you aboard the good ship *Shitstorm*." He snared the poker from the fire irons. "Because you're stupid," he said. "If I were limited to one word to describe you, it would be *stupid*."

Like a child I said, "Don't call me stupid."

Like a child he said, "Stupid, stupid, stupid." He tapped the iron on his palm, then against the side of his leg, and suddenly he came at me, swinging at my head, hell bent on adding injury to insult. I caught his wrist, twisted it hard counterclockwise. He dropped the iron as his elbow snapped. He cradled it tenderly against his chest with his left hand, as if he were handling china, howling in pain, in bursts, "I'll get you..." The pain had recast his voice into a raging falsetto. "I'll kill you dead," he went on. "I got a long arm. You'll never—"

"The arm I just broke?"

"I'll kill you dead!" he shrilled redundantly.

Suddenly I saw why Darlene was so afraid of him: his revved-up rhetoric was couched in a kind of gratuitous, bully-boy cruelty, a wacky malevolence.

I got to my feet, heading for the door in silence, trying to maintain what was left of my savaged dignity. Something glitched. I lurched into the table, overturning it. The food and the coffeepot went flying. I kicked a petit four into a corner, I ground caviar into the shag of the rug. Like a rudderless ship I sailed toward the door.

"You clumsy ape!" he yelled after me. "I'm going to get you!" he repeated, still in the clutch of his dementia.

My carotids were pumping like a sledge on an anvil. My heart raced. My left triceps throbbed. What was I to do about this unhinged bastard before he tried something again (and again and again)? He wouldn't stop until he'd succeeded in bashing me to pulp.

I would have to kill the hell out of him. Just thinking about it, I was shocked to find, gave me immense satisfaction. He had given me a permit to destroy him by trying to destroy me.

Which left me, then, with just one question: Could I still collect the ten–fifteen million Darlene had promised me?

That, too, I had to find out.

SIX

The waves snapped at the quay. The wind howled.

"I don't know," Scrap Iron Thompson said in his croupy rasp. "It's too durn blustery out there." Scrap Iron rented out a small craft at Marina del Rey. *Durn* was his only imprecation. He once told me swearing was lip filth.

"Christ sakes, Scrap, I can handle the boat, you know that."

"Maybe he's right," Gayle said. I ignored her. "I'm hungry," she went on. "I didn't have any breakfast."

Scrap Iron squinted, studying the sea with his one good eye, the other blind and milky since his last fight at the old Olympic Club many years ago. His corrugated face held that deep leather burnish peculiar to people buffeted by too much sun and wind and salt water. He sighed, shrugged, and said, "Now you be careful, you hear?" And Gayle and I were off in a cloud of spindrift.

Four Pines Point was, by the time we got there, relatively calm. I cut the engine and threw out the sea anchor.

"Why'd we come here?" Gayle asked. "I don't like all this kelp."

"I'm going in close," I told her, checking the valves. "I'll be nowhere near the kelp." I pulled on my wet suit and secured the leaded belt at my hips. "Why don't you eat something?"

"I'm not hungry. I was hungry before, but you were in such a hurry…"

My fault she had lost her appetite. I looked at her in her faded blue jeans with nothing between the imitation gold chain hugging her hips and that goofy hat she loved, made of raffia and flattened beer cans. Here she was, sullen and pouty, in the weird dishabille of a Hollywood Boulevard hooker, a slave to her own dismal thoughts. It was maddening. I never could tell what festered in that bangtail mind of hers.

"Will you for Christ sakes cover your tits?" I snarled. "You want the Coast Guard to come charging in and drag us off for indecent exposure?"

"This is a private boat. I can dress or undress any way I want. Moreover," she took a deep, angry breath and both nipples seemed to stare accusingly at me, "that's not the point."

"Oh, balls," I said eloquently, and went over the side.

It was the kelp I had to explore. Diving down, slashing with my knife through the otherwise impenetrable algae, I snaked passed the slimy tough coils of seaweed, a bobbing, weaving prison. It was as I thought. A cozy coffin for Tod.

I surfaced and swam south about five hundred yards to a public beach. Four roughly circular ramparts of piled rock, like the low fortifications of some prehistoric race, were scattered across the rise, thrown together I suppose by overnight campers for protection against wind and spray. A few people were on the beach, a few more around a smoky fire inside one of the protective shields. Beyond them, beyond the beach, their cars were parked along the shoulder of Pacific Coast Highway. Good. If I ever got that far, Phase II would be a piece of cake. The problem was getting that far. Phase I was going to be a bitch. I swam back to the boat, ready to phone Darlene at her tennis club.

SEVEN

The cemetery was a shimmery island set in the scorched hills beyond the Malibu cut-off. Dazzling white gravel walks meandered among the greenery and the flowering borders.

IN MEMORIAM
I hold it true, whate'er befall;
I feel it, when I sorrow most;
'Tis better to have loved and lost
Than never to have loved at all.

WHITEY
3-12-2001–4-1-2008
He did not know
He was a Rat

"How'd you find this place?" I asked her.
"I was out here once for a funeral."
"Whose?"
"A friend of mine's goldfish."
I squinted at her in the sunlight. She was serious.

I took her arm, steering her down the path, the gravel snarling softly under our feet, the sun sifting through the trees. We walked on, past the graves of horses, dogs, cats, canaries, and alligators, bats, boa constrictors, a hedgehog, a mountain lion, a vulture.

"What about your husband?"

"What about him?" She was being cagey.

"You still want him whacked?"

She nodded.

"Answer me."

"Yes."

"The money you offered me to do it? That still stand?"

"Ten million."

"You said ten or fifteen million. I prefer fifteen. And I'll take care of the taxes."

"Okay," she said.

"Okay." It was a deal. And now, the details: "You've got to have a party," I said. "At the beach house."

"Okay."

"When?" I said.

"Anytime. What difference does it make?"

"It *can't* be anytime; it does make a difference." She was nervous and no help. It was going to be tougher than I thought. "What you've got to do, you got to go out to the beach house, like for an afternoon. Then you decide, on the spur of the moment, to stay for a couple of days. *Then* you decide to have a party at the end of the week..."

"How about the sixteenth?"

"Is that a Sunday?"

"Saturday."

"It's got to be a Sunday." The police were busiest on Sunday nights, sorting out the twisted wreckage of people driving home with short fuses after a day of sunstroke. The longer it took a search-and-rescue squad to pull Hunt out of the sea, the better. I didn't want the blow on the head to be too easy to see—the coroner might view that sort of thing with suspicion.

"It's got to be a Sunday night," I repeated slowly, "at the beach, with your husband attending."

"I got to invite him? You'd better tell me what you're up to."

I wanted her to know as little as possible. The fewer details she knew, the less she could incriminate me. On the other hand, I wanted her involved, so as to make it more difficult for her to save her ass by sacrificing mine, in case some kind of predicament developed. I had to tell her something.

"He shows up at your beach party. At ten or so I come along, jimmy his car window if it's locked, coil onto the floor in the back. When he gets in the car to drive home, I'll stun him with a lead weight wrapped in a towel from my wetsuit. I want him thoroughly drowned before the cops can get to him."

"Drowned? You say drowned?"

"I'm going to drive the car off the cliff and into the sea with him in it."

A moment of silence. Then she said softly, "Okay, Sunday. In three weeks?" I nodded. She bit her lower lip, concentrating. "Suppose when he leaves, somebody decides to walk out with him?"

"You walk out with him."

"Suppose he's the last to leave?"

"Make sure he's not. Jesus," I said, "don't be so rigid. You've got to improvise."

"But..."

"If he hangs on, tell him you're tired, ask him to encourage the others to leave by setting a good example—that sort of thing. And at the same time, confide to another couple that you'd like them to stick around for a night-cap." She was still biting her lip. "What about your other guests?"

"Guests? Just some people we owe."

"Invite the dummies you owe. And the boozers, so they won't be too clear on what happens."

"It's going to look funny."

"What will?"

"Tod driving off the cliff. I mean, why would he do a thing like that?"

"Because his girlfriend brushed him."

"What?"

"He's got a big thing for your ex-maid..."

"Carmen? She turned him down? Nobody would believe that."

"I checked it out. You'd have no trouble proving it, if the coroner gets nosey."

"Carmen turned him down," she repeated dully. "That little bitch. I can't even remember her last name."

"Ochoa," I said. "She's fourteen years old."

"That bastard," she said, "Do you have to drive off the cliff with him?"

"There's no other way. We have to clear the rocks at high speed in order to land in the water. And it would look suspicious otherwise—you don't suicide yourself at ten miles an hour. Your guests might think he wasn't putting his heart in it."

She squeezed my arm. "I don't want anything to happen to you," she said. "That part of it worries me." I saw no reason to challenge the statement. Not at this time.

In a weary, faraway voice she said, "I wonder—is it worth it? What we're doing, when it all could be avoided. If only he'd just be reasonable. He wouldn't even miss the money, especially with this new deal he's got."

"What new deal?" I hadn't mentioned the merger.

"A few months ago, when I was working in his office, he was trying to put together some kind of big deal in Mexico. Enormous."

"Real estate?"

"I don't know the particulars—he was... very secretive about it. But I'm not as stupid as he thinks. One of his problems, he thinks that everybody's stupid and that everybody adores him, and..."

"What was the deal? Try to remember."

"It had something to do with an island."

"Where?"

A few feet away an old peckerwood in a tennis visor was weeping softly at the grave of a poodle named Cricket. ("So Much Love In So Small A Package.")

"An island off Baja," she said. "I don't know its name. It had something to do with a man called Voodoo."

"Voodoo? You ever see him?"

She shook her head. "This Voodoo called Tod constantly. I think he was a chemist or something." She narrowed her eyes in thought. "Once I remember Tod laughed at something this Voodoo must have said, and Tod said 'I'd call it monkey business. What do they call it in your chemistry textbooks?'—something like that. That's what he said—'monkey business.'" She frowned. "And there was another time Tod said, 'We'll have no trouble getting the girls. And some goons to keep order.' And once Tod mentioned curbs and restraints."

"Government restraints?"

"No. I think he meant like… restraining irons, leather thongs, that sort of thing."

"You think this Voodoo could be a code name? I mean it sounds like he's in business with the Marquis de Sade."

"Who's that?"

"Nothing," I said. "What do you mean, restraining irons?"

Her face twisted in puzzlement. "Well," she said, "in the office he won't let me do anything but open the mail for that old bag in charge. So one day I opened this bill and it's for chains, manacles, shackles and… and… What the hell do you suppose…?"

"I haven't a clue."

She sighed and twisted her face again. "I bet," she said, "the sonofabitch has gone off the deep end. Still, a big lump of that island should be mine. Yours too, like I said. That's where your end's coming from when you… you know."

"My end?"

"I can't—I can't just pay you in cash, Jack. It wouldn't look right. But I know that island's tied up in something—there's real money there, or Tod wouldn't give it half a glance. And you're an agent—you'd just have to work out the sale…"

"We'll keep in touch." I said. It all amounted to another complication I wasn't interested in just now. I brushed my lips against her forehead. She clung to me. Her yellow hair blew in my face. I felt a shiver run through her body.

"You're shivering," she said.

She was right. I'd have to get my ganglions in order, to shift into high gear for the task I'd set for myself. The melodrama I had pitched her—my crouching in the back of the bastard's car, bouncing a lead weight hard but not too hard off his patrician skull, speeding over the cliff and into the black sea, planting him behind the wheel of the Rolls as I twisted away from it, leaving him to drown in the kelp while I swam to the beach five hundred yards away, dragging myself through the sand and seaweed and broken glass, finding my car where I'd parked it—the script in its entirety was B-picture preposterous. But it was the best I could come up with, and Tod deserved every bit of it, as far as I was concerned.

That night brought nothing but Jerry Fleet. He dropped in on us bearing a coffee cake with the sales tag still on it, a bottle of slaughterhouse wine, and my severance check. He said that Senior would give me a glowing reference, that he hated to see me go, that at this juncture there was nothing they could do without blowing the merger. He was damned decent about the whole mess. But then the purpose of his house call dawned on me: Senior had no idea why Hunt had lowered the boom, particularly after we had gotten along so famously. He had sent Jerry to find out.

I let Jerry know that my dismissal had nothing to do with business. In view of Tod's imminent demise, I certainly didn't want to appear before Jerry as a prime suspect. So I spoke well and easily of Hunt, the dirty cocksucker, saying it was nothing really, simply that our styles didn't jell, and Jerry was impressed by my sturdy fortitude. After he drank the wine and ate three-fourths of the day-old cake, he shared with us his latest obsession: soap, which burned your eyes out, and why didn't some detergent smart-ass do something about it? Then he shook my hand like a little gentleman, repeating that he was sorry, that I was the only warm body in the office he could talk to.

"Anyhow, I'd just as soon bop off on my own," I told him.

Gayle was silent a long while after he left. Then: "What are you going to do?" she asked.

"Maybe I'll become an astronaut."

"I mean seriously."

"I don't know."

"Have you thought about maybe going back to college?"

"No." I glanced at her sharply.

"But that was a long time ago, what happened. Nobody'd remember." She walked over to the chair and stood looking down at me. "You were the hotshot of the English Department—"

"It wasn't much of an English Department."

"—with a vocabulary big as a rock. Piling up straight A's until the trouble. You would have had your degree in a few more months."

"I couldn't get back into college wherever I applied. They'd want a transcript. They'd find out what happened and I'd never get in."

"It wouldn't be in the transcript."

"A letter would accompany it."

"Then forget the transcript. Start again."

I said nothing.

"I'd work while you went to school," she said, melting into my lap.

"I don't think I could endure such saintly self-sacrifice."

"It's more like the repayment of an overdue debt. After all, I was responsible for—"

"It wasn't your fault."

"—what you did." She heaved a heavy sigh. "It was because of me."

"You're getting all anguished up over nothing."

"How can you say 'nothing'?"

"What I mean, I'm not going back to school. Case closed."

"What do you want to do?"

I didn't answer. Her undeflectable interrogation was getting increasingly painful.

"What about writing screenplays? Full time? We could move to a smaller place."

"I got a problem, Gayle. A secret I'll let you in on…"

She frowned, blinked.

"Thing is," I said, "I can't even come up with a springboard for a script. It's like I've got an incurable case of writer's block before I even start writing. So…"

"Something will come along," she said. "All you need is one good break."

We might have wallowed in the Trappist silence that followed for hours. But after not more than five minutes the phone shrieked.

I thought, That nut—calling me at home again. I scrambled for the phone, launching Gayle off my lap like a barrel of crabs.

"Hello!" I challenged, a rasp in my voice.

"Hello, Jack," Tod Hunt said smoothly. "How are you?"

"At what?" I managed to answer. "What do you want, Tod?"

"I want to tell you that my clearest thoughts come at this time of evening. And my cloudiest come late at night. I want you to know that all is forgiven, and my broken arm is healing nicely."

I didn't answer.

"Okay?"

A few hours ago, in a solid alliance with Darlene, I had committed to kill the hell out of him. I was going to take his wife and his money and everything he'd built. And now, suddenly, here he was troubling to hustle me back to an armchair beside his fireplace.

Patiently he said, "Jack, you still there?"

"Yeah."

"Well?"

"All right," I said.

"Good. And you hit it on the head, I must say."

"Hit what on the head?"

"About what precious little time we all have—carpe diem, gathering rosebuds—that sort of thing."

"Yeah?"

"So this is what I'd like you to do: See Miss Ochoa as soon as possible— tomorrow. Find out if she'd accept a Tijuana marriage. Come in tomorrow evening and let me know."

"All right," I said again.

"Good. See you tomorrow." He hung up.

I turned to Gayle. "We can forget screenplays," I said.

EIGHT

I took her to the finest Mexican restaurant in LA, which was a mistake. The food was Anglo-crisp-napkin Hispanic, not chili-scorched oilcloth. She ordered *huachinango*, took one bite, fluttered her tongue against her palate, and daintily put down her fork. Nothing; her taste buds had been burned out six months after she was weaned. And so we pressed onward to Thirty-One Flavors, where she packed away four vast scoops of green ice cream flecked with marshmallow, veined with taffy. A half hour later, driving down Sunset, she was still sucking contentedly at the caramel glued to her braces.

Where could I take her? Any public place, a bar, a coffee shop, was out. I was enjoined to introduce—reintroduce, to be precise—a certain sticky issue; how would she respond? I sidled a glance at her, sitting primly beside me in the compact, that glazed and dreamy look on her face (perhaps it was the four scoops of luscious zesty ambrosia mint honeycomb butter-brickle beatifiers). Nothing excites her, I thought; she carries a low pulse rate. Yet I was fearful of an ugly scene in public. Would the mere whisper of Hunt's name activate screams, sobs, the furious stomping of *huaraches*, her hot little claws branding scars on my cheek? Who wants to set off firecrackers under a fourteen-year-old sorceress with long nails?

So we drove on, I peering desperately through the neon night for a place to drop anchor.

"So you want to go to UCLA…" I ventured, my voice brimming with avuncular warmth.

"Yes."

"To be a nurse, right?"

"No. I don't know where he got that idea." She slouched in the far corner, quite relaxed, toying with a button on her blouse. Wearing an outfit of her own choosing, not Tod Hunt's, she was a sitting pinball machine. Her blouse of scarlet and cyanine swirls might have been used to clean old paintbrushes. A pair of burnt orange slacks and an intricate tangle of Woolworth jewelry completed the ensemble. It hit you between the eyes; it must have rattled the seismograph at Cal Tech.

"Are you rich?" she asked.

"God, no. What gave you that idea?"

"You do not laugh much. It would not surprise me if you were a real rich man."

I forced a cackle. "What do you want to be?" I asked. "I mean, if not a nurse…?"

"Do you watch the football and the basketball on the television?"

"Sometimes."

"I want to be a pom-pom girl, one who dances when there is the time-out. I would study to be a dancer on the TV."

"That's a large ambition."

"Yes," she said solemnly. "I am a sprightly dancer, fantastic. I have seen Anglo girls and black girls and Oriental girls do the football dancing, but never a Spanish girl. I would like to be the first of my country to dance with the pom-poms."

I turned north on Highland and cut sharply, for reasons I cannot explain, into the Hollywood High School parking lot. Night classes were in session. The lot was full. I jockeyed the car into an area with a sign on the fence reading AUTHORIZED VEHICLES ONLY. Three reserved spaces were empty, each with its stenciled legend: NURSE, VOCATIONAL GUIDANCE, and GIRLS VICE-PRINCIPAL. All three, I thought, were suitable in my case. I pulled into GIRLS VICE-PRINCIPAL, which felt singularly appropriate.

I twisted the ignition key and the engine gasped into silence. "This is

Hollywood High School," I said, "where Lana Turner was discovered."

"Oh?" She said. "What was she doing?" I looked at her quizzically. "Who," she went on, "is Lana Turner?"

"She was a great star of the cinema. The Señor Hunt could arrange for you to attend the school of Lana Turner and then UCLA..."

"Is that why you asked me to dinner? To start that up again?"

"What did you think?"

"I thought you were interested in seeing me. For yourself, and not for your patron."

"I'm too old for you."

"*You're* too old...?!" Her ebony eyes flashed scornfully.

I had anticipated a certain amount of resistance, of thrust and parry, but certainly not in this vein.

"Would you consider the Señor Hunt's most generous proposal if it included marriage?"

"Most assuredly not!"

"Why not?"

"He's a *gusano*." Her lips curled with loathing. "How do you say that in English?"

"*Worm*. Why is he a worm?"

"He is depraved. A pervert."

"What?"

"He wanted me..." She had bent forward in the seat, incurving her spine, dropping her head. I could not hear the mumble of words that followed.

"Tell me."

"...To... to p-put his... *miembro* in my mouth."

So that was it. There was something brutal and bizarre about Hunt's proposal, something deeply and disturbingly personal. Bainbridge and MacDevit scurried around my skull again. I shook my head violently to make the rats go away. "Suppose," I said, "the Señor Hunt were to give you his solemn word never to try that again? Would you consent to marry him?"

She shrugged. She said, "I do not know." And then, "The contract is for ten years, is it not?"

I nodded.

"In that case," she went on, "I would accept the contract without marriage. I do not wish to be a divorced woman in my twenties."

Carmen was staring at me through half-closed, unfocused eyes. "Although," she mumbled, "maybe… if I became the wedded wife of the Señor Hunt, would I not receive greater respect in his eyes and therefore gain greater control in my relationship with him?" She raised her finger to her mouth, little white teeth gnawing on the nail. "Then there is this to consider," she went on, like a sedulous philosopher dissecting twenty aspects of every premise. "Would not the Señor Hunt's authority be unrestricted if we were wed? I will not be his pawn for ten years."

"May I make a suggestion? As a friend?"

"Please."

"There is one way," I said, "that you might, as it is said, have your cake and eat it."

"There is no such thing as having your cake and eating it."

"What about a Mexican marriage in Tijuana? A marriage to enhance your security, and yet not a marriage, for it is outside your church."

"But is he not married? I have met his wife."

"He would be willing to get a divorce," I lied. She was silent for a moment.

Then: "It is good of you to think of me," she said. "I like that idea."

"I'm very fond of you," I said.

She took my hand and squeezed it.

"Now that it is settled," she said, "will you take me dancing?"

"I don't dance well."

"Good," she said. "I will teach you."

I turned on the engine. She slid across the seat, nestling against me, her head on my shoulder. "I am a fantastic dancer," she told me again.

"*Pervert*, she called me? *Depraved*?" Tod Hunt laughed pleasantly, fussing with the cast on his arm, the elephant in the room we both intended to ignore.

"She's not terribly sophisticated, sexually," I said.

"Or any other way. She's a poor, unenlightened member of a minority ethnic group. People like that are only interested in piledriver fucking—you know that."

"If you knew that," I said stiffly, "why'd you steamroll her for a head job?"

He switched on a tolerant grin. "You're a prude," he said. "And like most prudes, you're a romantic." He got to his feet, paced the length of his office, and leaned gracefully against the glossy wooden mantel of the fireplace. For a split second I thought he was on the trail of a fire iron, like old times. Instead, "You must understand," he went on, "getting laid in a car can be an acrobatic ordeal at my age. At my age, you begin to wonder, like a skier who breaks his leg, about whoever said it was fun in the first place. It never occurred to me that she was as prudish as you are."

"I'm not," I insisted. "And she's not exactly an ice maiden. She just felt your approach was an abnormal reduction of her dignity."

"Good lord," he scoffed. "She'll learn soon enough that the only sexual abnormality is abstinence." He looked at me peevishly. "Why are you being so counterproductive? You want me to say that I won't do it again?"

"That's what she wants you to say. I'm only the messenger."

"All right. I won't do it again."

"In that case, you've got yourself a bride. Congratulations."

He snorted.

"And now," I said, "what are you going to do about your old one?"

"What old one?"

"Your wife. You'll have to pay her off."

"Not me. I thought we'd been through all that. I told you—"

"You're flirting with bigamy. That could be more expensive than alimony payments."

He began to pace again, silently. Then, "About Mrs. Hunt," he said, absently picking up the riding crop on the mantel of the fireplace. The rays of the late-afternoon sun slanted through the window and caught him in their incandescence. "Once more, dear boy, I'm depending on you."

"What would you like?"

"What would I like? I'd like you to push something heavy on her. I'd like you to step on her neck, to send her a letter bomb."

"Seriously..."

He looked at me hard. "Seriously," he said. He lowered himself into the armchair. Carefully he crossed his legs, "I've been considering it," he went on, intertwining his long elegant fingers. He said, "I hear you can buy a hit in this town rather easily. I've been wondering what it might cost."

"I have no idea."

He looked at me. "You've done well in a sticky situation," he said.

"You'll be amply rewarded when the time comes."

"What time is that?"

"The time to erase her," he said.

I didn't answer. In the guarded silence each of us waited for feedback.

The phone rang. Tod picked it up at the coffee table. "Yes, Ms. Velasquez—I'll call him back." He listened for a moment. Then, "All right," with irritable resignation. "Put him on." Immediately, "Hello…? Why do they need the check today? Why do you want to take the… gear… south tonight? How much? Repeat the name—spell it." Then, "Okay, Voodoo, I'll send it by messenger." He hung up. Turning to me, he said, "You could do it. You have the mentality for it."

"What do you mean," I asked, "I have the mentality for it?"

"Before I go into business with a man," Tod said, "I want to learn a bit about him. Not unusual, you know. I found out, for instance, why you worked for Fleet—no truly legit company would touch you because of what happened when you came back from Iraq. Like a drink?"

I shook my head. He poured himself three fingers of yellow Canary. For a moment he rolled it on his tongue.

"When you came back," he said, "you went to a small, almost invisible college up north. Where you got into a brawl with two men you damn near beat to death with your bare hands."

"I didn't kill them," I said.

"It looked as if you sure as hell tried to. I don't know why, or why the whole mess was hushed up—it wasn't clear in my report. Whatever the reason, I'd say you were eminently qualified to… et cetera, et cetera, for which I would of course reward you handsomely. One million seems appropriate."

He crossed to his desk and opened the lower-right drawer. He pulled out a checkbook, wrote a check, recorded it on the attached voucher, split the two parts along the perforations, returned everything to the drawer but the check. He pressed a desk button; Ms. Velasquez floated in. He handed her the check and she floated out, closing the door behind her.

"Anything else?" I asked Tod.

"I don't think so," he said with a tight smile. "There's no one else I want put away just now."

He reached out with his cast-enclosed arm. We shook fingers with the hollow solemnity of undertakers.

*   *   *

I went to bed before midnight, bushed. I was afraid to close my eyes; I had to be up at two to meet the next exaction of my schedule. Staring into nothingness, I lay there on the bed until my eyes grew so accustomed to the dark I could make out the non-luminous face of my watch, the opaque spittle caking a corner of Gayle's sleep-swollen mouth.

I had, unhappily, no trouble staying awake; there was much to be troubled about. Hunt expected me to kill Darlene who expected me to kill Hunt who expected me to kill Darlene. Their faces blurred and dissolved, displaced by the bloody, broken faces of Donald MacDevitt and Carter Bainbridge. Out of the pursuing past they paraded across the night, plaguey ghosts exhumed by Tod Hunt... *two men you damn near beat to death with your bare hands.*

If only Gayle had walked away when they'd launched their attack on her. If only she'd ignored them. Instead, when the clowning began (if clowning it was) she had giggled, they thought, encouragingly. And if only they hadn't mistaken her nervous calliope laughter for sexual excitement (possibly their own). Or if she had feigned unawareness, or controlled her hysteria, or if it had found another outlet, or if she hadn't been so perturbed by her lousy grades. If she had stalled a bit to examine her predicament, if she had handled it (in any of a hundred ways), if she hadn't come running to me, so hurt and embarrassed, hot tears coursing down her cheeks. They had acted inappropriately, she sobbed.

Gayle Wyman was seventeen and a freshman when we met at our rather casual though accredited undergraduate academy, a gray muddle of stone and blinkered windows which rose on the edge of a prairie town hardly celebrated for a Rabelaisian variety of diversions. The county, of which it was the seat, boasted more bovines than people. The people who were there, town and gown, didn't find the school too stimulating, but they seemed to think that football was the most riveting of man's inventions and as bracing as their belief in God, their love of country, their reverence of motherhood, and their worship of cows.

Nature had never meant Gayle to be a student, although she did well in Introductory Spanish. Understandably, she spoke the language, having been raised by a succession of Chicana housekeepers. But at the end of her first semester she was hopelessly flunking two of her four solids, English and

Math. No amount of cramming or coaching on my part seemed to help. She was bright enough, much brighter in fact than most of the clods blithely cresting the academic waves. But Gayle at sixteen had a problem: she was one of those imperfectly beautiful girls who thought she was stupid and therefore at times responded as if she were.

She had gone to see Bainbridge, her English teacher, and found him with his friend MacDevitt, who taught math. They eyed her appreciatively. She always looked dishy, radiating sex the way most bodies emanate heat. Men were always casting her all wrong, and Bainbridge and MacDevitt were no exceptions.

"What have we here?" Bainbridge asked as she entered his office. "After all that fat meat and lumpy potatoes in class, here comes the dessert."

"The cherry on the parfait!" MacDevitt added. They were in their late twenties. Both of them were adept, they thought, at turning a phrase.

Bainbridge grinned at MacDevitt. "I am staggered," he said gleefully, "at Miss Wyman's resistance to the Romantic poets."

"It seems inconceivable," MacDevitt said, "that Miss Wyman could resist a romantic poet."

"Or peasant. Or plumber."

"Or mathematician." MacDevitt winked a beady eye. "Lead me into indiscretion, Miss Wyman," he pleaded.

They were beginning to get carried away, intoxicated by their own cleverness. Gayle forced a smile and looked from one to the other with bewildered deference. After all, they were teachers.

Bainbridge was a heavy dude. It might be said of him that he was in one respect the absolute opposite of Gayle: he thought he was sexy and he wasn't. He had a habit of standing in his tight Levi's with his thumbs hooked in his back pockets, body arched, leading with his crotch as though it were his center of gravity. His long, acned face was almost lipless. He wore so many rings on his left hand that he listed to port. Like so many bad teachers he had the omniscient air of a branch-bank manager.

"What can I do for you, Miss Wyman?" he asked.

"I was wondering..." Gayle hesitated, "...if there was anything I could do about my grades?"

Bainbridge threw up his hands in an exaggerated gesture of despair. MacDevitt exploded with a bark of appreciative laughter. He was a frail, triangular-shaped man with a small head, a trivial head. He had eyes that jutted out of his tallow-colored face like cupcakes.

"Tell you what I'll do," Bainbridge said thoughtfully. "That is—if you're in the mood for a little conspiracy?" Gayle looked at him uncomprehendingly.

"I'll pass you," he went on, "if you screw me."

"What about me?" MacDevitt barked excitedly. "I'll give you an A if you suck my dick."

He unzipped his fly and with his other hand reached out and touched the tip of her breast. She let out a cry and ran. MacDevitt's reduplicating laughter pursued her down the hall.

They were still there when I walked stiff-legged into the office. My expression must have told them what to expect. I was for some reason terribly aware of the electric clock making erratic tin noises on the bookcase. Like everything else in that damned school, there was something wrong with it. I moved in on Bainbridge like a gorilla with a blowtorch up its ass. He took a step backward, looking aggrieved. His face crumpled when I hit him. MacDevitt winced in sympathy. He threw himself excessively erect, as if he were in a trance, and then he bolted for the door. I low-bridged him and he went down against the side of the desk, hard. I turned back to Bainbridge. I hit him until my fists hurt. I jammed my thumbs in the corners of his mouth and pulled them apart. He screamed as the flesh split jaggedly and his blood spilled over my fingers. An untransmissible sound bubbled from the hole in his face and he closed his eyes and was unconscious.

I pulled MacDevitt to his feet. I had a good pop at him but I missed and he ran. I grabbed his shoulder and spun him around, a stunned plea for mercy in his eyes. He covered his face with his palms and blindly lurched forward, like a man running a gamut of broadswords. I hit him anyway. His breath struggled in his throat, a hoarse, scalded whistle. He gave off a smell like month-old crabmeat. It was not only fear; he had shit himself. I hit him again. He squirted across the room before he fell.

I stood there wheezing, surveying the remains of those two presumptuous fleas. I walked away, the smell of blood and shit commingling, clinging to me. Gayle and I left school that same afternoon.

So much for flashbacks. But the nightmare—the savagery of it all— was still on me when I pulled into a side street near Hunt Realty. I walked half a block, listing to my left; inside my trench-coat pocket were the tools I'd need to break into Tod's office and nail down a few facts about the island off Baja that Darlene had offered me a piece of, providing she could grab a piece of the monkey business her husband and Voodoo were conducting down there. That was the missing fact, that island. If Tod wasn't going to let me go straight, all the dirt he had on me didn't mean I couldn't still just do him in. Even if everyone expected me to be a killer, I could still choose who to kill. Caught as I was now between opposing schemes, the island, and the ten million Darlene claimed it represented, would be the determinant.

I pulled on a pair of rubber gloves. To jimmy the imposing street door, I started with twisting a credit card. I didn't think it would work; I was right. Then I tried the putty knife. It sprang the door with a tiny jingle.

I followed the pale milky beam of my flashlight to Ms. Velasquez's desk. Opened her log to the day and date.

There it was, under incoming calls: *5:15—Vudukovich*. I moved on to Hunt's desk. His black leather address book was on it, and in it: *Vudukovich, Luther*, with a Westwood address, a phone number, and a second lodging: *Isla San Dismaso, Baja California, D.F., Mexico*. The top-center drawer yielded Tod's checkbook. Beside what would have been the last executed voucher was recorded the payment of $6,383.20 to Bianchi TV Wardrobe and Party Sales, covering the purchase of chains, manacles, canvas fetters, iron shackles, leather thongs, whips and gauntlets, pony harness, and brass-studded dog collars.

I turned to the lower-right double drawer of Tod's desk. In it was a safe, a squat, overweight iron box, locked of course, and refusing to yield to my putty knife. I slipped the sharp steel edge of my chisel into the slit between the front panel and the frame, tugged, jiggled, and Holy God Sweet Jesus Christ, I flew on sheer terror straight up in the agitated air, blasted by the mad clangor of the security system that pounded me temples to toenails. Panic later, I told myself.

With deliberate speed I got the hell out of there. I could still hear the din an hour afterward, in the kip with the covers pulled over my head. I couldn't believe Gayle could continue to sleep through its intensity.

NINE

The morning after my semi-successful raid I returned to the scene. Double-parked in front of the building were two Beverly Hills police cars, their cherry beacons rotating on the light bar.

Inside the reception room were two uniformed cops, a detective in mufti, and a technician in a jumpsuit with MASTER SECURITY CORP. emblazoned on the back. I stutter-stepped through the throng and ducked into Tod's sanctum.

He said, "Close the door."

"What's going on?"

"Some oaf tried to break in here last night."

"Get anything?"

"I don't think so." He gestured to an empty armchair. "Sit down."

I sat, uncomfortably aware of the cops in the next room.

"The time has come—" He was interrupted by a sharp knock on the door. It opened without invitation. In the threshold stood a ginger-colored man in a grungy suit. He had stiff red hair and skin like a bad cut of beef. The mouth was large, thin-lipped, the eyes flat and brown. A small, crescent-shaped scar on the right temple. He wore a short-sleeved shirt and a tie. Three or four ballpoint pens protruded from a transparent plastic case in his shirt pocket.

"I'm Detective Sergeant Joseph Laudermilk," he said, "Beverly Hills

Police." He held up his wallet to prove it. "I want to check your bathroom."

"Why?" Tod asked crossly, annoyed at the intrusion.

"Because," Laudermilk explained, "we leave no stone unturned. Also, I got to take a leak." He disappeared through the far door.

Tod glowered after him, silent. Discourse couldn't compete against the sound of Laudermilk's monstrous piss, followed by the fierce cascade of the toilet flushing.

The bathroom door opened. Laudermilk zipped his fly and wiped a thick hand on his pants. Without a word he went through the door to the outer office.

"About Mrs. Hunt," Tod said…

"Hold it a minute." I found his engrossment a bit disturbing with a swarm of cops in the next room, but their proximity did little except to outrage Tod. He seemed to think his attitude toward their presence should be defiant, as if they were invaders violating his privacy.

"I'd like you to do it tonight."

"Let's not be hasty."

"Why not?"

"An operation like this we have to discuss…"

"All right. Let's discuss. Where do you intend to do it?"

"Your place? In Beverly Hills?"

"Most definitely not. She's spending a few days at our house in Malibu." He wrote a number on a piece of paper. "Here's where you find her," he said.

I reached out for the slip. He pulled back. "Commit it to memory," he said, and I made some slight pretense of complying, as if I didn't know Darlene's address.

"What's she doing there?" I asked, still trying to decelerate.

"What she always does. Plants her ass on the edge of the cliff, communing with nature. She's got a thing about the beach—the kelp bed, whales."

Again I stalled, but the best I could come up with was, "Hmmm…"

Irritably he said, "It's your call. You can hack her to death with a machete, step on her neck, bludgeon her or squash her like a bug or put holes in her with dumdums—but I'd like to know."

His eyes held a sheen of excitement; rather than cut short our parley he wanted to extend it with details, minutiae. What could I come up with that would seem lurid enough to satisfy his bloodlust?

Suddenly I knew what to tell him—a certain exquisite departure from what I told her I'd do to him. I'd break into the beach house, take care of her, then go back to the car, slip on my wetsuit, secure the regulator to the air tank, and belt the weights around my hips. Then, returning to Darlene, I'd peel off her nightclothes—it would best be done in the middle of a foggy night. I'd carry her down the steep path snaking to the sea. I'd swim with her to the kelp bed. Holding her by the hair, I'd dive deep among the windrows, thick and intertwined, like shackles of steel flex. And there...

"Well?" Tod asked.

"In that kelp bed you mentioned," I said, and when I finished he stared at me for a long time.

"Imprisoned," he said finally, "in the kelp. She'll be safe—if that's the word—and nothing can spring her loose—"

"Not even a seaquake."

"—before the fish have at her. That's good," he went on, "Christ, that's good." He leaned back, thoughtfully tweaking the tip of his regal nose.

"Not even a corpus delicti." His grin turned into a frown. "You said it should be a foggy night?"

"It would be better."

"When's the next foggy night?"

I shrugged.

He went to his desk, opened the LA *Times* to the weather page. "Not tonight," he said. "Not tomorrow."

"It could change fast. You know the beach."

Again the frown. "Okay," he said, "so would you please phone Miss Ochoa, pick her up, and settle her in her new digs?"

I tooled toward the inner city enshrouded in smog to the Casa Ochoa. Confined to an insipid fifty mph, I was overtaken, cut off, yawped at, fingered, and otherwise violated by the kamikazes of the freeway. And then I damned near racked up the car as my phone buzzed louder than it had ever buzzed before.

"Jack," Jerry Fleet hollered, "we got to take a meet."

"What's up?"

"Where are you?"

"Ten minutes from the office. Can't it wait?"

"I'll meet you in ten minutes at… Swanson's."

"Where?"

"The ice cream store across from the office."

"What are we going to do there? Play unnatural games?"

"Where do you want to meet?"

"I don't. What about the bar a couple doors from Swanson's?"

"I thought you didn't drink."

"You bring out the worst in me."

"Okay. In ten minutes." He hung up.

TEN

I stood inside the door, afflicted by a bad case of snow-blindness until my eyes adjusted to the palpable darkness of the bar. An unmistakable voice called, "Over here." Slowly Jerry took shape, his body canted forward over a drink, the skinny forearms shielding it as if he were afraid Senior might stride in and take it away from him. Beside him where he sat was an attaché case of imitation oilcloth.

Jerry pushed his bull-rider hat back on his forehead, revealing the pistol-grip sideburns like parentheses enclosing his mad little eyes. He pinched one cigarette from a pack in the smile pocket of his piped and darted shirt and scratched a wooden match on the sole of a wing-tipped, two-toned boot with an inlaid shaft of red stitchwork. It was difficult to determine the nexus between the western threads and the attaché case, but Jerry was fond of both. Poor bastard, yearning for clean air and tumbleweed, unwittingly born in Baltimore and set down in LA, that hotbed of batshit and vanity. He blew a cloud of smoke in my face.

He said, "Just what the fuck you up to?"

"What do you mean?"

"I mean," he leaned across the table, "I know things that could make you pale." His bolo tie, dangling over his glass, dove in. The aglets clinked dully on the ice and submerged. He fished them out, dried them on a paper napkin. "I mean Mrs. George Norton, that's what I mean."

"What about her?"

"You on the ball or are you stumbling over your own prick?"

"Jerry," I said, "you trying to jack me up? Who the hell you think you are?"

"You're fulla shit, that's who I am!" He reached down, fumbled with the catch of the attaché case. He took a large, unwieldy volume by the paper spine and dropped it on the table with a thud that rattled his bowl of nachos. "You familiar with this?" he asked.

I squinted in the gloom. "The telephone book?"

He nodded. "You ought to be. The office subscribes to it."

"Jesus," I said.

"You wouldn't give me the time of day about Mrs. Norton—what's going on. If I asked you once I must've asked you twenny times. So I called her." He looked at me and smiled nastily. "Don't drop your teeth—I couldn't get her number. 'Not listed,' the operator said, unlisted, like so many of those fuckheads in Malibu. So I call a friend in the business office of the phone company. She's not unlisted—she's not listed at all. He patted the volume between us on the table. "So I look her up in our street directory, the back-wards book." He was relishing his moment of glory—Jerry Fleet, nonesuch cowboy-detective. "Shall I go on?" he asked.

I said nothing.

"You know and I know there ain't no Mrs. Norton," he continued. "That house is occupied by Mrs. Tod Hunt and it's owned by *Mr.* Tod Hunt." He took a bite out of his drink and leaned back, enormously pleased with himself. "What's the matter?" he grinned. "Cat got your tongue?"

The son of a bitch was trying to take me over, and such was the tilt of his mind that he wanted me to add my kudos to his self-congratulatory tale. Fuck him. But—

"Jerry," I said, "I got to hand it to you."

"Don't give me that horse-hocky."

"You solved the mystery."

"What're you tryna pull?"

"She's fucking bonkers. That's why he keeps her in the deep freeze, way the hell and gone up the coast."

He was staring at me, puzzled. "What's the matter with her?"

"Manic-depressive. Paranoid."

"How'd you find out?"

"She also has delusions of omnipotence, grandiosity."

"What's that mean?"

"It means five minutes after I got there she was dropping Tod Hunt's name all over the rug. Playing the lady. Mrs. Tod Hunt this and Mrs. Tod—"

"He know?"

"That she's nuts? I just told you—"

"That she's trying to sell their house?"

"Sure. It pains him. He hates to talk about it."

"How do you know that?"

"How do I know? Because that's why he fired me—remember? I thought I'd better let him know, but it pained him so he didn't ever want to see me again. So he canned me."

"Why'd he take you back?"

"He realized he was being unfair. He's a decent man."

"Decent!" Jerry snorted. "That pigfucker wants everything and gives nothing. A hundred and ten percenter. You don't know how tough it's been trying to close the Mexico deal with him. Shitfire," he went on, "you got me going around in circles."

I hoped so. "I hope you haven't told Senior..."

"I told nobody. I wanted to check it out with you." He glowered at me—eyeballs blazing out of that tame, forgettable face, the face of a windup toy, a bed-wetter—as if he were trying to mesmerize the resistant truth out of me. He asked, "You sure it's not something else?"

"What else could it be?"

"How the hell do I know? I thought maybe you were humping her." He snickered. "Eating off Hunt's plate."

"Jesus, Jerry..." I saddened my voice and shook my head, keenly disappointed in him.

"What'll I tell Hunt now?"

"Why should you tell him anything? It could blow the whole deal for Fleet and Fleet, if he gets pained again."

"But I got to tell him something," he said uncomfortably. "The bastard was bragging on the mint properties he's bringing into the deal, and I told him we had a few piss-elegant listings of our own—you know, for leverage.

And he said What for instance and I said I'd let him know."

"Tell him something else."

"What? Without Four Pines—which it turns out he owns—we got a choice collection of crap houses." He sighed in quiet torment. "That prick owns everything," he said enviously. "Christ knows what else he's got."

"You'll think of something." I got to my feet. "Something in Mexico," I suggested. "Some island off Baja he's never heard of. That should arouse his interest. But before you do anything, let's the two of us discuss it, okay? We don't want to cock up the deal for Senior, right?"

"Where you going? What's up?"

"Jer," I said, losing my patience, "My job is to close the deal with Hunt. It's an ongoing gig, with no such thing as a day off."

He grunted, scowled, downed his drink, waved to the waitress to order another, changed his mind, threw a bill on the table, and together, like good old drinking buddies, we sallied forth to the parking lot. He got into his car, I got into mine. A block away I was still in a sweat.

Driving. Up the ramp onto the thrombotic freeway. Carmen Ochoa beside me and, on the back seat in a cardboard carton, all the treasures and trappings of her fourteen years.

"Have you seen the place?" I asked her.

"I have seen neither the place nor the Señor Hunt."

"It is most pleasant," I said.

"Does it have the television?"

"A magnificent television, with an ingenious implementation for the Spanish broadcasts." She was not impressed. A blankness, even dreaminess, seemed to possess her.

"You may divert yourself with the Spanish cinema."

"The speech of actors is not diverting," she said flatly. "It is an absurdity."

I shot off the freeway at Vineland, hung a right on Ventura Boulevard. Heavy traffic, the drones homing to their hives.

"How is your family?"

She shrugged.

"I didn't see them when I gathered you up."

"My father is at the shop for the sports, to buy a good knife."

"In case something needs cutting?"

Again she shrugged. "He is a rich man now. He must protect his wealth. And every man should have a good knife—you never can tell when..."

"Your mother?"

"She visits her cousins. We have an abundance of cousins." She paused, her eyes casing the dreary street for something of interest. "Napoleon is gone," she said, "since last week. I do not know where."

"He left no word?"

"He never does. It is not the first time."

He's partying, I thought. Celebrating his good fortune. The old man buys a knife, the old lady brags to her *primas*, and Napoleon splits. He wouldn't be back until all the tequila was gone.

"It is his way," Carmen said with a sister's tolerance. "It is the way he enlarges his capacity—by traveling." She was staring fixedly through the windshield, watching the neon signs explode in the sky like tired fireworks:

MORE MONEY MAX

THE BEST USED CARS

and in pygmy letters under it—

ARE IN LOVERS LANE

SE HABLA ESPANOL

"Your indulgence, please. Over there..." It was the bottom line that caught Carmen's attention. "About what is Spanish spoken?"

"About the autos. The buying and selling."

"Your permission?" She hesitated, her hand on the radio knob. I nodded. She twisted the dial to a Spanish station and we were drowned in a lachrymose love song. She sang along in a sugary whisper, unconsciously imitating the soloist until: "Your indulgence—" she pointed a slim finger toward a fast-food shack plastered with more signs of self-praise than there seemed space to hold them.

ANDY'S CASA GRANDE

THE BEST MEAT IN TOWN

IF YOU CAN'T EAT IT—BEAT IT

MIXED GRILL—TACOS AND CHOP SUEY

WHERE ALL THE CHINESE TRUCK DRIVERS EAT

"Why is that place so denominated?"

"Casa Grande?"

"Only to midgets is it a casa grande."

"It is a joke."

"I do not find hilarity in it." And then, "Hola!" Her eyes held on an animated monstrosity, a neon girl high in the sky churning her pelvis and tossing her overwrought hips. There was something painfully harsh and rachitic about her exertions, reminiscent of a silent movie. Beneath her the pulsating ruby red letters proclaimed

THE FRENCH LICK

TOPLESS-LIVE-BOTTOMLESS

OPEN ALL NIGHT

A HOT FISTFUL OF ENTERTAINMENT

"The girl has a nervous disorder?"

"Possibly."

"The place is a clinic for such maladies?"

"It is a cantina. The girl dances."

"What kind of dancing is that?"

"It is an art form not unlike the basketball dancing, but without the pom-poms. Or much else, for that matter."

She stared at the parking lot full of cars with welts of chrome.

"Would they do Coca-Cola in the cantina?"

"Coca-Cola and other things."

"It is a *lupanar*?"

"No."

"Then I would have there a Coca-Cola."

"I am sorry, Carmen. I am in a large hurry. There is an infinity of Coca-Cola in the new house." I turned the car up into the hills. It panted with the climb.

"Are there eggs and milk and sugar?"

"Are you hungry?"

"I would like to bake a cake."

"There is a plenitude of eggs and such." I smiled at her. "It will be a happy house for you."

"There are no happy houses."

Poor kid, I thought. She'd been through plenty. "A house can be," I said. "It is not impossible."

"A house can only feel sadness," she persisted. "It shows."

"How?"

"By the way it looks—blind and paralyzed, reproachful. Of a certainty you have noticed."

"It *feels*, you say?"

"All things feel. Trees, rocks, streams, houses."

"How do houses feel?"

"Very bad," she said.

Jesus. Another masquerade personality, prime candidate for the asylum. A child, and already she was beginning to sound as squirrelly as Darlene with her seals. "Why do they feel so bad?"

"Because they know that we are people and they are only houses."

We drove up to the house. I swear it looked at me reproachfully. I unlocked the door, handed Carmen the key, then followed her in, carrying the carton. I pulled the curtains. Happy or not, the house had a spectacular view of the Valley; unfortunately it focused on the neon of Ventura Boulevard far below. There was the electric-chair blue of Andy's Casa Grande, the pyrotechnics of More Money Max's, the animated dancer of The French Lick.

Carmen ignored the vista. She didn't so much as glance at the room for longer than it took her to locate the television set. She zeroed in on the Dodgers and the Giants, studying the picture, and then: "I do not understand..." Another moment of dark reverie. "How can it be that the pom-pom girls dance at the football and the basketball but not at the baseball?"

"One of life's imponderables," I said. "I must go now, Carmen."

"Will I see you again?"

"But of course."

"Might I be permitted sometimes to engage you at the telephone and inquire after your health?"

"I'll call you, okay?" I had to get going.

She stared at me for a long moment. "You," she said softly, "are one cold fish." And then she disappeared into the kitchen, and I set out again for the highway. The fog was coming in after all.

ELEVEN

I rang the beach-house bell. In answer the desolate cry of a gull fell out of the black night air.

I had phoned Darlene that afternoon, telling her I'd be over. The announcement was greeted by a bark of mirthless laughter. "I thought you had copped out," she said. Then, "All right," as if she had more important demands on her time, but might manage to squeeze me in for ten minutes.

The door opened. She was wearing a housecoat of red silk slit up the sides, revealing her long slim legs almost to her waist, while a third slit, front and center, started at her shoulders, sloshed over her breasts, and tapered to a V at her waist. Her feet were bare and between her toes were rhinestones, each the size of a purple grape. I was unprepared for all that glitter and flesh. Transfixed.

"Well?" she said sulkily. "Come on in."

The house smelled of brine and dampness despite the heat thrown off by the fire popping and cackling in the fireplace, spewing corkscrews of smoke. The living room was full of driftwood, as if a grove of old trees had shit all over the floor.

In a corner was a deep ceramic bowl on its side, still holding a dozen shoots of gray arthritic timber the way a more gifted person might arrange flowers. It seemed to have been displaced to make room on the coffee table for a clutter of playing cards, sheets of paper marked with untidy Xs and Os, a bungle of red and black checkers on a board, a pair of dice and pachisi discs. She stared at me and I stared at the mess.

Suddenly she broke into tears. She stumbled across the rug to the bowl in the corner and kicked a deep crack in it. "It's k-killing me out here," she sniffed. "It's like I'm in s-solitary c-confinement." Her unhappiness erupted into hysteria. "I've been p-playing solitaire," she wept, "shuffling cards till my hands hurt. I've been p-playing tic-tac-toe and, and checkers and pachisi, taking b-both sides like I'm some kind of deranged. I got an—an allergy. I sneeze and sneeze, that's how I lost some of the checkers someplace, prolly under the goddam couch."

Her body shook, and I wrapped her in my arms. I couldn't even decipher the next rash of words that poured out of her. How could I kill this dopey, over/underdressed, pathetically sad, lonely, lost girl with a petrified bubble hanging out of one nostril and from the other a clot of mucus bouncing off the lapel of her housecoat?

I thought about it. I tried to will myself into whacking her. I could cut short the whole rigmarole if I just did as Tod asked. I could get out of the middle of everything, all the competing agendas, take his seven figures and be done with it, Mexico or no...

She stopped sobbing as quickly as she had started. Again, her face was flushed and sullen. "You're laughing at my bowl of twigs," she said. "Go ahead, laugh, but I did have talent. I did all this research about seals. I was going to do a book or something. And I had other talents. I speak Spanish, sort of, from when I was a little girl in Texas. I had a screen test at Paramount. They said my face didn't hold enough light. I told them to take their light and stick it up their boom box."

She was fast regaining her wildfire petulance. It made her in my eyes a more palatable target than had her tears.

A solitary fly buzzed, dipping and wheeling across the room, then disappeared like Darlene's unrealized potential. A gust of wind billowed the curtains on the open window facing the sea.

Sadly she said, "I could have been something. It bothers me on and off, all the time. All I needed was a push, but he couldn't have given less of a damn. So full of himself there was no room for anybody else, the way rich people get when they get richer and richer and... I wonder," she said in a fraudulent whisper, "I wonder if I'll ever get to be like that?"

"Not a chance," I said.

"What makes you so sure?"

"A carnival swami told me."

She was not amused. "Once," Darlene said, "when I was very young, I went to this fortune teller. 'My dear,' she said, 'I predict great suffering for you.'" She heaved a great actressy sigh. "Yup," Darlene went on, "she hit the goddam nail on the head."

Another gust of foggy wind curled the curtains and demolished the smoke, and I saw what was wrong. She had opened the window to clear the air, which iced the house which spiked the fire which was built to dispatch the cold in the first place.

Why had I come? When I phoned, when I drove over, it hadn't been with any kind of malice aforethought. In fact it had practically been automatic. I'd wanted to see her, I realized. Her husband had ordered me to off her only a few hours ago and instead I'd zombied over here in hopes of another hour or two of easy bliss. I stepped toward her. She ignored me, seemingly unaware of my intentions. She crossed to the bar, poured herself a large shot of gin. As she sipped, "You're screwing it up," she said, recovering her tinderbox voice.

"Screwing what up?" I asked. Her words hit like cold runoff.

"About Tod's exit. You had it all wrong. The idea of me throwing a party—that's what's wrong. I shouldn't be anywhere around when you do it. I have to be above suspicion." She finished off the gin, poured herself another. "You find out anything about Tod's Mexican island?"

"Just its name. San Dismaso," I heard myself saying.

"You've got to go down there," she said.

I stopped. I thought. "I think you're right," I said. She was—

But then a scream of terror rose from her lips, cross-fading into a long hoarse eerie whine of protest. She pointed to the window, wringing her hands at the same time, and in a trance of disbelief we watched the snake as it slithered from under the curtain and crawled sluggishly toward the warmth of the fire.

It was the biggest reptile I had ever seen. The damn thing poured across the hearth with nothing between it and the heat but Darlene. I yelled to her to get out of the way, but my voice was no longer subject to my will. She stood there, rigid, hypnotized. I grabbed a captain's chair, legs pointing at the monster, holding it in one hand while with the other I snared Darlene's wrist and yanked her out of its path. She squealed in pain and came out of her coma, then ran the length of the room and stood there while I switched my attack to the primary target. I raised the chair to bring it down on the wide flat head and out of the corner of my eye another snake, blue and grimy, dipped over the ledge of the window. I looked again—Jesus, I'm up to my ass in snakes—and the blue snake became a long leg in ragged Levi's. And that's how we met young Ralph Farkleberry.

Ralph is an unkempt, bristly-coated animal, all hair and parted in the middle—on his head, on each side of his little mercurochrome eyes, nose, and mouth. Long and thin, the way a barracuda might be considered long and thin, and dressed like a secondhand-store dummy on safari. Pith helmet, belted jacket, bush boots, with a skinning knife strapped to his waist on a thong of rawhide. Stains of coffee, grease, sweat everywhere. Before I'd finished taking it all in he'd draped the boa around his neck with a twisted smile that Darlene somehow found attractive.

Introductions were made, once we caught our breath. A wanderer on the earth, Ralph was presently residing at Zodiac Ridge, the hippie commune on top of Yerba Verde Canyon, he told us. He had infiltrated Four Pines Point to borrow some firewood because Leo was freezing. I could see he was a grifter adept at borrowing anything not tied down, but Darlene was sympathetic— suddenly she was worried about the snake's health.

"Leo?" she asked. "That's his name?"

The grifter nodded. He removed his jacket, feeling right at home, revealing a red and white T-shirt of Raggedy Ann and Andy fucking.

"That's a weird name for a snake," I pointed out. "Leo's a lion."

"Leo's a Leo, zodiac-wise." I didn't think he liked me either.

"That's his *sign*," Darlene explained, as if I lived in a tree. And turning to Farkleberry, "What's yours?"

"Pisces."

"I'm Virgo," she allowed. "You and Leo hungry?"

"Well, I am," Ralph said. "Leo only eats like two-three times a year."

She turned to me. "We'll talk about what we talked about later," she said. "Right now I've got this terrible headache."

It was scattering time; I was being dismissed. Which was all right with me. I'd had enough excitement for one evening. As I was leaving, Ralph announced that he was leaving too, but that he'd be right back.

"Where're you going?" Darlene asked.

"To get my heap parked down by the beach. It's not exactly a heap," he added proudly. "It's a vintage hearse."

"A what?" Tod's eyes narrowed disbelievingly.

"He drives a broken-down hearse," I repeated.

"Clyde Farkleberry." He shook his head incredulously.

"Not Clyde. Ralph."

"Ralph, Clyde." He shrugged indifferently. "I wonder what his name was before he changed it to Farkleberry. And, Lord—with a boa called Leo."

We were at Tod's imperial seat. The living room was roughly the size of the Superdome.

I had called him at midnight from a pay phone, as per instructions, beside a gas station on Pacific Coast Highway. He asked in the code we had agreed upon, "Have you checked out the property on Dribble Drive?"

If Darlene had been thoroughly dispatched I was to have answered yes. But Darlene was alive and full of juice and, by this time, rolling in that mirrored kip with the vagabond. I swallowed hard and said no.

"You'd better come over," Tod said, and here we sat, broken-hearted, in the Superdome at 1:30 a.m., surrounded by more than a dozen dark portraits of antecedent Hunts, each identified by a little brass plaque centered along the base of the frame. Ezra, Thomas, Lawrence, Abraham, many of them peruked, most of them, I thought, severely handsome, all of them evil-eyed.

Tod looked up from his wine, meeting the malevolent leer of an ancestor in the robe of a judge who seemed to be enjoying our little tableau.

"Once again," he said in a low voice, "we seem to be swamped by the flukiness of life." Then, as though he had suddenly impacted the significance of my report, "Is it possible," he said in a voice of astounding mockery, "that I am being fucked over?"

I shrugged, reluctant to comment further. Anything I said, yea or nay, could spark an explosion of his wrath, which would again be directed at me, the messenger of ill tidings, just as it had been when Carmen had rebuffed his overtures. His snottiness would intensify—it was because of my dilatoriness or my ineptitude or my negligence that his wife was shacking with the kid inside that incongruous Raggedy Ann and Andy T-shirt. His eyes clouded; despite his loathing, his contempt for Darlene, he could not accept the idea that the failure of his marriage might have been based on mutual deception.

"You're sure?" he asked again.

I nodded solemnly.

"Maybe you're jumping to untidy conclusions."

"Maybe."

"I mean, maybe he was applying for a job. A houseboy or a handyman or..."

I couldn't believe it. Here he was insisting that Darlene—*Darlene*—led an exemplary life of virtuous self-denial, simply because she was spliced to him.

"Don't take it so hard," I said consolingly.

He stared at me without comprehension. "Take *what* so hard? What are you babbling about?"

"We're stalemated for the moment. We'll just have to regroup."

"Why?"

"The fact that Mrs. Hunt and this kid are..." I hesitated over the operative word.

"Fucking?" He supplied it for me. He chuckled, having a high old time, and shook his handsome head. "You fracture me," he grinned, "although I'm touched by your concern."

"But you seemed..." my voice trailed off in a croak. I felt myself flushing.

"I don't give a damn if she's screwing the kid's snake. I just hope the relationship lasts a bit longer than a one-night stand."

I glanced at him quizzically.

"I want to make sure that the neighbors notice him. That they catch at least some of his sparkle." He sipped his wine thoughtfully. "This Ralph with his hearse is a nutcase—even without the snake, he'd be the obvious suspect for doing her in. He'll take the heat, if there is any, off us."

For a long time he simply sat there, slowly twirling the stem of his wine glass. "Couple of other things," he said. "How did you manage to catch so much of the action at midnight?"

"Well, first I saw the hearse in the driveway; if it was hers, you'd have mentioned it."

He raised foxy questions, but I had expected he would. "There was a flickering light," I went on, "coming from what turned out to be the bedroom. The window was open enough to stir the curtains about. A fire was banked down but still burning in the fireplace."

"They didn't see you?"

"They were busy."

"How'd you know his name?"

"I went through the papers in the glove compartment of the hearse."

"How'd you see the snake?"

I hesitated.

"Tell me," he said, "was the snake in bed too?"

"The snake was... it was in a cage. In front of the fireplace."

Again he paused. Finally, "Question is, how do we get to her with him around?"

"We can't. We've got to wait. Maybe a week, ten days..."

"Ten days!"

"Until she kicks them out, or he and the snake split on their own."

"Jesus," he said, "let's not make a career out of this."

"You think I find it a million laughs? I feel like I got an icebox on my back." I heaved a great stressful sigh.

"That bitch," he said, as if he hadn't heard me. "If this weren't California, I could cut her off without a sou. But here, adultery doesn't cost her a dollar." Grimly he sipped his wine. And then, "How much time off were you thinking of?" he asked.

"I don't know. A few days. A week, maybe. Till things simmer down."

"Things usually come to a boil before they simmer down," he said stiffly. He gave me an appraising stare. Then he said, "Okay. Three days, but no longer. Just remember we've got unfinished business."

"I'll finish it."

"Sure," he said. "When that happens, I'll slide down a banister waving a glass of champagne."

"All right. But what's the hurry?"

"Miss Ochoa. She's getting antsy. She hungers for a wedding band."

"That's a good sign."

"Is it? She won't let me near her till she gets it." He shook his head wearily. "Of all the women on earth," he said, "I get hooked on a caricature straight out of yesteryear."

TWELVE

I had to tell Gayle I was going away—tidings she could hardly be expected to greet with a standing ovation.

No matter how pissed off she gets, I told myself, be nice to her, considerate. Soothe her, stroke her. So I waited till she'd settled in with her latest potboiler after dinner, then bent over the back of her chair and kissed the top of her head.

Her body stiffened. "Don't," she said. Her lips quivered.

I backed off fast.

"You don't have to look so relieved," she said.

"What's that supposed to mean?" I asked.

Instead of answering she eased herself out of the chair and meandered to a point of the wall where the paper had been scraped off, leaving an irregular little excavation that looked like it had been nibbled by a sloppy mouse. Expressionlessly she inserted a fingernail, prying loose a chunk of plaster the size of a quarter. She brought it to her mouth.

"Goddammit!" I said. "You'll poison yourself eating that stuff."

"Screw you," she said primly. "I eat what I want."

"The whole fucking wall's going to fall down. It makes me sick—" Abruptly I clamped my mouth shut. Be calm, don't get riled, I had told myself, and here I was ignoring my own storm warning. "What I mean," I said lamely, "it could make *you* sick."

"I read in a book it's healthy." She rolled her tongue around the plaster as if it were candy. "Full of vitamins. You look like you could use some."

"What I could use is some time off. I'm beat. I got to get away."

"Fine. Where'll we go?"

"Look, Gayle—I got to be by myself."

"I need time off more than you do."

"Okay. We'll both go away."

Slowly she returned to her chair. "You mean separately," she said. She pulled the pink wrapper tight around her chest. She asked, "Where are you going?"

"I don't know."

"You'd better make up your mind." Her voice climbed to a falsetto. "God forbid we should happen to go to the same place." She was watching me closely. "Are you having an affair?" she asked.

"Of course not."

"Yes, you are. I know who she is, too. Not her name exactly, but she's been calling when you're not here."

"Then how can I be with her?"

"When you're with another one of your bimbos."

"Who's been calling? Katz's secretary? I told you—"

"Not Katz's secretary. This one speaks Spanish."

That stupid Carmen. I'd have to talk to her. I'd have to...

A fist the size of a hardboiled egg slammed into my face.

"Cut it out!" I said, trying to grab those flailing knuckles.

"You make me... *miserable*," she snarled between punches. "You put me... into a *turmoil*..."

I'll put you into a fucking cast... but no, don't even think that way, I cautioned myself, don't *ever*.

She was still now, spent and gasping for breath. She turned abruptly and disappeared into the bedroom.

I fell onto the couch. Jesus, what a mess I was making of everything. Jack Hopkins, messmaker. She stormed out of the bedroom and headed for the door. "Where are you going?" I asked.

"A goose for the gosling," she proclaimed, "is a goose for the gander." And slammed the door behind her.

I lay there on the couch. My body hurt, my arms and shoulders, as if I had been throwing punches. I reached for the phone. When Carmen Ochoa answered I didn't get past "Hi" before she said, "Can you come right over?"

What now? I wondered. Reluctantly I said I would, and dialed again.

"Yeah? What you want?" Scrap Iron Thompson said.

"Listen, Scrap, I'm going away for a little while..."

"You want a boat?"

"And you to sail it for me."

"Where to?"

"Baja. You know an island called San Dismaso?"

"Never heard of it."

"Find it on the chart, okay?"

He grunted. "You sure that's the name?"

"I'm sure. San Dismaso."

"I knew you would come," Carmen said. I didn't know what the hell she was talking about.

"I phoned and phoned," she said, "and always no answer, except for that *puta*." Her dark eyes probed me. "Who bloodied you?" she asked. "Who fattened your lip? The *puta*? You live with that *puta*?"

"She's not a *puta*."

"No? All she says is, 'Allo! Allo!' and calls me filthy names. Still, I knew you'd be receptive..."

"But you extinguished the phone before any message was left. How could I have guessed it was you?"

"*You knew*," she insisted. "Because you are receptive."

We were going around in circles. She seemed rather pleased about it. I studied her face, her eyes calm and deep, her hair shining. How different she was in her weightless beauty from her thick-jawed, goat-shouldered clod of a brother. How was it possible that they were wrenched from the same womb?

"Why did you call?" I asked.

"There was a prowler. Late, two nights ago..."

She had been undressing for bed. She felt someone was watching her—"I am also receptive to such vibrations." She doused the lights, peered through the curtains. A man was in the shadows. A rapist.

"He raped you?"

"But of course not."

"How do you know he was a rapist?"

"I know such things."

I wasn't going to argue with her. "What did you do?"

"I go to the kitchen. I get the bread knife. I return to the window. He is gone. You hungry?" she asked.

"I will have the Señor Hunt supply a bodyguard."

"I do not want a man always in my proximity."

"What do you suggest?"

"A gun. The rapist shall find I am a dangerous woman to fall foul of."

"You'll have to ask the Señor Hunt."

"Why cannot you provide me? Is it so much to ask?"

"I don't have a gun. And I'll be away for some days."

"Where are you going?"

Jesus. Here we go again. "Canada."

"Where is this Canada?"

"A country to the north."

"I will wait. If before then the rapist reappears, I will stick him with the bread knife."

"Would it not be preferable to see the Señor Hunt? Perhaps he can provide a better solution."

"I wish not to see him until the time of the marriage."

"But you must..."

"Where is it so nominated in the bond?"

"He will make with you the marriage as soon as is humanly possible."

"Speaking with a frankness, I dote on his absence. I do not care if I never see him. When he comes here it is only to knead my flesh, like dough in the hands of a baker. I am not the fat lady at the fair," she mixed metaphors so fast it made my head swim, "and he the guesser of my weight."

"It is that you excite him irresistibly."

"If he touches me again, I hope the good Lord Jesus excites him with a heart attack. I wish to speak more of the gun." Now her eyes were blazing in their persistence. "You must see that my need for it is imperative. It is not only for the rapist."

"Now wait a minute," I said. "You will not use a gun on the Señor Hunt.

It is prohibited." As if I could stop her.

She snorted, "I can temper the transports of the Señor Hunt with but the flick of a finger. The gun is for the school."

"School? The school of Lana Turner?"

"Not the school of Lana Turner, which is of a bruising distance, and in another district. I speak of the school down the hill, a journey of insignificance, but—"

"You have registered?"

"I have attended. But it is a school of gang fighters and of guns secreted under the skirts of their *cholas*. Because of them I cannot go to the bathroom where they deny me admission as they smoke the marijuana. I will not go back without a gun."

"But what of the pom-pom dancing?"

"It is not worth it. I cannot dance if I am a corpse on the bathroom floor."

"All right," I said. "I make you this commitment: When I return I shall go to your school and talk to the principal, and then you will have admission to the bathroom, and you will dance with the pom-poms."

"You are of a possibility correct about the pom-poms," she said, "but the principal herself will not brave the bathroom."

"Then I shall go even higher," I said righteously. "Beyond the principal."

She shook her head. "You will not be happy," she said, "until there are corpses all over the tiles."

"Only if unavoidable."

"You are a good friend. You try to help, and I am not without appreciation."

"I am your friend. Is there anything else before I go?"

"Just a small infinitesimal favor, if I may be emboldened to ask. A whetstone," she said, "for the bread knife."

She was hell-bent on sticking somebody. Perhaps she wasn't so different from Napoleon after all. Siblings under the skin.

Gayle had gone out by the time I got back from Carmen's, which was not unexpected. I was sure she was with Jerry Fleet, sharing a cozy Naugahyde booth at the Vegetable Patch (a favorite nightspot), gorging herself on an imitation hamburger made of carrots and spinach and bumblebees, seasoned with cilantro, on a bacteria bun, and swilling it down with a tarantula-juice julep (specialty of the house).

The phone rang at midnight, while I was packing. Christ, I thought, Carmen. Raped, staggering to the horn. Hoist on her own bread knife. But when I answered there was nobody there.

THIRTEEN

Scrap Iron Thompson stood at the wheel, his stocky form half-dissolved in a solid mass of heat. The wind whipped the water, the boat crashed and staggered.

The heat didn't seem to affect Scrap Iron; he was a weather-resistant man. There was a tilt to his face suggesting sadism, because of his blind eye. He had lost it after a fight when an appreciative crowd had showered the ring with money. A fifty-cent piece had caught him unawares and that was the end of his career, but Scrap Iron climbed out of the ring glowing with the intelligence of the oppressed. He had saved a little money: now he'd put it into a boat for hire, and then another, until he had four. "The fleet," he called them.

In the bright and gusty evenings when the red sun dipped into the sea we would sit around and break the long day's silence with a few pleasantries. The night before landfall he was (for him) positively loquacious. "How's Gayle?" he asked.

"Fine."

"You ought to marry up with her."

"You're a great one to talk. I've never seen you with a woman." I grinned. "Don't you like girls?"

"Oh, I like wimmen," he said vaguely.

"At a distance?"

"No. I like..." he frowned, and the big busted nose on his wrinkled face twitched like the flaring nostrils of a horse. "What I like," he went on gravely, "is to smell 'em. Never knew a girl to smell bad in my life. If you just smell 'em," Scrap Iron said, "they don't expect nothing from you. Most times they don't even know they're being smelt."

"What happens if it kind of dawns on them?"

"You got to be careful," he said. "They could raise a stink—wimmen are funny—and you could get your tee-tee throwed in jail."

"Just for smelling?"

He nodded sagely.

The beach at San Dismaso was glaring white, beautiful, until it gave way, forty yards inland, to a desolation that lacked grass and trees. A few angular shrubs, neither lush nor green, sprouted among the rocks and the buckbush, foraged by a flock of scrawny goats. Beyond them was what seemed to be a colony of rusted tin huts.

Signs the size of billboards sprang up like thickets of weeds along the littoral. The lettering was slipshod, but the message was clear:

¡PRIVADO!

¡NO ENTRAR!

¡PROHIBIDA LA ENTRADA!

And in English:

NOTRES

PASSING

Now and then the dun-colored apparition of a man materialized out of nowhere, moving sluggishly for a moment before he faded back into the jungle.

All this from the boat, via binoculars, about a mile offshore. Slowly we circled San Dismaso; its roachiness was evident from any angle. The wild goats were everywhere. A couple of buildings, as rickety as the huts but much larger, appeared now and then before the passage of the boat or an upthrust of topography blocked them out. They seemed to be occupied by a silent scattering of men. From the larger shanty rose a brackish column of smoke. It lumbered straight into the sky; not a breath of air stirred. I raised the binoculars, but I couldn't zero in on anything but goats. It was worrisome, as was everything about that bleb on the face of the sea, that lump of real estate for which I had a promissory note. I would have liked to explore each stony inch of it under the uncompromising light of the sun, but discretion insisted that I postpone my survey until nightfall. Best to get on and off that unpromising rock without detection; Tod Hunt might view my reconnaissance with something less than approval.

My worries lengthened as the sun declined. When night fell the idiot bleating of the goats was joined in eerie concert by the shrill disconsolate screech of something wild and shambling and uncombed in that jungle.

We dropped anchor when darkness fell, a hundred yards offshore. I asked Scrap casually if he'd like to come along. I didn't like the screech of those things that seemed to be slouching through the forest.

He said no. I asked him where was his sense of adventure, wasn't he interested in exploring a tropical island at night? Not even in the daytime, he said. I told him I had reason to believe there were girls on the island. You can smell them, I promised.

Scrap looked at me with his unmatched eyes, one grave and blue, the other moist and milky. He didn't know what I was up to, he said, and he wasn't asking any questions. I offered him an additional fifty bucks for the pleasure of his company. He said he'd wait on the boat.

And so, feeling rejected, I eased myself over the side and into the water. What the hell, I told myself, there was nothing to fear. All day I had seen men walking around unarmed among the goats, and they didn't seem to be worried.

Of course, it was the men I should have worried about.

The surf carried me ashore and tossed me gently in the shallows. I untied the sneakers from my neck, put them on, and moved inland. There was no trail, at least none that I could detect in the night. I got snagged, scragged, pierced, and concussed by shrubs, vines, thorns, rocks. I even staggered into nothing, with that sense of panic that always precedes the foot in its abrupt descent to the bottom of a pit, even when the pit is no more than a few inches deep. I was heading for the large shed in the middle of the island, the one marked by that column of smoke. It couldn't be seen, but it could be heard; it was from there that all the yelping of the dogs and the screeching of the forest banshees seemed to emanate.

I slogged on, it seemed, for hours. I climbed a steep rise, looked back, was astounded to see the phorescent waves breaking on the beach not more than two hundred yards away. I started down. My feet went out from under me. I bounced painfully on my ass and slid the rest of the way like a man on a toboggan without a toboggan.

I got to my feet. Sweat streamed down my face, burning the cuts and scratches. Then everything unaccountably went orange and red and yellow: the beam of an electric torch was glued on me. Out of the darkness maybe a dozen enormous men came toward me, and a moment later two dozen hoof-like fists closed the gap.

I screamed. I continued screaming as I fought back. Some son of a bitch even pummeled me with the flashlight.

My breath was a harsh, lung-clogged whistle. My nose ran with blood and mucus. Still I managed to keep bellowing.

And miracle of miracles, my pitiful cries were answered. Someone else had swarmed into the fray, and on my side, throwing short, evil punches. Fear must have sharpened my vision, for I could see old Scrap Iron working methodically, a wooden expression on his tilted face, a trace of sullenness around the set lines of his mouth, his eyes (even the milky one) gentle, dreamy, while he used his astonishing fists with all the cunning of a samurai with two swords.

We were turning the tide when an authoritative figure appeared. Looming up like a tornado, Napoleon Ochoa waded in to restore order, screaming Spanish insults at his countrymen, bisonic shoulders and forepaws blocking their increasingly feeble punches.

"You dumb fucks!" he screamed at them. "Your mother fucks monkeys! You got clap in your assholes! You got chili for brains!" As a peacemaker he was a bit too enthusiastic. I wondered how long he had been watching before he stepped in.

When they were properly subdued he stood back, taut as a pistol hammer, and surveyed the wreckage. "I will kick their whole fucking heads off," he said to me by way of apology. He jabbed a finger in my general direction and turned back to the wounded on the forest floor. "You stupid shiteaters," he said, "he's my good friend."

"Who's in charge here?" I asked him.

"You want to see him?" He patted my shoulder and added importantly, "I can arrange it."

The bat-eared young man got up from behind a desk piebald with fungus. He was one of those people whose lips become moist when they talk. He seemed moist all over, in fact, thanks to the oily repellent he used to calm the bugs that buzzed about his head like a halo.

He crossed the room, hand extended. Napoleon had given him a knockdown on me, and then disappeared through another rickety door before I entered. "I'm Vudukovich," he said. "Thank you for coming and please leave." He dropped the hand before I could shake it, then lifted it up again to glance at his watch.

"What business are you in, Vudukovich?"

His mouth clamped shut, a moist, bloodless slash in the long oily face. He had no intention of answering.

"Why would you want your apes to kill me?"

"You did come stomping in here," he said, "unannounced in the middle of the night."

"You in real estate?" I asked. "A developer?"

The room was still; outside day was about to break and, closer now, the whatever-they-were yowled and the cicadas chirped their thin silvery complaint about the heat.

"You mind if I look around myself, then?" I asked.

"Sorry," he said, "not without the express permission of Mr. Hunt."

"I work for Hunt," I said.

He raised an eyebrow.

"I know about the manacles and all already," I went on. "I've seen worse, you know. The projects he's got me on…"

The eyebrow flickered.

"Look, why don't you call Hunt in LA?" I suggested. "Tell him I'm here. Get his permission to show me the dungeon…" Hunt would soon enough find out from Vudukovich about my surprise visit. I might as well break the news first.

"I already have," he said. "He says to tell you your vacation's over. It's time for you to go, Mr. Hopkins." And then he gave me a pat on the arm and went back to his desk.

In the clearing outside Voodoo's office was a single dwarfed tree, the only animal, vegetable, or mineral on San Dismaso which looked comfortable, for it rested in the shade of Napoleon Ochoa. He stood there, the biggest beast in the forest, scarfing refried beans from a tin plate. Beside him on a rock was a bottle of tequila.

A few of his bravos lounged nearby. Removed from the group with his own plate of beans was Scrap Iron, basking in quiet self-satisfaction now that he had kicked the revolving shit out of so many Mexicans.

Napoleon's jaws worked like a reptile's, engulfing his food. He took a long swig from the bottle, twisting his mouth around the taste of it. He too seemed self-satisfied. Why not? He never had it so powerful. Full of largesse and secret knowledge, he offered me a drink. I tilted the bottle and coughed. It had a raw laboratory flavor.

I'd struck out once, but the eternal optimist in me responded to the dime-store agave. Maybe a subtler approach at interrogation would work on Napoleon. I wiped my mouth and tried to grin. "Your sister misses you," I said.

Napoleon grinned. "Have another drink," he said graciously, shaking a cigarette from a pack. He struck a wooden match on a tooth and inhaled deeply. Then he set the tin plate on a rock, plucked a bright and silky butterfly from a leaf of the tree, and held it squirming over the match.

"What're you doing here, anyway?" I asked, all out of subtlety.

Napoleon turned back to the tequila. "This juice'll send you to the moon," he said appreciatively. "Why mess with spaceships?"

The bravos stirred, rousing themselves out of their early-morning lethargy. They refilled their tin plates at an iron pot hooked to a crossbar above a smoldering brushfire and carried them across the dusty compound to the large barnlike structure fifty yards away. A din went up—that spine-chilling ululation of the whatever-they-were—from inside.

"What's in the barn?" I practically pleaded.

He shrugged dismissively. "*Una cosa gringada*," he said. He stood there blinking like an underground animal.

"What kind of gringo thing?"

Again he shook his head.

"What's making that noise?" I persisted.

"Goats," he said. "The fucking island's full of goats."

I looked at him disbelievingly.

"Pain in the ass," he said. "Hunt wants me to round 'em up."

"And you keep them in *there?*"

Imperturbably he said, "That's right."

"Napoleon—you wouldn't bullshit a buddy, would you?"

"Jack—" he looked hurt. "Christ strike me dead if I..." His voice trailed off. His puddled eyes, brimming with vacant, false sincerity went suddenly ablaze. "Just look at that," he whispered hoarsely, staring past my shoulder.

I turned. Out of the tangled wilderness came a clutch of teenaged girls. Their lilting Spanish, punctuated with laughter, rose like soft music over the clearing. There was something lovely and fresh and spirited about them in their bright-colored skirts.

"Just look at all that pussy," Napoleon crooned.

Leggy, dark hair shining, they clustered around the barn door like a big bowl of flowers. One of the bravos inserted a heavy brass key into a padlock that would have been more appropriate on a Ruritanian keep.

Everybody was watching, solemn and breathless, as they filed through the door. Scrap Iron gazed after them with idle lust, nostrils distended, smelling away.

I took a few steps after the girls before Napoleon put a lock on my arm.

"Hey," he said. "You can't go there."

"Why not?"

"Orders." He jerked his head toward Voodoo's office. "He wants you off the island."

"I'm going. Just—you've got to tell me, Napoleon. What are those girls doing in the barn?"

"Taking care of the goats. Matter of fact..." His grip on my arm tightened, adding pressure to the lie.

I suppose I could have made a run for it, dashed to the shed, scooped up a rock and heaved it through a black window and seen for myself—providing of course Napoleon and his amigos didn't pounce on me like a plate of refried beans. But I let him guide me toward the beach. Scrap Iron followed us.

Napoleon was saying, "Maybe we can do a little business together."

"What kind of business?"

"Well," he said, "I'm supposed to get them goats off the island. Sure, I could ship 'em to the mainland and let 'em run free. But I figure I could maybe squeeze a short buck out of it if… you're in the real-estate business, right?"

I nodded warily.

"I could sell them goats in California if I had a place to keep 'em. Nothing elaborate. Some out of the way little place not far from LA."

"I don't know any goat farms," I said firmly. "That's a little off my beat."

He nodded, disappointed. "You mind letting go of my arm?" I asked. He did so; slowly the circulation returned. And then it hit me.

"Hey!" I snapped my fingers. "I think I got just the place for you."

"Great," Napoleon said. "Where?"

"Just over the line in Ventura County. A tree farm owned by this old guy, Mr. Dickens. I saw it just a couple weeks ago."

"How much?"

"We'll work it out when you get to LA. You'll be able to live with it."

"You'll gimme a break, right? Screw the old fucker a little?"

Sure I would. But Napoleon Ochoa was the fucker I'd screw. I'd take him for every peso in his kick—this avaricious dinosaur with a brain too small for his body, this sadistic *piojo*, this cremator of butterflies. And I'd pass it all on to Mr. Dickens. I wouldn't even take a commission.

And then maybe on top of that I'd finally get Napoleon to talk.

FOURTEEN

The long voyage home. Scrap Iron even less communicative than usual, and I grappling with disconnected thoughts.

To postpone the face-off with Hunt, it seemed to me, could only have prolonged a sticky situation. I drove directly to Tod's office, where Ms. Velasquez was properly agitated by my fierce, unheralded appearance. My shirt and dungarees were bloodstained, my beard was a thicket, my wind-burned eyes were wild.

Unlike Ms. Velasquez, Tod regarded me with no outward show of shock, although his greeting was less than tepid. His bearing sustained an unfamiliar rigidity, as if he was having difficulty holding himself in check.

"You look fresh off a lost boat," he said coldly. "Have a nice holiday?"

"I've been to San Dismaso."

"So I've been informed. How'd you even know the place existed?"

"I saw something on Ms. Velasquez's desk."

"In the middle of the night, I presume. At least that solves the mystery of the break-in." He sighed audibly. "And your conduct down there..." He shook his head in a parody of disappointment. "You seem to have a genius for slubbering everything you touch."

"Just what are you up to? That's all I want to know."

He looked pained. "It's not always good to ask questions," he said. "Moreover—"

"You mean, it's not always safe to answer them."

"—Moreover," he repeated, "your attitude fails to captivate."

"Tough," I said. "I damn near got my balls nailed to the floorboards, and you're not captivated. Well," my voice was rasping like static, "neither am I."

Tod's face fell. He bit his lower lip. "Everything we do," he said, "seems to have a strain upon it. Perhaps it's inevitable, considering the nature of our enterprise. Still..." he added wearily, "let's not get unmoored. Let's not get bogged down in ugly recriminations. Let's try to... coalesce."

My hand was on the doorknob.

"Wait a minute," he said, a few octaves above his usual register. Did I detect a note of panic in his voice? Then, evenly, "When I want something, I want it desperately..."

"It's a trait we seem to share."

"Yes," he said, managing a grin. "A chip off the old block. If I'm hard on you it's because, well, I think of you as a son..."

I turned. A son.

"Please sit down," he said. Slowly, like a sleepwalker, I went to the chair and sat. He leaned back and closed his eyes, and for once in his exalted presence, his silence didn't discomfit me; I felt no need to fill it.

Then he said, "Let me try to dispel your concern by sharing a confidence." He paused. Through the open window came the sad abrasive rustle of palm fronds.

He said, "I don't really enjoy being... immersed in the debasing pursuit of wealth. My interest in San Dismaso has nothing to do with economic diversification. Nor is it an attempt to extend my imperium, as it were."

Imperium. It was unbelievable. Suddenly he was all sweetness and light, shedding his nastiness, regaining his amazing grace, and with it that flamboyance with words, that unique, indecipherable air of his, half scholar, half huckster. What was he trying to sell me now?

"No," he went on, "real estate is not the most inspiriting of activities. I've derived little satisfaction from it. And so what's left? Not retirement, not withdrawal, but something, some kind of commitment." He grinned. "I'd like to do something of value before Jesus takes me for a sunbeam."

"What? What has it to do with San Dismaso?"

"Well," he said, "I've had this itch for years. It's about time I scratched it. What I want..." His eyes held a soft dry shine. "It goes back, I suppose, to my father. He had high hopes for me. All I wanted was to follow him into his business—the cone business."

"The what?"

"Ice cream cones. But he had something else in mind. He wanted to believe that some day I'd find a cure for the common cold, or Alzheimer's, or..." Again he lapsed into a long, crippling silence. Finally he said, "He died of cancer the same year I quit med school." He blinked, making a visceral effort to dislodge those painful memories from his mind. "About the San Dismaso project..."

So here it came, at long last. I waited for him to go on... and waited... and waited. He seemed to be grappling to pluck some elucidating comment from a source that wouldn't part with it. Finally, "Dismaso," he said, "is not commercial property, it has nothing to do with the Fleet deal. It's..." he lowered his voice, as if he were about to share a secret of great consequence. "I'm trying to develop some manner or means of... purifying, extracting from or eradicating certain imperfections of, of... by the application of remedials to ensure what we hope will be a significant departure..."

"Could you be a bit more explicit?"

"Why should I?" he asked irritably. "If it doesn't concern the Fleets, what concern is it to you?"

It was of great concern to me.

"Just trust me," he added.

I've always hated that expression. Of all the paltry bromides in the language, "Trust me" is the most disaffecting, possibly because it is mouthed so abundantly by the least trustworthy people I know. Tod had tied himself in a knot of words, a meaningless tangle of batshit. It wasn't enough. I wanted something, anything that might have explained the roachy hut with the blackened windows, Napoleon and his thugs, Voodoo in charge. And the thongs and restraints and the bouncy young girls...

"Look, I think I deserve some smidge of enlightenment about—"

"All in good time," he cut in. "I hate to badger you, but our primary enterprise is still unresolved."

"I'll get around to it."

"When?"

"Hell, I just got back."

"From your holiday," he said dryly. "Now it's time for work. Which, I hope, hasn't lost its savor?"

"Of course not."

"Good. You'll do it tonight."

"That's out of the question. I'm exhausted."

He said, "So am I," stressing each syllable, somehow freighting them with foreboding. "You exhaust me," he went on. "I'm tired of your tampering, including the disorder you created on Dismaso. Do it tonight," he ordered.

Tod got to his feet, signaling my dismissal, and suddenly I was as bone tired as I had claimed to be. All I wanted was to peel off my filthy jeans, shave the stubble from my face, sink to my ears in a steaming tub, and see Gayle. I hadn't thought of her, not once, while I had been away, but now I yearned for her. Those calm, unastonished eyes, the color of dewy forget-me-nots—how could I ever have thought them vacant? That long-limbed body, a willowy miracle—how could I ever have thought it graceless? Her concern for my irregularities—how could I ever have considered her intrusive? Even her wackiness, filtered through my florid sentimentality (or was it lust?), seemed endearing.

I hurried home.

In the tub I lay like flotsam, my mind a faulty projector reeling off flashbacks to San Dismaso and flashforwards to Darlene. Gayle should have been home by now, but there was no sign of her. I was resigned to passing out alone, maybe just sinking under the waterline and succumbing, when the phone rang. I sped to the receiver, balls-ass naked.

"Jack!" Gayle's voice was flat and anguished. "Jerry's dead! Somebody shot his whole stomach off!"

She sat in a small room with a shirt-sleeved detective, a steaming mug of black coffee clutched in her trembling hands. He looked disconcertingly familiar—the red hair, the flat eyes, all those ballpoint pens. Sergeant Joseph Laudermilk, BHPD. He had me pegged, too.

Jerry and Gayle had gone to a movie on Wilshire Boulevard. To save three bucks he had parked on a side street three blocks from the theater. Returning to the car, they were followed by a man, his features and his clothes indistinguishable on the dark street. She wasn't even aware of him until he pushed a gun into Jerry's spine and fired twice. Gayle screamed, ran, looked back. The man did not follow her. Instead, he stood bent over the body for what seemed to be an inordinately long time, as if he were examining the fruits of his labor. He left, in the opposite direction, only after lights went on in a few apartments along the street. No one came out to investigate. Gayle ran to the corner of Olympic, crashed into a mom-and-pop deli, called the police.

Laudermilk said there were no suspects, but prowl cars were still dragging the neighborhood. Jerry's father had been notified, had arrived a few minutes before I got there, was in the morgue at the back of the building with the victim.

The detective was not talking; there was nothing to talk about. Although Jerry's empty wallet was found next to the body, Laudermilk intimated that the murder conformed to a pattern, the mindless, unmotivated malignity of a badass kid who pumps slugs into a stranger just to see which way he'd fall, and then as an afterthought ransacks the billfold. Random violence, he said, is not uncommon these days.

The police never found Jerry's killer.

The day of the funeral the Fleet office, authorized by a memo from Senior, suspended all business for one minute of mourning and reflection.

That night we paid a condolence call on the old man. Only a few people were there. Gayle sat in one corner with two or three anonymous women, their voices muted yet somehow overripe. In another corner I sat drinking with a few men in subdued polyester suits while Senior talked about his son.

The apartment house on Doheny smelled of sauerkraut. Senior's flat was dusty and haggard. The walls were uncontaminated by pictures, but above the chair where he sat was a framed poster in gothic script. *When I Walk Through the Valley of the Shadow of Death I Shall Fear No Evil* (it read) *because I am the Meanest Son of a Bitch in the Valley.*

He wasn't mean now, but even in his sorrow he was the incessant salesman.

What he was flogging was Jerry, and his memories of his son bore little resemblance to the Jerry I knew.

"Yessir," Senior was saying, "he was always the fiddle of the company. Always bubbling over, so enthusiastic, always saying 'Out of sight!' and 'Wow!' and 'Mellow!' and 'Dynamite!' So full of life. Why, just to look at him made people laugh. Yet he never expected much; he was just happy by himself, with a little Limburger for breakfast, and Twinkies. I used to reward him with Twinkies when he was a kid, and he never got over his love for them."

His eyes were bright with tears. "Goddammit," Senior went on, "he had class." He looked from one polyester suit to another. The polyester men rearranged their faces to an even greater degree of solemnity. Senior blew his nose. I wished I had followed Tod Hunt's advice.

"Don't go to the wake, or whatever it is," Tod had said. "You'll regret it."

"I've got to go," I'd said. "So should you." We'd agreed to wait a couple more days on other endeavors, in view of events.

"Not me," he'd said. "Even under less straining circumstances my sympathy is never very convincing. And in this case..." He shook his head emphatically.

"But when a man dies, you can't just ignore it..."

"I'll write Senior a note and enclose a donation for Jerry's favorite charity. What could that be? The Salvation Army, where he bought his clothes? Or the soup kitchen of the Main Street Tabernacle, where he got his Limburger?"

"Is that what you want when you die? A donation to your favorite charity?"

"Not particularly."

"What do you want?"

"Presents," he said.

"He had this sensitive stomach," Senior said. "What with the Limburger and the Twinkies and all. That's why he was all the time passing wind. He didn't mean it, you know what I mean?" The polyesters nodded with understanding.

"And he'd always apologize. 'Parm me,' he'd say. 'I guess I just committed a social indiscretion.' Thing was, he couldn't help it."

He couldn't help it all right. Jerry had been programmed as if by a higher authority to be an asshole. Farting was the way he expressed himself.

"You know," Senior said bitterly, "it never rains but it shits. I mean a downfall. You realize this has to happen just two days before my birthday?"

He closed his eyes and constricted his face. "I keep thinking I'll have to clean out his desk—it's a father's duty, but I know I'll just fall apart." He shook his head and leaned it on his hands, "Why is it," he sighed, "the good go young"—his eyes locked chillingly, accusingly, with mine—"and the shitheels go on forever?"

Then, only then, did the thought occur: was it possible that the slugs that killed Jerry had been meant for me? It was a dark street. He was with my *amiga*. Who else beside Senior considered me a shitheel, had cause, or mustered a hatred so deep that he'd resort to murder? It was a harsh and desolate issue I would have preferred to ignore.

But I couldn't. Driving home from Senior's with Gayle, "Let me ask you a question," I began. "Do you suppose whoever shot Jerry might have thought he was shooting me?"

"Good God…" she said.

"What's that mean?"

"It means, do you always think you're the center of the universe—in this case the focus of the whole damn shooting match?"

"No, but—"

"Then drop it." She curled stiffly up in the seat, pulling the collar of her coat up to her ears.

And then it hit me. "You think *I* did it?"

There was a long, uncomfortable silence. "Not you personally," she said. "But, I don't know, lately there's been something so angry about everything you do. You could have put out a whatchacallit—a contract, with the person who did."

"Why would I?"

She turned to face me. "Jack…" I could feel her eyes cutting through the darkness of the car. "You know me—I'd rather look the other way than cause a fuss. But…"

"You're causing a fuss right now. Give me one good reason why I'd kill Jerry."

She said, "Jealousy."

I shot her an incredulous glance.

"Jealousy," she repeated. "What made you try to kill Bainbridge and MacDevitt."

"I *didn't* try to kill them. And it wasn't jealousy."

"Why are you yelling?"

"You drive me crazy."

"See?" she said wisely. "That's what jealousy does."

"Listen carefully. You heard what the detective, Laudermilk, said. Jerry was killed by some nut with an advanced case of..." There was a phrase for it... "...unbound aggression. Just a wanton, senseless murder."

"There was something funny about it."

"Tell me. I could use a laugh."

"I mean funny-peculiar. I can't put my finger..." She sat very still, concentrating. "There was something about the way Jerry was dressed. Something weird..."

"He always dressed weird. From his twelve-gallon hat to those idiot boots."

"That's it!" she said. "The boots. You know—ostrich, with the red trim. He was wearing them that night, but later, when they wheeled him into the morgue, they were gone."

"Somebody took his boots off?"

"The somebody who killed him. *Traded* with him. Jerry was wearing some beat-up old Wellingtons, from like Sears. The kind," she went on, "Jerry wouldn't be caught dead in." A statement inconsistent with the facts.

"Maybe you should tell the cops."

"I will."

"Only, for Christ sakes, don't mention your theory."

"About jealousy? I wouldn't do anything to hurt you."

"That's not the point. I didn't kill Jerry. You understand?"

She nodded. "I guess I wanted you to be jealous."

"I am," I lied stoutly. And after a second I realized I was.

The next morning I readied myself for another day of it, the whole mess. Gayle had left early, leaving me to a cold shower and a cup of coffee. But when I opened the door to walk out to my car, in the threshold stood Detective Sergeant Joseph Laudermilk.

"Come in," I said. I tried to sound hospitable.

"We've been trying to get some information about Mr. Fleet." He crossed the carpet and eased himself onto the couch.

"Senior or Junior?"

"The victim."

"Got any leads?"

"Not a clue. Might as well try reading the entrails of a duck. Anything that comes to mind might help."

"Anything at all?"

"Anything. To help us put the find-out on him. To see how he ticked and tocked. You worked with him?" he asked. I nodded.

"Real estate, right?"

"Right."

"How would you describe him? Good at the job? A fuck-up?"

"A little of both."

"What kind of a fuck-up?"

I looked at him quizzically.

"A whip? A dildo? A pomegranate?"

Whether Sergeant Laudermilk enjoyed his craft was a moot question, but he certainly relished the fractured vocabulary that went with it. "Want to smooth that out for me?" I said.

"A whip—a badass fuck-up. A dildo—a nut fuck-up. Pomegranate—a dope fuck-up."

"A pomegranate, I guess."

He nodded understandingly. There was about him a sort of gravity, the total absorption of a child at play or a scientist at work.

"He run on his own motor?"

"What?"

"A loner?"

"Kind of."

"Odd, kind of, wouldn't you say? A loner in the real-estate dodge? I thought all you people come on like a nose guard for the Raiders."

"Not all of us."

"He get along with people in the office?"

"Far as I know."

"You and he were friends?"

"Business acquaintances, really."

"That's all?"

What was he driving at, this Class B cut of meat? "What more should there be?"

"It seems, according to Miss Wyman, she stepped out with him once in a while."

"That's right."

"But she's your steady, right? She was flopping with you?"

"They were friends."

He eyed me skeptically.

"They'd go to dinner, or a movie sometimes when I was working."

"You work nights?"

"Once in a while."

He was pensive for a moment. "You handle homes in Beverly Hills?" he asked.

"I have."

"I could use a small house."

An interesting overture.

"Maybe I can help you," I offered. "What's your price range?"

"I'll go as high as sixty grand."

Sixty grand in Beverly Hills. The son of a bitch, looking for a free lunch. If we took lucky, that might get him an outhouse with a Dutch door on rusty hinges. Not even a two-seater. But in the affairs of men there is always the skew factor, and if anything went awry, I could use a Beverly Hills cop in my corner. "Let me look around, see what I can come up with."

"I'd appreciate it." He plucked a card from an overloaded wallet. "Here," he said, handing it to me. "Where I can be reached if something comes up. And the sooner the better." He paused, then, "About the victim..."

"Jerry?"

"You were working the night he was offed?"

"Yeah." I nodded dumbly, but I was thinking fast. "Not exactly working, but I was busy." I couldn't mention San Dismaso. The island led to Hunt, Hunt to Darlene. What answers she might supply to Laudermilk's questions I shuddered to contemplate.

"Busy doing what?"

"I had some time off from work. I was going deep-sea fishing—I had chartered a boat for a few days from a man called Scrap Iron Thompson at Marina del Rey…"

"Scrap Iron? Used to be a fighter? What's his righteous name?"

"I don't know. We were out on the water when it happened, anyway."

He looked around, staring at the blank eye of the television set across the room.

"Nice apartment," he said.

"I prefer it to a house. No worry about upkeep."

"I hate apartments," he said flatly. "Thin walls. They're every one of 'em fucking boxes surrounded by noise and bad smells."

"Where do you live?"

"Torrance. All that freeway driving, I'm bushed before I get to work. And then there's the price of gas."

"Damn shame," I commiserated, "working in a town where you can't afford to live. And a police officer to boot…" Pour it on, baby, I told myself, "…your life on the line…"

"It's a lousy life," he said, "only good for pumping adrenaline. What about the victim?"

"Jerry?"

"Didn't he have a small house in Beverly Hills?"

"Yeah. But it's pure silk. In today's market that house'll go for more than two mil."

"I was hoping we could work out some kind of a deal."

Did I detect the insinuation of some oblique, subterranean threat in his words? "It's owned by the company—Jerry's father."

He was silent; I had punctured his balloon.

"I'll have to find you something south of Wilshire."

"South of Wilshire is for shlubs," he said, stiffening as if I had insulted him. "It's got to be north of Santa Monica." Sergeant Laudermilk was not making a request; it was a demand.

Fuck him. "I'll do the best I can," I said coldly.

"I know," he said with a relenting sigh, as if he realized he had gone too far. "I didn't mean Miss Wyman was a shlub."

"Miss Wyman…?"

"I mean with her living south of Wilshire and all."

"She lives *where?*"

He stared at me as if the answer were too obvious for words. Taking a small notebook from a pocket, he moistened a thumb and flipped a few pages. "She stopped by the station this morning—she gave me her residence, in case I had any more questions. Twenty twenty-eight and a half El Camino."

I must say I took the ugly news with some semblance of equanimity. But I felt like I had caught a wet flounder across the mouth. The bearer of good tidings looked around like a man wondering what to bludgeon next. He unleashed his ass from the chair and left.

FIFTEEN

2028½ El Camino. A second-floor duplex with the name MS. SHELLEY WILDE on the tarnished brass mailslot. Ms. Wilde answered the door wearing a black and brown Nubian sheath. She was a thick column emblazoned with stars and stripes, additionally resplendent with rings on her fingers and on two stubby toes. Her red hair fell from her head like the thrums of a particularly unruly mop.

The few words we exchanged were mutually unintelligible, made so by a toy bulldog nipping at my heels and yipping hysterically. The little bastard had a bark that could grow hair on the palm of your hand, the menace of a much bigger animal. His breath, wafting upward like a miasma, was enough to sour pickles.

Gayle appeared, as solemn as only she could be in pink cord slacks and a candy-striped shirt. We settled down on the couch in silence—we had no choice, since that fucking dog kept barking at me.

"Shelley's a friend from the office," Gayle shouted, "and this is Blossom." At the sound of his name, Blossom came trotting over, grinning lewdly. "Watch out," Gayle said.

Too late. He charged and humped my leg. I kicked him in the very bull's-eye of his lust. He thudded to a landing halfway across the room, shook it off, came back and tried again. I cracked him across the ass with the only weapon handy, a copy of *Ms.* He looked shocked, emotionally bruised. He curled up in a corner and went to sleep.

Gayle began talking, ever so softly, looking straight ahead, never meeting my gaze. I tried willing her into eye contact, but it didn't work. Hearing her was equally difficult, for Shelley, having retreated to the bedroom, was playing an Andalusian folk tune on a cassette and, from the sound of it, staggering around like a moose in clogs. Other evidence of chaos penetrated the walls. Screeching, shouting, wailing, stomping, as if she were possessed.

"She all right in there?" I asked.

"Shelley? She's practicing her flamenco dance."

"Oh."

Gayle said, "I can't take it anymore."

"Neither can I. Let's get out of here."

"I don't mean Shelley. I mean you."

She said she was so pissed off at me she could faint. She said I didn't share with her—not even a hill of beans. "There are parts of you," she said, "that I'm not supposed to question. I got to pretend not to notice. Well," she said, "the hell with that."

"Ask me. Ask me anything. I'll tell you."

"You want to know what I want to ask you, is that it? All right—*what are you up to?*"

"It's very simple. It's…"

"Well?"

"I can't tell you."

"Ha!"

"It's… a big deal. My whole future."

"*Your* whole future…"

"*Ours.* We could be fixed for life."

"Does it have something to do with Jerry's death?"

"Of course not, absolutely not. If you could only accept things for a while. Adapt a little."

"You want me to change. Is that it?"

"Just for a short time."

"God," she said, "why is it, when people speak of changing, it's always other people they're talking about?"

"It won't be long—I promise. And in the meantime, if you could just try to enjoy—"

"Enjoy what? Being ignored, feeling invisible, taken for granted?"

"Listen to me, Gayle—"

"How can I enjoy feeling jealous of whoever you spend your time with, never knowing where you are or who I'm jealous of?" Her eyes held the wild, fixed stare of a wounded animal. "You think I'm some kind of mindless toy. Wind her up and she walks, she talks, she screws, but only when you want to."

"Gayle, listen—everything will be all right as soon as—"

"Well, that's good news," she snapped. But then her anger faded like breath off a mirror, and sadness took its place. "In the middle of the night," she said softly, "when you're out God knows where, I feel so frightened and lonely. That's what your love does to me."

"I'm not very good at showing it."

She shrugged. "People aren't very good at just about everything. Don't you see?" she asked imploringly, "that's what love is for. When things go bad, love is what holds you together."

"Listen to me. I love you."

She shook her head. "You went away when I needed you…"

"I came back."

"Too late. It's all over between us, don't you see? That's when it really hurts, when it's all over."

"I missed you when I was away."

"I miss you most when we're together. God," she said, "the world's a messy place."

A clicking sound came from the bedroom. The uproar was implemented by castanets.

"Let's get out of here," I repeated.

"I can't," she said, standing, straightening the belt of her slacks. "I've got to go someplace."

"Where?"

"Out."

"Who with?"

"You don't know him. Stanley Crump."

"The guy in your office? The supervisor?"

She nodded.

"Goddammit, you told me he's a married man."

"And you're not," she said. "And you never will be."

I drove slowly into the sunset, toward Four Pines Point.

Protectively, I tried to dwell on something besides my departed cohabitant, but Gayle would not be upstaged. I kept returning to her and her tooting around with Crump. Wretchedness clung heavily to me like wet seaweed.

The next thing I realized I was at the wrought-iron gate and the wilted roses row on row. Parked just inside was Ralph Farkleberry's hearse.

I drove on, up the dark coast, until I was jouncing down a narrow dirt road under a cathedral of trees. At the end of the track was the Dickens nursery, with saplings and potted plants and wooden flats of ground cover strewn about with so little regard to geometry that they appeared uncultivated; it was like a garden agreeably neglected. And there in the moon glow stood Mr. Dickens, as if he had been waiting for me.

His great age had marked small havoc on his large hickory frame—he was still upright and handsome, with an open, ponderous brow around which clung, like the locks of a noble Roman, a shag of fine white hair. He wore chinos and scuffed Wellington boots, and at his throat was a polka-dot neckerchief like a great bright butterfly. He was polite, graciously polite, as if he knew of no other option open to him, despite my unheralded intrusion. In the tradition of country people he forthwith offered me a cup of coffee, leading the way to a percolator in the potting shed. He took a crumpled paper sack from a pocket in his jeans and pressed me to accept a horehound drop.

His wife had died just a week ago, he told me in answer to my question. I murmured condolences. He accepted them without despair or the natural melancholy of one whose own life was drawing to an end. I wondered if I'd ever live to be a tranquil old man. I doubted it; I had too many bad memories. But I couldn't help remarking on his equanimity.

"It's almost as though you look forward to… to…"

"To death? No," he said, "the thing is, I've stopped looking any which way—it's a waste of time."

"All in all, how'd you like the ride?"

"Sometimes it was as rough as a stucco roller-coaster. But all in all…" he looked off like a man on the beach, serenely recollecting the days when he used to go into the water.

"You don't mind talking about yourself?" I confirmed, in case he did.

"The older I get, the more I like it. But still," he frowned, "there are times when I lapse into long silences. And why not? Nobody ever listens. People are endlessly interesting, but on the other hand," he said, "they can be mean, miserable pains in the ass."

"What do you believe in? Anything?"

"Moderation," he said emphatically, "although I've found you don't really learn anything until you do it to excess."

"What's worth striving for?"

"Peace of mind," he answered. "Still, nothing is duller or *dumber* than peace of mind. The brain goes dead. You acquire bad habits. In a way that's what life is—a collection of bad habits."

"Do you have any?"

"All old men have. And the worst of them is dying."

"But you seem so calm in facing it."

"I'm not facing it," he said irritably. "It's following me around like a fucking beggar."

Things were going turvy. I looked around at the dappled earth, the acid ingredient of fertilizer in my nostrils.

"You like your work?" I asked.

"Yep," he said. "Always have. And yet there are times that I think I should be doing something else."

"What?"

He didn't answer. "Anything else for your readers?" he asked. "Don't you want a picture?"

"Picture of what? What readers?"

"Aren't you the young feller from the Oxnard *News*? You were up here about a year ago, on my ninetieth birthday?"

I told him who I was and why I was there—about Napoleon Ochoa's interest in renting the place. I asked if he was open to it.

He said yes, and then again no.

"You have something better in mind?"

"I don't know. Let me ask you—why'd you ask me all those questions?"

"I was interested."

"In me? Or in the farm?"

"Both, I guess. But about the rental…"

"I suppose I'm amenable. Unless… you see, if you're that interested in me and the farm and all, maybe I got a better idea." Those mild, arcane, and totally fraudulent eyes latched with mine. "How'd you like to have this spread, after I'm gone?"

"Me?"

"Well, you can have it. Just come on up now, I'll teach you all you'll have to know, and when I pass on it's yours. I'll put it in writing."

I didn't answer.

"All I need is five thousand dollars to save the place—pay the debts and start in again."

"I haven't got five thousand," I said. I might have added that if I had, I'd stay up all night watching it rather than sink it into this arboreal sump hole. It's not that I can't live without the brights or that I take comfort in crowds, or that the closest population to Mr. Dickens's farm was in a town I couldn't believe they built that small anymore. It was just that at that moment the old man's offer had no appeal whatsoever. I had no intention of spending the rest of my days at grunt labor, a grove ape scratching the earth.

"Well," said Mr. Dickens, "keep in touch. Maybe you'll change your mind."

SIXTEEN

It had been too long since I'd last checked in at the Fleet office. Time, I figured, to put in an appearance; technically I was still in Senior's employ. I didn't want to drop totally out of his humdrummery. Perhaps he might harbor the dopey notion that I was conspiring with Tod against him. If I didn't need his good regard, I certainly didn't want his suspicion.

The same scabby sign was still above the door. FLEET & FLEET. I walked into the old man's office.

He was bent over his cluttered desk; he had aged considerably but not well since the last time we met. The skin of his face and throat were crumpled, loose as a lizard's. His gray-veined hand trembled intermittently. He seemed to be staring at nothing. When he looked up, blankly, it was as though he didn't recognize me, and when he did his gaze was malevolent, as if he were about to rebuke me in advance for the folly and presumption of anything I might say. I said hello, playing it safe.

"And to what do we owe your exalted presence?" he asked with a sneer in his eyes.

"Wanted to see how you were getting along," I said.

He grunted. "There's a lot of messages for you," he said expressionlessly. "All from the same guy." He rummaged about the talus slope of junk on the desk. "Wouldn't talk to me," he said, wounded. "Just wanted you. Here it is." He squinted at the note.

"Shit," he went on, "can't read my own writing." He tilted his hand, moved the slip toward his rheumy eyes, then away from them. "Kady," he said.

"Kady?"

He looked again, blinking, holding his breath in concentration as though his scrawl contained an alchemist's secret. "Katz?" he asked me. "That ring a bell?"

I nodded. "No big deal," I said.

"His secretary sounded like it was. She said Katz wants to see you soon as possible." He crumpled the slip and tossed it toward the wastepaper basket, missing by three feet. "She sounded nervous."

"You know how it is," I shrugged dismissively. "Katz has a broken-down duplex, with a second. The less chance they have of moving it, the more frantic they get."

He nodded disinterestedly. "You want to do me a favor?" he asked. "You mind cleaning out Jerry's desk?"

"Jesus. Haven't you done that yet?"

"It's hard. I mean if you could see your way clear..."

"Okay, okay." Goddammit, who knew what lurked in there? Year-old Twinkies trading microbes with a herring or two. I turned to leave.

"Jack..."

"Yeah?" My hand was on the doorknob.

"Forget it," he said grimly. "It's my job. I'll do it. One of these days."

It was the kind of Southern California day so many transplanted Easterners love—cold, dark, and overcast. The blistering sun that beat down so ostentatiously month after month unhinges New Yorkers the way the full moon addles lunatics.

I had to see Darlene. She was "nervous"; if Senior in his state of dilapidation had noticed it, anybody would. But that was the least of my problems, no more than an indication of what could follow. With Laudermilk floating around and Tod no doubt on his last drop of patience once again, Mrs. Hunt's nervousness could signal calamity.

And now she was waiting for me beside the shining big sea water. I hurried to her side; I had no news to offer about San Dismaso, and as a result I'd begun to feel that the time had come to negotiate a settlement between Tod and Darlene. Let us hope for a propitious alignment of the planets, for I had had enough of their schemes and complications. I had had enough of them. I was over it.

The roses in the garden, their long stems brittle with neglect, dipped stiffly in the wind which flattened the dry grass, emitting a faint sound of tiny blades being sharpened. She was wearing a belted white jumpsuit with the winged insignia of the U.S. Air Force. There were pearls at her throat and sergeant's stripes on the sleeves. What spoiled the pert illusion of a chorus girl on stage for a military number were smudges of paint, from knees to shoulders, that covered every shade of the spectrum.

"Well," she greeted me sardonically at the open door, "at long last. If it isn't the always elusive Jack Hopkins."

She gestured me in, extending an elegant slim arm like the maître d' of a posh restaurant. Something sparkled and flashed: on her paint-stained fingers a couple of gems writhed with colored light. She smiled amiably, noting my noting them. "My daytime diamonds," she said, wiggling the two rings, then led me to the couch in the living room.

I sank into the deep pile. Just take it easy, I told myself, set the stage, reconnoiter, gas away with my sparkling hostess (who smelled musky with perfume and pungent with oil paint).

"I'm glad you called," I began on a note of approbation, "I've been meaning to call you."

She settled down on a cushion, which emitted a soft sigh as it yielded under her firm little behind. There was about her an unsettled duality, an alliance of mild complacency and sinister portents.

"I have something to tell *you*," she said. "Thing is, Tod hasn't been bugging me at all lately. It's a big relief. Usually, you know, everything I do he blames on me." She took a deep breath. "So I've decided to forgive him." She put her warm little paint-stained hand on mine. "I don't want his blood on my hands, Jack, and I'm sure, deep down, you don't want it on yours either. You see," she smiled at me as if she were some sainted paragon preaching the

Good Word from her golden seat in heaven, "I've learned there's more to life than I'd been led to believe. A quick buck won't make me happy, and anyway happiness is a paltry goal. You know who said that?"

"Henry Thoreau? Karl Marx? Tokyo Rose?"

"George Bernard Shaw. He said..." She closed her eyes, absorbed in concentration. "'The thing is to be used, spent, squandered in the splendor of one of life's consuming causes.'" She beamed another moist, angelic smile at me, making the utmost of her redemption, hogging the scene, a reformed sinner bathed in the lamb-blood light of the Lord, and eager to share her born-again beatitude with me.

Well, all this hardly sounded like the Darlene I knew. What was this metamorphosis that had transformed her into a wispy, conciliatory, Shaw-spouting nun? What was this hair shirt she was wearing under the pearls and the linen blouse?

She sat there, Queen of the Seraphim, eager to accept some kind of unassertive, unspectacular divorce settlement that wouldn't make a dent in Tod's fortune. And I was the factor, it could be made to appear, responsible for Darlene's capitulation. Certainly I stood to benefit in Tod's eyes for accomplishing precisely what he wanted without the messiness of bloodshed. Avoiding all that otherwise inevitable ugliness and discomfort should be worth something.

"Don't you want to know why?" she prompted with sweet modesty.

"Sure," I said. "Why?"

"Come. I'll show you."

She led me to a side room I had never seen before. In it was a high stool, an easel, a kitchen table full of acrylic paint cans and brushes. Against the walls were stretched canvases, large paintings that might have been the work of a retarded gorilla. The kindergarten colors were painful to the eye. The compositions were all quite similar—squarish but ill-defined, as if the gorilla had used the same garish jukebox, over and over again, for his model.

How do you like them?" she asked shyly.

"Hmm," I said, narrowing my eyes, standing close, moving back, play-ing Theo, astounded by Vincent's mad, inspired brushwork.

"Phenomenal," I said.

"I'm so glad to hear you say so," she said, squirming with pleasure. "It's called stochastic painting, Ralph told me. I do it blindfolded."

"Unbelievable." I hadn't seen the hearse, but it seemed like that gutter-snipe was still hanging around.

The paintings were numerous. They were forthrightly numbered 16, 17, 29, 37, all of them unsigned. But of course she couldn't write blindfolded. She engulfed me in a glistening smile. The trace of sullenness around her mouth, so evident in the past, was gone. And there was about her a vibrancy, a bounciness that was adorable, and more so when she said, "I'm happy now. I'm *thinking*—somehow the blindfold helps. I still have to master technique, but I'm on a steep learning curve. The thing is to develop creativity and flow with it."

Now a peculiar thing happened. Two peculiar things—three—which I can only explain by an overwhelming sensation of relief in not having to respond, one way or another, to Tod's expectations of my whacking her (or to hers of whacking Tod); and by the additional extraordinary awareness (given the time and place) that happiness is sexy (at least I've found it so). And then the third: I wanted to pull her into my arms. But instead I said, "I'm glad you're happy."

"It's not only my painting," she said, "I've been seeing someone."

"Ralph?" Who else?

She nodded.

"He's a painter, too?"

"He does jewelry. You know—African stuff—out of watermelon seeds and like pork chop bones. He's a very remarkable person."

Now I knew where the Shaw quote came from. "Where is he?" I asked.

"Surfing."

Outside fast flowed the evening tide, and the shades of night were falling. "He surfs in the dark?"

"Of course not. He promised to pick up some groceries on the way home. He'll be back any minute." Then, as if I had asked, she said, "He's fine—Ralph."

"And how's Leo?"

"You want to see?"

What I wanted was to get out of there fast, to tell Hunt that he had a deal that beat the hell out of homicide.

"You're lucky, " she said. "This is Leo's big day."

"Great. How's that make me lucky?"

"Today he gets to eat—it's kind of unusual. You can watch." She took my arm. Without enthusiasm I walked with her to the adjoining room. The heat in there had a pungent aridity that seemed to scorch the eyeballs. On a table was a large wire cage that bottomed out in a sandbox, and in it was Leo. He raised his heavy head like a periscope and flicked his tongue in greeting. He settled down again.

Darlene went to another cage. She opened the trap and stuck her hand in. The rat scurried to avoid it, squeaking. Her fingers closed over the tail. For a moment the rat struggled, a flailing gray ball bobbing like a spent yo-yo. And then it hung still.

"I couldn't have done this even a month ago," Darlene marveled at her accomplishment.

She carried the rat to Leo's cage. She paused and looked at the snake, about seven feet of lethargy. He was spread out on the sand like a lead pipe twisted into a loose 8.

Darlene slipped open the hinged lid and dropped the rat inside. It scampered across the sand like a mechanical toy, as far as possible from the python, and lay there alert and trembling. Darlene stood mesmerized. Tentatively, as if propelled by hypnosis, I crossed the room to stand beside her.

The boa constrictor raised its head. Sluggishly it curled its pale brown body, the tail flicking slowly, brick red with black and yellow markings. The head quivered almost imperceptibly, and then the body lunged. The rat streaked to the diagonal corner and the python flopped heavily on the sand.

I felt distinctly uncomfortable.

Darlene's face held a taut vacancy. She stood still as a stone watching the cage.

Leo wound himself up for another shot at his dinner. It took a lot of time.

"Jesus," Darlene said huskily. "Would you look at that? Leo's like in slow motion..."

The python had pulled himself into striking position like a conical beehive. Now he lurched forward, epileptic and implausible as a papier-mâché serpent on a string. Again the rat dodged, and, with an air of indifference, as though this deadly game engaged some other rat, certainly not him, it slithered across the sand, back to its original post.

"You might as well pull up a chair," Darlene said. "This could take some time."

Silence, heavy as the heat, hung over the room. The snake hissed softly. The rat squealed as Leo sprang. A thudding noise, like a moldy tree falling. He had missed again.

"You'd better get him glasses," I said, "or he'll starve to death." I felt better now that I wasn't going to witness an execution.

"He doesn't eat much." She continued to stare at the cage. "Sometimes he goes two or three months without, Ralph says…"

"It'll take him two or three months to catch up with that rat." I had to acknowledge that old Ralph cut a wide swath. An authority on snakes and Shaw, painting and Christ knows what else. "Maybe," I suggested, "you ought to cook Leo a steak."

"He's just not hungry. Ralph had one that didn't eat for over a year."

Leo, possibly out of sheer exhaustion, lay where he had fallen. Now he curled up in a tight witless ball and went to sleep.

"You ever see anything like it?" Darlene asked. "He sleeps with his eyes open. He doesn't have eyelids."

"He doesn't have much of a brain, either."

She turned slowly to face me. "You don't like Leo, do you?" she said accusingly.

"I never thought much about him, one way or the other."

"It's unfair. I mean, just because you don't like Ralph. You don't know anything about him."

"Do you?"

She sighed theatrically, "Who knows anything about anybody?" she asked. Her voice rose a few operatic decibels. "Who can fathom the human fucking heart?"

"All I know, he's a dip-shitty drifter—"

"He's seeking alternatives."

"—off a spaced-out commune for the overaged."

"He's a philosopher and an artist."

"Whatever you say." I moved toward the door. I had to get out of there, get far away from Darlene, Ralph, and that fucking snake—the weirdest *ménage à trois* this side of Krafft-Ebing. "If you could see your way clear to take a few notes on some of the pearls old Ralph drops—just jot them down on the back of an envelope—we'll run through them the next time you call."

"Don't be such a smart-ass," she murmured. "And about that 'next time'—you might as well know we won't ever be calling each other again. Or seeing each other. Ever." The blood seemed to have drained from her face, leaving a patchwork of gray and white, the tincture of panic. "If you dare call me," she said thickly, "or come out here again, I'll have you castrated with a blowtorch."

"That," I said, bristling, "would be a hell of a way to refuse a well-meaning phone call."

"You think I'm fucking stupid…?" (What was she so upset about?) "A push-over? 'A well-meaning phone call,'" she repeated hatefully.

"What's so painful about—"

"I know why you're so pissed," she raged. "It's like Ralph says…"

"What's he saying now?"

"He said you'd get bent all out of shape if I lay off Tod money-wise, 'cause you wouldn't be getting the money we discussed. I just hope you don't intend to do anything about it."

"Like what?"

"Like tryna shakedown me, which you'd have reason to regret."

I didn't answer.

"Just try it," she said, "and I'll… I'll…" Fury held her tongue, but only for an instant. "You think," she rampaged, "I'll stand still for your black-mail?" She turned abruptly back to Leo.

And then a barren, strangulated cry tore the air. I saw her run—shamble— to the cage, the terrible rattling noise caught in her throat. Her eyes were flinty, her mouth was twisted and hung open like a dog's in midsummer.

In the cage the rat had gnawed a neat excavation in Leo's head. Now it sat on the edge of the concavity as on a little throne, high on the coiled dead body, feasting.

SEVENTEEN

At home, alone in bed, I tried to think of how to pitch it to Tod. Darlene was game for a settlement, sure—but how did I know about it? "She asked me in," I pictured myself beginning... and pictured Tod slamming a chalcedonic paperweight against my head.

Stymied, I stared up at the chunks of plaster Gayle had clawed from the wall to chew like stale taffy. The luminous hands of the clock read a few minutes after one. Gayle. What was she up to? Probably in a plastic orange booth at some bluegrass bar, rubbing knees with Mr. Crump, her goatish supervisor. Shit. I pounded the pillow and thought seriously of jerking off. Instead I hurled myself out of bed and lurched toward the kitchen for a beer.

The phone rang. "Listen," Tod Hunt said, "I couldn't sleep..." The tortured wail of a blood brother in the haunted forest of the night. Was I going to have to come up with something on the fly? "...so I went over to see Carmen. I thought maybe if I whimpered a little I might get lucky and she'd give me a sympathy fuck..." He was speaking fast, the words running together.

It sounded like a reprieve. "How'd you make out?" I asked.

"She's not there. Where is she?"

"How should I know?"

"Can't you find her?"

Was he out of his mind? I said, "You think she's back with her parents?"

"I can't barge in there in the middle of the night. They'll think something's happened. *I* think something's happened."

"Is her place okay? Nobody's trashed it or..."

"No. Everything's battened down, but the drapes in the living room are wide open. Someone might have been watching her." His voice trailed off. The silence was concussive. Then: "I wouldn't ask you, but I can't get involved..."

The shitmobile coughed and clanked—its sleep had been interrupted. Where could she be? Something Tod said on the phone had touched a nerve, but whatever it was lay imprisoned in some part of my mind; I couldn't shake it loose. Over and over again I reviewed his every word... something... imprisoned... something locked... the doors, the windows... the drapes—that was it! The open drapes. Looking down on The French Lick.

The place was empty, except for a few men slouching at the bar or curled around the spongecake tables. No one acknowledged my presence, so I walked to a stool about the size of an aspirin and flopped.

A sequined backdrop flew the length of a small, slightly raised stage, its glitter long lost. A waitress slouched at the bar with a pair of twin volcanoes on her bare chest. She bounced toward me like a showboating athlete dribbling two basketballs.

"Hi," she said flatly, bending over the table, dangling the basketballs in my face. A little swastika was tattooed above a nipple.

"Hi. Scotch and water, please," I said, adding, "Who owns this place?"

"Beats hell out of me. I just work here."

"Who runs it?"

"S'not around."

"All right. Who's in charge?"

She stared at me with an animal's limited concentration.

"I'll get him," she said, and with a tired toss of her tits headed back toward the bar. She walked—trudged—with a curious incurving of the spine, possibly caused by the forward drag of her counterweights.

The door leading to the kitchen swung open. The voices of two men slashed through, arguing in explosive Italian. It flapped shut again, and at my shoulder stood a slim wraith of a man in black slacks and a black short-sleeved shirt. His pockmarked face was the color and texture of cottage cheese. He looked like he had recently climbed out of a sporty grave at Forest Lawn.

"Frank Magenti," he whispered. His handshake was the brush of a moth. He repeated my name and looked as if he were trying to place me, and couldn't.

"You got a girl here named Carmen Ochoa?"

"Can I see your badge?" Neither his voice nor his manner was antipatico. Just cautious.

"I'm not a cop."

"A relative?"

"No."

"Then why you want to know? This girl do something you don't like?"

"What I don't like is what she's doing around here."

"Mister..." he reached into his shirt pocket for an unfiltered cigarette. The flame of his lighter was as bright and as brief as a tracer bullet. "...We run a legit operation in the leisure business."

"She..." The word was drowned out by a flash flood of hard rock on a scratchy cassette. It was loud enough to give you cauliflower ears, to break crystal. Just as suddenly the little stage was overrun by a quintet of screeching girls in fringed white leather bikinis about the size of Band-Aids, and sequined white leather boots. They bounced and slithered to the shooting sparks of the music.

Four of the five dancers were tree-tall, monadnocks of sex. The fifth was Carmen, waving, of all things, pom-poms. She waved them like whips, as if she were a lion tamer. Her caramel body rippled with a grace that defied gravity, her round little ass switching in a ridiculous parody of a dance so frenzied and swift I could hardly have followed her feet, if they had been what I was staring at. Astonishing. When finally the music boiled to a climax and she with the others ran off the stage, I was a limp rag.

"The kid with the pom-poms," I told Magenti. "Ochoa."

"So?" His shallow eyes held a flicker of menace. "You tryna tell me who I should hire?" He snared the swizzle stick next to my drink and broke it between his fingers, as if he would have found it more gratifying had it been my neck. "You ever hear of the First Amendment? Which what you call guarantees freedom of expression? That includes artistic—"

"She's fourteen years old."

Without pause, without even the smallest shift of inflection, Magenti said, "Get her out of here."

We sat in the car, separated by maybe a couple of million light years. She had not gone gently into the night. A lustrous dark red pallor consumed her lovely face, and she was furious, refusing to talk, mumbling to herself (but loud enough for me to hear) in a spasm of rustic maledictions. It was unending, and she never repeated herself. A pestilential rat, she called me, a ruinous worm. A thieving magpie, a vulture, a syphilitic blue pig.

I could understand her rage. Canned before she got started and far too young to assume the emeritus. When finally the storm subsided: "Would you like something to eat?" I asked.

In perfectly enunciated English she said, "Fuck you."

"You learn that at The French Lick?"

"I have learned much English," she said in Spanish.

"Such as what, if it pleases you to say?"

She took a deep breath, "Lifestyle," she said. "Heightened consciousness. Horrendous. Up your jebobo, badvibes, dummass, fucker, farout, wow." She had a hell of an ear.

"Would you like some ice cream?"

"No," she shook her head sharply. "Why have you made me redundant?"

"For a thousand reasons. First, you're underage. Second, you could be deported..."

"And what would you care?"

"You would go hungry. The papers say Mexico has raised the price of bread."

"All countries have a sameness in that regard," she said. "They have all the money, but they swallow it into their own stomachs." She seemed to calm down a bit, displacing her anger from me to politics.

I turned off Ventura Boulevard and up into the foothills.

"Where are you taking me?"

"Home."

"I am not tired. For a favor, can we drive to the beach?"

It was—I glanced at my watch—a quarter to two, and I was whipped.

"The girls at The French Lick talked much of the beach. They frolic in the sun, before they come to work."

I sighed. I picked up the phone and called Tod. "I found your stray lamb," I said, "at her parents' for the night. She'll be back tomorrow."

"Jesus, Jack, thanks," he said. "I really appreciate... tell you what—why don't you sleep late in the morning? We can set back the agenda a day or so."

On to the beach, past the dark houses and the spectral cars rushing by like meteors tumbling through space.

"I thank you," she said gravely.

We were barefooted, kicking the cool sand under the blackness of the sky.

"It was a good idea," I said. The lights of Pacific Coast Highway curved like a necklace across Santa Monica Bay.

"I do not speak of the beach," she said, "but of The French Lick. The people who came there were totally without appreciation of art."

"Philistines, eh?"

"No. Americans. But slobs, peasants. They looked like something out of the test tube of the Doctor Frankenstein. Like they escaped from the zoo. One of them—I would swear he had a tail. I kept waiting for him to order bananas. And even the clean ones, with the hair combed in a nice ducktail, you had to stay out of the dark corners. They would follow a girl off a freeway bridge, and give her the zig-zig, you will pardon me, before she hit the ground."

"I'm sure it was most difficult."

She shrugged, sighed, and then her smile lit up the night. "But it is all behind me." She collapsed in the sand. "You are a good friend."

"Sometimes it takes an incident like this for one to appreciate school."

"I would not say that the experience has enflamed in me any such yearning. I do not like school."

"What do you like?"

"I think," the wick of her tongue curved over an upper tooth, "I would like to live on a ranch. I am a phenomenon with crops and animals. I am a fantastic cook, a baker of breads and delicate pastries."

She stared out at the ocean, at the gold path on the water drifting toward us from the moon.

"I would like to dance in the evening," she continued. "And grow things on the ranch during the day."

"Would that not be tiring?"

"To do something well is not tiring. To do two things well is a refreshment, each for the other." She smiled. "Would you care to see where I was kicked by a cow when I was four?"

She twisted her body, holding her breath with the rapt concentration of a child. The scar was on her elbow, a small white crescent. I examined it respectfully.

There seemed nothing more to do for the moment except shiver in the wind that whistled around us. The surf pounded the sand pebbles, popping like a salvo of a damp musket.

"We shall build a fire," she said.

We gathered driftwood, she doing most of the gathering, piling the moist harvest in my arms. Expertly she lighted the fire. I lay back and she tumbled against me. Her hair smelled bittersweet, of iodine, her breath like strawberry milkshake. For a long time neither of us moved. "I have an idea," she said in a strange, silky voice.

"Oh?" I limned aimless doodles in the sand with my finger.

"Would it please you," she asked, "if I took off my clothes?"

I shot up off my back, propelling her with me. "No," I said sternly.

"You refuse to sleep with me?" she asked, glowering.

"That's right."

"You are no gentleman," she declared. "Even those apes at The French Lick were in that respect men of honor. If I had asked them to sleep with me, I'm sure they would have obliged."

I bet they would have, I thought. Not that I wasn't tempted. From the moment I had seen her frisking around the boards in Magenti's cave my heart had looped. Hell, it wasn't my heart at all; my reaction was centered in my groin, and now, here on this windswept shore, with the smoke of the fire drifting over us, she was swiftly reducing me to a perspiring jelly.

But I couldn't do it. We all know that one good turn in the kip or the sand deserves another. Tod might well be the last to know, as was so often noted in the lore of cuckoldry, but it was only a question of time before he did. I'd just barely extricated myself from his first wife—I didn't need to get in any deeper with his second.

And Carmen was fourteen years old. Not even past her quinceañera, I told myself.

She was crying. Her slim torso was curled womb-like against her knees, her arms enfolding them, her head bowed under the swirl of dark hair. I put my arm around her. "Carmen." Quietly, sternly I said, "I can't sleep with you."

"And I thought you were my benefactor," she said scornfully. "That you would not treat me with less respect because I am in distress."

"Your benefactor is the Señor Hunt."

She shook her head. "You and he want the same thing—for me to be compliant. A toy for him to play with."

"No. He likes you better for having a mind of your own."

"I am not at all sure what he likes. It is galling that I am expected to be what he likes."

"He is much taken by the way you are."

"He speaks of marriage, but all he wants is the zig-zig. He has no love for me that is not half contempt. I hold in his eyes a glaring insignificance."

"I cannot agree with you."

"That is because you are afraid of him." She chewed on a knuckle. "You are afraid for your employment—whatever it is that you do." Derisively she asked, "Are you a pimp?"

I said nothing.

"Well," fire leaped and curled in her eyes, "you will not have the employment unless you... you... do you not understand?"

"You are giving yourself unnecessary pain."

"It is not so much the pain as it is an absence of joy. If I cannot find happiness when I am young, when can I find it?" She shook her head sadly, gulped a sobby deep breath, then: "I would do much for my papa and my mama—you know this—but the thought of defloration by that old man is unbearable."

I looked at her disbelievingly. "You're a *virgin*?"

The knuckles which a moment before had been in her mouth slammed into mine.

"You think I am a *puta*?" she snarled. "Then I act like one!"

Her fists pummeled me like toy pile-drivers. I grabbed at them, snared them. She struggled, and then went limp in my arms. But she was adamant.

"You do as I say," she insisted, "or I will never see Hunt again."

"Suit yourself. But," I added lamely, "he can do much for you."

"So you have said, an infinity of times. This thing between that old man and me—don't you see?" she said hopelessly, "It cannot work."

"He's not old. He's autumnal."

"We are as different as chalk and cheese," she hesitated, groping for words. "Even if I were to take rich with Hunt in America, still there is this distance between us."

"You could change. You could learn the new ways."

"No. It is like a social... a social malnutrition. It is like the fighters of my country, who live in Mexican slums even after they become champions. It would be better to live in a mansion, but we lack preparation for it."

"Don't you enjoy your new home?"

She shrugged. "It is a confinement." She rubbed the big slow tears away with the back of her hand. "Are you going to sleep with me or not?"

The question hung chillingly in the night air. The fire had sunk to a bed of lascivious scarlet that waned, then waxed again in the wind sweeping over the beach like a sinister bird. For a moment I tried to imagine a way to set Carmen up with Ralph Farkleberry.

It was ridiculous. Here with irrefutable logic she's begging for a bounce and I'm playing hard to get.

That pig-iron pestle in my pants decided for me. I leaped toward her in a spray of sand and she met me halfway, and we were thrashing around, tearing off our clothes. I pressed into her. She gasped and gasped again. O-h-h-h Jesus Mary and Joseph, she gasped, throwing back her head, her sweet panting breath coming dry and hoarse. Her nails sank into my shoulders. She was getting the hang of it, her body arching, her stare dull and blank... a little grimace on the molded lips... her tail whipping.

She lay there trembling, the silvery fire washing over her, throwing a glaze on her face, giving it the look of a stained-glass saint. Her black eyes held a kind of drowsy satiety.

Finally she said, "So that's it. What makes the world go round. Some big deal." She leaned over and brushed a gossamer kiss on my mouth. "You sure you did it right?" she asked.

* * *

I lay in my bed exhausted, as if I had run a great distance in a cold rain. I hadn't slept in twenty-four hours.

We had come back to Carmen's chalet drained, frozen, and silent. Her postcoital crack about my, shall we say, lack of prowess still bugged me. What she didn't know about zig-zig could fill a tome. And yet...

"You are much woman," I had told her, yearning for some crumb of endearment in return.

"And you are much man," she answered, yawning. She glanced through the open door to her bedroom. "Maybe," she said, "it would work better in a bed?"

"Maybe. But not tonight."

The phone damned near blew me out of the sack. Darlene's unnerving voice made no attempt to suppress her anxiety. "What are you doing?" she demanded.

"Oh, sitting around cracking sunflower seeds." What in the hell did she think I was doing at six forty-five in the morning?

She said, "You were right. I got to see you."

"Right about what? See about what?"

"That bastard Farkleberry. He had me brainwashed. We had a terrible fight last night about the goddamn snake. I don't know what to do with him."

"Call the SPCA."

"Not the snake. Farkleberry. I'm afraid of him."

A little nerve began to pulse arrhythmically on the side of my head. "Where is he now?"

"Surfing. But he'll be back any minute."

"Get in your car. Take off for... for..."

"He's got my car. The hearse wouldn't start."

"I'll pick you up."

"Not here." She paused, and then she said, "Where, goddamnit?"

"I don't know," I said, "let me think..."

And then I remembered. The switchback road leading up to the camp Ralph had told Darlene and me about, above the gorge where he had been squatting, just east of the beach house. What was the name of the fucking road?

"Jack?"

"Listen. There's a road leading up to the hills, just east of the beach house…"

"Yerba Verde Canyon?"

"That's it. Exactly one mile up."

"I'll be there," she said. "I'll start now."

"Wait a minute. Why now? It'll take me an hour to…"

"I'll have to walk. I'll be off the road, in the woods."

"How will you judge the distance—the mile?"

"I have a pedometer. I'll pile up three stones where I go off the road."

"See you in an hour," I said.

EIGHTEEN

The three flat stones were balanced on the berm of the road where a steep path descended into the gorge, surrounded by a girdle of hills, severe and brooding and shaggy with chaparral. It was hard to believe that human beings were no more than a mile away. I started down the path and promptly stumbled over a rock, but my weariness rather than the terrain was to blame. I felt light-headed from lack of sleep, suddenly old, an alien in this tilted landscape.

The path continued downward. A jackrabbit streaked through the stunted sagebrush as if it had been kicked. He vanished as swiftly, as mysteriously, as he had seconds ago appeared.

I was in a sunless clearing within a maze of tangled shrubs. No one was there. Behind me a dry branch cracked. I spun around. Facing me, a dozen feet away, with nothing between us but his beard and the knife in his hand, was Ralph Farkleberry.

I took a deep breath. "Hi, Ralph," I said in a voice I hoped was soothing. "Sorry I missed you yesterday."

He got straight to the point: "She never wants to see you again. But I'm gonna dead you up, just to make sure."

He was as nervous as I was, flexing his vocal cords to fuel his waning courage. The giveaway was his breathing, the rib cage going in and out like a concertina. Keep talking, I told myself.

"She's as changeable as a prairie fire—"

"Shut up," he snapped. "One more peep outta your bill and I open your neck at the bleeding place."

His inventory of ferocious bromides was relentless, but I had little time to dwell on style. He came on, moving as if he had a broken spring, that shuddersome knife slashing the air.

"Only this morning she called. Couldn't wait to see me."

"Couldn't wait to get rid of you," he said. "Why you think I'm here, and not her?"

Because, I realized, she wasn't satisfied with our last interview. Because she wanted me dead; I knew too much. Because Ralph was the new boy on her block, so she sics him on me like a mad dog.

He was on the verge of panic, not that I could tell from his face with all that hair on it. But his grip on the knife was too tight. The hand holding it shook perceptibly. He came at me, the shiv moving in a short slow plane across his body.

"All right, Ralph," I said, "I get your message. Why don't we leave it at that?"

"There's more." His unblinking mercurochrome eyes were shot with purpose. "She said to cut your dick off."

"Anything else she say? She tell you she's married?"

"She's separated."

"It takes two to separate, Ralph. You know who I am?"

"She told me. A nosey real-estate wimp."

"She told you a lot of things."

"Shut up!"

His knife continued to trace an invisible parabola in the air—and then an odd thing happened. Which proved that his untidy head was not totally impenetrable to suggestion.

"Jesus," he pulled up short. "You her husband?"

The knife wavered unsteadily and dropped a fraction, and in that irresolute instant I splashed my fist on his nose, my only visible target. I could feel it, hear it snap. I twisted the knife from his limp fingers and threw it into the thicket. I must have hit him twenty times before he fell like a dead tree.

Blood gushed from his nose and from his open mouth, dyeing his beard, and his eyes sought out mine in a look of dull astonishment. I reached down and shook him until they regained a semblance of awareness. He began to cry, a racking, hoarse strangulation. His hands with the blood seeping through them covered his nose and his mouth as I pulled him to his feet.

"Listen, assface, can you listen?"

He seemed to nod through the red beard.

"To answer your question: No, I'm not her husband. You hear me?"

Again that uncoordinated nod, like one of those idiot dolls perched at the rear window of a car, the head bobbing on a wire.

"Open your fucking eyes. Look at me." I reached in my pocket, peeled a card from my wallet. He opened his eyes. They were rimmed with fear.

"I'm not going to hit you again, okay? I want you to read something." I flashed the card before his grotesque face. He tried hard to unblock the neurons that carried the message to his brain.

"Sergeant Joseph Laudermilk," he said spongily.

"Beverly Hills Police," I prompted. "I'm doing a little job for her husband. Get it?"

"Yes, sir," he said. *Sir.* "Can I ask a question?" Humbly.

I nodded.

"How come," he mumbled, "you didn't pull your piece on me? You're a police officer...?"

He wasn't as groggy as I thought. "Because, Ralph, I'd rather use my fists on a pissant like you." I stared him down and pressed the advantage. "You just attacked a police officer with a deadly weapon. That's a rap you're not going to beat, unless you get the fuck out of this county."

"Okay," he said. "I'm splitting."

"Now. This minute. Where's your hearse?"

"Up the road. Beyond the next turn."

"Get in it and drive. And don't look back." I took his arm and together we struggled up the thickety hill. "You got a key to the house?"

He nodded.

"Give it to me."

He handed it over.

"Can you drive?" I asked as he fell into the hearse, revving the engine. He nodded again, dully. I reached through the window and laid a heavy hand on his shoulder. "One other thing, Ralph—don't ever fuck up again. I'll know every move you make and I'll be all over you. We cops got ways of finding shitheads like you."

Again he nodded, and the hearse took off like a scalded-assed rat. Up the rise, around the bend, and out of my life forever. Or so I thought. I should have known that a pest like Ralph was not to be disposed of so easily. I exhaled sharply. There was nothing in this disorderly world that I wanted more than to go home, sink between the cool sheets, and sleep. But the day was just beginning. What it would hold had been unabashedly determined by Darlene, my sanguinary butterfly, on the dark edge of the ocean. She had steered her blustering pseudo-assassin on me; I had to counterattack before she launched her next offensive.

I crossed the rose garden and passed the Rolls in the driveway. The house was still, waiting patiently for me to slip Ralph's key into the latch. The door opened quietly. I entered the living room.

Darlene was not there. I climbed the stairs in the stillness. The door of her bedroom was half-closed. I pushed it open and stared at the room in total disbelief.

Everything in it was trashed. The mattress had been ripped open, the ticking scattered like tufts of dirty snow. The pillows had been sliced with a knife, creating a havoc of feathers. The drawers and contents of Darlene's writing desk, of a bureau, a chest, and a chiffonnier had been dumped on the floor, like windrows in the path of a doomsday machine. Untidy mounds of clothing, a pyramid of shoes, all were scattered. They dwarfed the dimensions of the room, and on top of one ungainly heap was an overturned leather-tooled jewel box. Beside it was a miscellany of early treasures. A skate key, a bean bag, a rabbit's foot, a half-dozen jacks, a frayed yellow ribbon—the precious harvest of Darlene's years in West Texas, much of it tagged in a laboriously childish hand; a few gray and black pebbles *"from Sour Springs Lake,"* the rattles of a diamondback *"from Rattlesnake Round-up,"* the brownish petals of a gardenia, *"Mustang Prom Night, Sweetwater High,"* a trilobite fossil *"found over on Stink Creek Road near Merkel,"* a lacquered sand crab that *"bit me on Rivera Beach, Corpus Christi,"* a birthday card of faded hearts and flowers:

It's great to be Eight,
There's nothing so fine,

So just make the best of it
'Til you are Nine.
Daddy

But no jewelry. That son of a bitch Ralph. I should have emptied his pockets, glanced at least in the back of the hearse. Or maybe Darlene was wearing all of it. But where was she? I dashed down the stairs, out the front door, and ran to the edge of the cliff. A painfully luminous light hung over the water. Something sparkled among the rocks on the face of the cliff, an infinitesimal splinter abnormally sharp and bright, and then it was gone. I squinted at where it had been and again it burst, a swift intensity, and then I saw it was attached to a finger of a hand partially exposed in a rocky crevice.

Darlene's daytime diamond. I hurled myself down the cliff.

Her body was wedged between two great boulders, planted tighter than if she had six feet of dirt weighing her down. She looked strangely pointless, like a cracked doll. I stood there, staring down at her deadness. Knouts of water and the high wind pounded the rocky coast, abrading her as if she had been snagged by an angry Leviathan with claws. Soon, a matter of days, and she would be reduced to something less than human. Whoever was to find her might regret the discovery if he came too close.

And then the wind ate its way into my lungs. Loitering there, I realized, was strictly forbidden by all the rules of self-preservation. I scurried back up the precipice, leaving my future buried under those rocks with Darlene. I had to call Tod and tell him I had ganged agley, that somebody had gotten to Darlene before me. I pulled up before a phone booth at a roadside joint. My hand shook as I dropped coins into the slot.

"Tod?" I said, "Jack here."

"Hello," he said placidly, "how are you?"

"Fine. And you?"

"Fine." Casually, he asked, "Have you checked out the Fleet property on Dribble Drive?"

I took a deep breath and... and then I said, "Yes."

"Good," he said, "good."

NINETEEN

It was almost a week later that Darlene was found. An adolescent boy and girl, foraging after sex among the sheltering rocks, stumbled upon her body.

The discovery rated no more than a quarter of a column in the Metro section of the *Times*. After all, it was the third of the day, the five hundred and ninety-seventh homicide of an annum (the previous year had piled up 1,023) that had run but half its lethal course.

Tod maintained a glacial reserve in dealing with the police and the press. Only once was he quoted in the papers; a reporter who approached him for a statement was dismissed in one caustic sentence. "I do not," Tod said, "have a capacity for public mourning."

Nevertheless, it seemed to me that he was secretly miffed by the paucity of print. That the press found her negligible was to him a diminishment of his own importance.

Indeed, he wanted the best of everything, good press along with the admiration of the bored, frenetic men and women thrusting tape recorders and mikes in his mouth, demanding photos of his wife, which he claimed he didn't have—so even her loveliness was reduced to a dismissive rumor. Whatever that remarkable face had looked like, with the mask of sea maggots upon it she was not in her present state a beauty. The police meanwhile were pursuing the usual unspecific evidence, but the restlessly inattentive world didn't give much of a damn.

The leads themselves were as elusive as foxfire in the deep California night. No one volunteered information. No one mentioned a bearded stranger or a hearse parked in the driveway of Four Pines Point. And as the days slipped by, Darlene evolved into a non-person.

Still I stayed clear of Tod. Two days after Darlene was found I returned to my desk at Fleet Realty (the sign had at last been repainted), where unfortunately I couldn't avoid Senior. He too was altered far beyond the decline I had noted less than a month ago. The sockets of his eyes were deep melancholy cavities in the pinkish face of an old man, a withered baby's face.

A feeble passivity about all things seemed to possess him; all things save one. He was obsessed by Darlene's death. He questioned me closely about Tod—how was he taking it? What were the details of the murder? Anything that wasn't in the papers?

Nothing, I assured him, that I knew of. I hadn't seen Hunt, who sought isolation in his sorrow. And he had never been one to confide in me.

"She must have been a mess when they found her," Senior said in hushed, scholarly tones.

"How so?"

"It says here..." he rummaged through a desk drawer, eased out a wrinkled copy of a national weekly, one of those sensational journals dedicated to human kinkiness—sadistic mayhem, masochistic diets, astrological divination, and the sexual appetites of celebrities. Two short columns on page three were devoted (in a way Tod would not have appreciated had he read such publications) to the murder. "It says the waves and the wind had ripped all the clothes off her body. She was balls-ass naked when they found her, except for the ring on her finger and the shoes on her feet." He ran his rheumy eyes over a paragraph. "Blue and white sneakers, it says. You think the motive was robbery?"

"That's what the papers said."

"What about the ring? The sapphire?"

"All I know, the cops were quoted as saying the thief must've panicked when she appeared, killed her, and without further inspection tossed her off the cliff."

Senior sighed. He tossed the magazine back in its drawer. "I don't give a fuck about Mrs. Hunt," he said, "or Tod Hunt either. It's Jerry…" His flow of words was like a choppy, uneasy current, hard to navigate.

"What about Jerry?"

"You shafted him, Jack. You fucked both of us over. After all we done for you."

"What are you talking about?"

He opened another drawer and took out a vinyl notebook with a Western motif on the cover—saddles and spurs, a branding iron, smoking six-guns. It was the kind of loose-leaf a third-grader might carry to school, only it had Jerry's name on the spine.

Senior opened it to a sheet of company stationery lodged between two pages. "I cleaned out Jerry's desk," he said in a dry monotone. His eyes with their watery glitter ran over the childish scrawl before he handed it to me. "Read it," he ordered.

The letter was dated a few days before Jerry's death. *"Dear Daddy,"* it began,

Birthdays are a time for praising the birth day boy but Ive been thinking maybe its even better on such an occasion that your only son was to pay you the very highest compliment of being really honest with you. You probably dont remember that when I was a little kid we were so close together that that friend of yours Kenny Zierler called us conspirators. I was so little at the time that you had to tell me what that word meant which made me real proud. I dont know how it happened but it was only a little later about the time Mommie passed that you commenced hollering at me. It got so bad that when I would look out the window in the evening and see you coming down the street home from work that even before you came into the house Id get penis pains and when I told you about them youd holler at me some more. Well Daddy there are times now when I see you coming into the office or walking up to my desk that I still get those penis pains. Of course I never told you about them I figure what good would it do but I wish we would get along better. I just wish we were like we used to be when we were conspirators and we would laugh over something and you would give me Twinkies, but I know as things stand now you dont like the way I dress or my eating habits and sometimes I think you wouldnt like it no matter how I dressed or what I ate. You think I dont pull my weight but you dont know how hard I try and youre always throwing Jack Hopkins up to me as a crackerjack gogetter and when I tell you whats going on with him you dont believe me as if I would lie to you Daddy. Still I think you're the best father in the world and on this occasion I really want to sincerely wish you many happy returns of the day

That was as far as Jerry had gotten. The poor bastard, yearning for the Twinkies and endearments of yesteryear... I handed the letter back to Senior. He slipped it into Jerry's notebook.

"What's he referring to?" I asked. "The business of what's going on with me?"

"You know fucking well," Senior's dry voice snapped. "Four Pines Point. You did a knockdown on the property for a Mrs. George Norton. Only it was Jerry's impression that she was Mrs. Tod Hunt."

That prick. He had promised not to tell Senior...

"Something funny's going on," he said. "Something fucking stinks like fish rot in an alley."

"What, for instance?" I glared back at him.

"Whatever it was, you should of told me," he said reproachfully. "I been like a father to you, goddammit. And Jerry was like a brother. He knew you thought he was an ass-wipe and it hurt him deep."

"Look, Senior. This is easily explained. Mrs. Hunt—"

"Jerry told me the explanation you gave him," he said skeptically. "I only mention it because that's what started Jerry not trusting you. He figures you're jerking us around, he don't know exactly how. He figures we better find out."

Senior plucked his gold toothpick from the desk pad and plunged it into an ear before he went on: "You been telling that girl you been shacking with that you're away nights on business, which she confides to Jerry. What kind of business can that be, Jerry figures, at night? Are you really with Hunt, or are you fucking him over too?

"So Jerry commences tailing you"—here we go again. Jerry the cowboy sleuth—"downtown, where you pick up a spic kid and take her up in the hills. He notes the house and drives on. He comes back to stake out the joint, a couple of nights before he's... killed. He sees this girl through the window, figures she might see him—"

He figured right: he was her "prowler," her "rapist."

"—so he hauls ass. He figures you're getting a little nooky on the side, paying the rent. Then he figures maybe you own the house, maybe you're in business for yourself while you're picking up a salary from us. Maybe you're siphoning off a good buy here and there, fucking us over.

"But Jerry ain't one to jump at conclusions. He wants proof. He goes down to the Hall of Records, to ascertain whose name the house is in. He damn near craps hisself when he finds out it's owned by Tod Hunt"—he glowered at me—"who never reports it when he listed his holdings with us."

"What'd Jerry make of that?"

"The way Jerry reads it, he figures Hunt figures the house is chickenshit, not even worth mentioning in his inventory. He figures that with you and Hunt farting around together, getting as tight as Dick's hatband, he loans it to you for your doxie."

"So he was satisfied?"

"Hell, no. What's chickenshit for Hunt is bonbons for us. He shoulda mentioned it, and he didn't, which is a lack of business integrity, fair play and all that shit. Jerry was I mean pissed off. He had principles."

"What did he do? Jerry?"

"Jerry? He told me." His icy eyes pierced mine. He was getting close to the truth, the hammer ready to strike. Don't squirm, I told myself. Meet the challenge.

"And what did you decide?"

"Me? Nothing."

"Didn't you believe him?"

"I didn't want to," he said bitterly. "I didn't want to do anything that might cock up the deal with Hunt. There were larger things at stake than making a big noise about a craphouse in the hills. But then..." his old pink cherub face shriveled; I thought he was going to cry. "Then I read my birthday letter and I felt like dog shit." He sidled a downcast confessional glance at me. "I felt ashamed because that boy was right. He was doing the ethical thing and I let him down."

Senior blew his nose; it sounded like coal rattling down a chute. He stared into his handkerchief.

"Nobody was doing anything unethical," I said, "certainly not you."

"I was too hard on him," he insisted, begging for rebuttal.

"No. You were trying to help him grow up."

Senior nodded agreement, and I had him, I thought, I had him. The moral philosopher who first coined that lapidary postulate about flattery getting you nowhere must have lived on the moon. Mankind thrives on soft soap.

"You were trying to teach him the facts of life," I went on.

"Of course I tried. But hellfire, he was thirty-four years old, school was out forever." He shook his head and put the toothpick in his mouth for solace.

"It's just he was too sensitive for the rough and tumble..."

"Yeah." He nodded, feeling much better. "He was afraid of you, too."

"What?"

"You used to shiver the piss out of him."

"I can't believe it."

He cackled, happy to shift the onus onto me. "There's something about you, Jack, that's—I dunno—you're so fucking unpredictable. Hell, there's been times when you gave me a gallstone or two. And you were a Marine."

It took a little time for me to digest this new hairball.

"What's that got to do with—"

"Everybody knows those Marines in Iraq came back crazy. You see," Senior went on, "Jerry thought maybe if you figured out what all he told me, you'd wax his ass." And then he said, with unmistakable clarity, "Or worse."

"What did he think? I'd shoot off his kneecap?"

His response was silence, but that was answer enough.

"Do you think I killed Jerry?"

Senior said, "No." For a moment he studied his toothpick. "If you did, you'd of made damn sure no evidence was left around that pointed to you. I mean, if you thought you had a reason to kill him, you might think that he thought you might be thinking about doing it. You follow me?"

"Kind of."

"You'd of found some excuse to go through his desk." He brushed his fingers over Jerry's loose-leaf. "Go through his appointment book to see what might be in there of a suspicious nature—the Four Pines Point appraisal, frinstance. Well," he went on, "you didn't do it. Although I gave you every chance, you never took me up on it. And anyway..." he paused for a moment. "If there was anybody I was going to accuse you of killing—"

"What're you—"

"You met Mrs. Hunt. You told Jerry you knew who she was. Hell, you've known her for"—he flipped the loose-leaf open, turned a few pages to the entry he wanted—"for a couple of months. And now according to the papers somebody puts a shiv in her five-six times and drops her off a cliff."

"You're out of your mind. Why would I...?"

He shrugged. "Coulda been a lover's quarrel. Jerry figured you were boffing her. I don't think that's an unreasonable conclusion."

"Christ..." Now I was squirming. Senior took up the slack.

"I know you, Jack. You'd fuck a snake if somebody held its head—not that I give a shit. Whoever killed Hunt's wife is Hunt's prollem. My prollem..." He leaned toward me across the desk. "Lemme put it this way. Maybe I should of done what Jerry wanted me to when he was alive—face up to Hunt, insist on him being as fair-square with us as we were with him. But Jerry's dead, and facing Hunt now won't bring him back. And anyway, the deal's done." He leaned back in his chair, his eyes nailed on mine. "We signed two days ago."

"You what?"

"The merger. It's a go, Jack. Tod's heading to Mexico tomorrow to oversee the switchover. And clear his head, I guess. And it's only when I start packing up the office that I find Jerry's letter. Too late to even get our fair share straight."

I was barely listening anymore. Somehow, amidst everything else, I'd let Senior hand off my old retirement plan. Tod was going to Mexico. The bastard was pulling up stakes.

TWENTY

Or was he? Maybe I'd jumped to conclusions—maybe Hunt would be back in a day or two. Maybe it was all a matter of waiting until things cooled down. It gave me a modicum of comfort that I knew where to find him, but I didn't like hearing about his travel plans secondhand. After I left Senior I must've stopped at half a dozen pay phones, trying to decide whether to break radio silence. I'd already dropped a nickel in the last one when I resolved to hold off. It was no time to be making noise, and Hunt wouldn't be fool enough to leave me in the lurch. I was a cold-blooded killer in his eyes, after all.

And meanwhile—who killed Darlene Hunt? Ralph? But if he had, why didn't he take off immediately, rather than drive up Yerba Verde Canyon to confront me in the ravine? Because he had to eliminate me as a witness; I knew he'd been living in that house with her. She steered him to me—the nosey real estate wimp, as he put it.

But now he had reason to believe I was a cop. Would he find it suspicious, now that Darlene's body had been found, that I wasn't beating a path to the hole he was hiding in? What would he do—confess something that could somehow recriminate me?

And something else: Even as I phoned Tod from that gas station on the

Coast road, the eyes of two unsmiling adolescent boys were on me. They wore identical cut-offs and T-shirts, red and blue, with yellow lettering across the chest: I'M SO HAPPY I COULD SHIT.

I climbed into the car and drove off, thinking, had they noted my license plate? Would they report it? With the finding of Darlene's body, would an all-points bulletin go out to every precinct in the county? Would it come to the attention of Laudermilk? Could he put the find out on me? It seemed impossible that anything could be known only to me.

And what about Carmen? I would have to talk to her, and soon, for I was Tod's envoy, designated to tell the next Mrs. Hunt of the last Mrs. Hunt's demise. And of Mr. Hunt's imminent relocation. It was a task made more unpleasant by the altered relationship between us.

There is a certain tentative stickiness in meeting a girl for the first time after you sleep with her, especially if, for whatever reason, you've sworn on a stack of Kama Sutras that you'll never sleep with her again. That sort of confrontation is attended by extreme discomfort, coupled with a frightening sense of imminent explosion. Hell hath no fury like a woman scorned, okay, but ten thousand hells cannot contain the congealed rage of a woman screwed and cast aside.

There was no telling how Carmen would react. Suppose she snitched to Napoleon? Suppose he decided to avenge the family honor? It was a shuddery thought. But I was obsessing again. There was no reason to expect any of these things to happen until they did.

Napoleon. What was going down with him and Mr. Dickens? I had sent him a contract, addressing it to San Dismaso, for a six-month lease on the tree farm, and never heard from him. Probably, with his limited attention span, he had by now forgotten about the goats and was into God knows what—Mexican jumping beans or French ticklers.

I was being drawn into bad thoughts by sheer suction. There must be some way to reverse the switch. Try thinking of...

Gayle. I missed her. You can only tell by the amount it hurts, she had said, after it's all over. It was beginning to hurt. Oh, Gayle, come back to me. Lie with me once again and pull the hair out of my legs. Have a bite of plaster.

TWENTY-ONE

I found Gayle in a tree in the backyard, a dryad in cut-offs eating an apple and reading a book.

"Hi."

She looked down at me dubiously.

"Can I come up?"

She shrugged.

I worked my way through the branches. They looked cool and inviting, the limbs of veined silver, the bark of velvet, the leaves as fragile and soft as fine linen.

A delusion and a snare. The trunk was full of sharp little warty protuberances which cut my hands. The boughs were pustuled with oozing sap. The foliage was coated with viscid dust. Why is it that trees, venerated by poets and peasants alike, are so fucking filthy? I made it, finally, to the side of my darling, to be greeted by an unruffled silence.

"How are you?"

Still no answer. Try again. "How's Shelley? What's she up to?"

"Washing the dog."

I knew that. He was in a bubble bath when I had arrived at the apartment. He had damned near drowned in the tub, in his frenzy to get at me.

"You like living with Shelley and that sex maniac of a dog?"

She shrugged disconsolately. "It's shelter."

"How's Mr. Crunt?"

"Who? You mean Crump. He's a pain in the ass."

"Come on back with me."

"You're a pain in the ass, too. What have you been up to? With your other girls?"

"What other girls?"

She said, "Jerry wasn't as dumb as you think."

"Jerry imagined things. He'd tell you anything to get into you."

She stiffened.

"What I mean," I said indignantly, "he was trying to discredit me in your eyes."

"What about the one who called herself Mr. Katz's secretary?"

"That was business, for God's sake. She was Mr. Katz's secretary. I swear."

"And the other one? The Spanish one?"

"Oh, that," I said dismissively. "Hunt rented her a house. Something was wrong with the plumbing."

"Why didn't you tell me? You knew how upset I was."

"You were so upset you wouldn't have believed me."

"I don't believe you now. Why do you have to take care of Hunt's plumbing?"

"I work for him."

"He's got you by the bongs. Jerry had twice the guts you've got."

Oh, Jesus. What's the use? "Jerry was a foul-up," I said. "He was always pissing in his own bucket."

"Not always. Jerry went to see Hunt and did something. He said I'd find out soon enough."

"Come on. Jerry was full of shit, Gayle." That son of a bitch, dead as dog shit and still making trouble.

Her eyes were aghast. She seemed to retreat within herself, pulling her legs to her body and sending me a sparkling flash of thigh.

"You make all these accusations," I said, "but you can't back them up any more than Jerry can—could. How do you think I felt, every time I had to go out on business you were off somewhere with Jerry or Grump?"

"Crump. They meant nothing. I was lonesome."

"Don't you think I was lonesome? Jesus," I whined, "you're my girl. If you do come back…"

"I don't know," she said.

"I said *if*. Can't we explore? What we got to do is lay down some ground rules."

She frowned. "What about ground rules for you?" she asked accusingly. "You're the one who—"

"No more Crump."

"No more going off for a week without me. No more going out for the night, even for business."

"Suppose I want to like play poker with the boys?"

"What boys? You never played poker in your life. No more criticizing—"

"Me—?"

"—what I wear, the way I walk…"

"When did I ever say anything…?"

"You don't have to. You make faces. You look pained. No more yelling about what I eat. Including plaster—as if you're so fastidious in your eating habits."

"Me?"

"You eat paper clips."

"*Okay.* They're all little things."

"Ha!" she snorted with such violent derision she almost fell out of the tree. "They… they're *indicative*," she said grandly, "of larger issues. Like whatever you want I've got to put up with."

"We've got to consider what we *both* want. Hell, I got feelings too."

"I know. It's about the third time you told me." Her eyes narrowed. Her jaw squared. "Whatever your feelings, from now on they're going to be otherwise."

"All right. You want me to sign a paper?"

She hesitated, unsure, still, I thought, unswayed. Then she shrugged. "What the hell," she said, "if we're going, we might as well go." She twisted her rump off a gnarly branch. "Before Blossom gets out of the bath and does his thing again."

TWENTY-TWO

Slowly I opened my eyes and stretched my cramped legs. Gayle in her nappy bathrobe was crocheting a doily.

I sighed contentedly and stretched some more. There was a kind of peace about the place. She was more relaxed than she had ever been. Since she had come back we had gone to a couple of movies, where she held my hand in the darkness. We had gone to a couple of restaurants, where she never spilled the soup or talked with a mouth full of salad. Not once had she pigged out on plaster.

When she did talk, I listened, just as she listened to me. Our undemanding conversation was pleasant if unexhilarating. Not once did I resort to a lie and, to tell the truth, I found an unexpected satisfaction in my own guilelessness.

I was keeping my head down. Tod would send up a flare before too long, I was sure. And until then, I wasn't ready to rush into another beating from Napoleon's *compas.* The job was done, I told myself, and it was just a matter of waiting to collect.

Thus we spent our days and nights in a kind of quietude. No mean accomplishment when you come to think of it—day upon day without alarums or calamities. And then it was shattered. The telephone knelled, and I was back in the battle, up to my ass in the filthy thick of things.

TWENTY-THREE

The ground was stained dark with dried blood and beaded with animal excrement. An evil smell hung over the clearing. Wisps of smoke spiraled up from the flue; the firebrick walls of the crematory were still warm to the touch.

"Some old Chicano built it about a week ago," Mr. Dickens said. "I thought it was a kiln."

I nodded. "Napoleon's father. He's a stonemason."

"But what for?" he asked plaintively, popping a horehound lozenge into his mouth. "What's he trying to do? I mean, he brings a flock of goats up here from Mexico—and burns 'em to ashes?" He glowered at me, as if his gimlet eye might shake loose an answer. When it did not, he said, "Tell him he can have his down payment back. I want him off my property, or else I'm going to the cops. You tell him that."

Tell him? First I had to find him.

Carmen was painting fat acrylic flowers on the mailbox. "So it will feel at home," she explained. "I will put my name on it, so it will know it belongs to me, and that I will take care of it."

I would have preferred not to involve Carmen in the Napoleon neck of my life, but I had no choice. "How are your parents?" I began.

"Splendid. My papa brought me a knife of an alert and wondrous beauty, in case the rapist reappears. My mama has a mother-of-pearl crucifix on a chain of gold linkage to wear at her throat. My papa contemplates the purchase of an auto. Would you recommend the repository of Señor More Money Max?"

"Absolutely not."

"Who then?"

"Why don't you ask Napoleon?"

She shook her head. "Napoleon observes no more than a careless devotion to his family. He has no time for his papa, occupied as he is in the discharge of his duties for the Señor Hunt."

"About him..." I said. "His wife... his wife has died."

"The Señora Hunt is dead?" she asked. Abstractedly she shoveled a glob of gum into her mouth and chewed on it slowly. "When I knew the Señora Hunt, her arrogance stomped me like dirt beneath her feet. But now that she is dead..." Her black eyes flashed. "One should never die if one can help it. But of course she couldn't."

"Those things happen every day."

"Of course. But," she insisted, "not as often to the rich. They are protected. Much more often to the poor."

"In America to everyone."

"America is truly a democracy," she observed sardonically, "even in death."

Her talk was getting to me. I had to remind myself that I didn't kill Darlene.

"Lorenzo the Half-wit," Carmen was saying in a hushed voice, as if to herself.

"What? I'm sorry...?"

"Nothing. It reawakens the sadness of another death, a friend. He too died young."

"The half-wit? Your friend?"

"Lorenzo. In our village of Vileza. He always dressed like a soldier, in a suit of camouflage cloth and a black belt and boots his brother who was in the army had given him. A toy plastic rifle slung on his shoulder. The tourists of winter who lodged at Guanajuato nearby, they were afraid of him, the way his head lolled around and his mouth hung open and the spittle ran down the corners, but mostly because he would discomfort them, pleading pitifully for *pulque*. Do you know of *pulque*?" she asked.

I did indeed. *Pulque* was made from fermented sap of the maguey, the spiked century plant. It had the sour, unsavory smell of rotten apples. Cloudy as smoke in a bottle, it tasted like curdled milk mixed indelicately with Limburger cheese and gunpowder. It was vile, and it could whang you.

"The tourists, of course, had nothing to fear," she went on. "Lorenzo was very gentle. He never did anything except once a year, when we honored Santa Maria, our patron saint and Queen of Heaven. There were fireworks and the four lion heads of the fountain in the square, with their great snaky manes and their round empty eyes, were coated for the fiesta with plaster of Paris and turned into astonishing likenesses of Pope John, Juarez, Lenin, and Jennifer Lopez. The likenesses were even more remarkable with water gushing from their mouths.

"It was at this time that Lorenzo would lead the band imported from Guanajuato, and then he would repair to the cantina, with the hope in his fool's eyes that somebody would buy him *pulque*."

She looked away, her oval face in profile shadowed by sadness.

I waited for her to go on. Finally, "What happened to Lorenzo?" I asked.

"Nothing happened." She was watching me narrowly. "He died."

I clicked my tongue sympathetically. "All that *pulque* catch up with him?"

"Yes. In a way…" Her mouth was drawn tight. Then she smiled and relaxed, but it didn't quite dispel her pallor. "It's just," she said offhandedly, "it was the night of the fiesta, and he had done very well with the tourists. He staggered out with all that *pulque* sloshing around inside him, and he fell in the fountain and drowned, right between Lenin and Jennifer Lopez." She shuddered. "That's how you might say we came to California."

What was she trying to tell me? "Did *you* find him?" I asked.

"Napoleon did." She asked, "Do you know the expression—it is gutter Spanish—the *dicho*, '*Hallar es guardar, perder es llorar*'?"

"It's much the same as English," I said. "'Finders keepers, losers weepers.' A child's rhyme."

She nodded. "Well, Napoleon reasoned that he found Lorenzo, so…"

"He wanted to keep Lorenzo? What for?"

"He wanted his boots. He had never owned a fine pair of boots before, so he—" She caught her breath, staring sharply at me. "What is it?" she asked anxiously. "You have turned green."

"It's okay," I said. "What happened with the boots?"

"Lorenzo's brother was coming home for the funeral. He had an army gun, and we were afraid. But Napoleon would not yield. He took the boots and went to the States. Not long after, my father followed, with my mother and me."

"Lorenzo's brother would have killed for the boots?"

She shrugged. "It was an affair of honor. One does such things in Vileza. You will not tell anyone about Napoleon?"

"Assuredly not."

"Then come," she said, taking my hand, leading me into the house, "I will make you a strong cup of coffee, to cure your greenness."

I went along shakily, my mind a jumble of incoherent thoughts, one of which insisted on taking over, like an unwelcome, immovable houseguest. Had Napoleon drowned Lorenzo for a pair of boots, and then seven years later snuffed another half-wit for the same purpose? Could he have beaten me back from San Dismaso the day I left, and come after *me* in that alley?

I had to track him down, I realized, and not just for Mr. Dickens. "Which reminds me," I said casually, "Napoleon asked me to find him an apartment."

"But," she said uncertainly, "he has an apartment."

"Oh? Where?"

"I do not know." Nervously she twisted a ring on her finger. Why do you not ask the Señor Hunt? Surely he must know…?"

"I would, but…" It was my turn to hesitate, as if I were trying to shield her from an unpleasant truth. Which I was. "If I mention Napoleon, Hunt would associate it with you. And again he would be all over you like a blanket of wool."

She nodded gravely. "You are a man of exquisite sensibilities. Anyway, I do not know where he is, although it would not be difficult to find out from another of your colleagues."

"Who's that?"

"A man…" she paused. "What was his name…? Flea…? Flick…?"

"Fleet?"

"That's it," she said.

One of my knees turned to butter and collapsed. I clutched at the mailbox for support and got a handful of wet paint.

"Jesus Maria," she said. "Why are you acting convulsively?"

"Sorry. Foot went to sleep." Clearly, she didn't know of Jerry's death.

She wiped the pigment from my palm with a rag.

"Who told you of this?" I asked.

"Napoleon, of course. He was bragging of the regard he enjoyed in the eyes of the Señor Hunt. He asked his patron about an apartment and was referred to this Jerry Fleet."

If that were true, why had Tod not sent him to me? Why hand the deal over to Jerry? Did Jerry, despite his protestations to his father about Tod, have some little thing going with the man he so vigorously claimed to distrust? Or was there something stewing on the back burner between Jerry and Napoleon?

"Carmen," I said, "we have always spoken the truth together, have we not?"

She nodded solemnly. "There is," she said, "an entanglement between my horoscope and yours. I trust you as I trust no other. At night in my bed I have illusions. I am engulfed in flames and you burst through the door and I fling myself into your open arms and you carry me to safety..."

Her eyes were on me, holding a glaze of brightness. I felt distinctly ill at ease. "Don't get carried away," I mumbled. "I'm full of imperfections."

"I do not think so." She studied my face with a kind of somber serenity. "If I had a picture of you, I would burn a candle before it. I would carry a lock of your hair, or a fingernail paring, in a little black silk bag around my neck..." And then, suddenly, she smiled, realizing the extravagance of her Latin hyperbole—"To ward off gas pains. At school," she giggled, "if I ever get there, I shall say the multiplication table in your name."

"*Excelente*," I said. Now where the hell was her goddamned brother?

TWENTY-FOUR

People of all ages paraded along the Venice boardwalk on rollerblades. Under the faded awning of a corner store, I stood watching a little house behind a picket fence halfway down the block. It was the second time today I had stood on a corner, the first about a hundred feet from the Fleet office. Just after noon, Senior had appeared, sucking on his gold toothpick in anticipation of lunch. He walked down the street in a kind of plodding jut, as if he were leaning into a hurricane, climbed into his Lincoln, and drove away. I went into the office, opened the cross-file of rentals, found Napoleon's address in the contract. It was probably the last Jerry had executed.

105 Dogwood Ave. The fence and every house on the street was slanted with decay and sagging with exhaustion, the clapboards pocked with dry rot, the paint flecked and blistered. Not a sprig of dogwood sprouted anywhere; it was one of those streets christened, as is the case of so many enclaves carved out of the California wilderness, by some émigré from the East, nostalgic for the flora of his homeland.

The skaters whirled past like dervishes consecrated to flux, although they seemed to derive no joy from it. A few ships cooked slowly on the horizon, moving as if in a dream. I glanced back at 105 Dogwood for the fiftieth time. And then I saw him, climbing out of an old rust-bucket of a flatbed truck. He grinned when he saw me and slammed one paw into my shoulder with jovial ferocity.

The other paw held a beer can. He tilted it into his mouth, gurgled it dry, squeezed it out of shape while it squeaked in anguish. He tossed the can into the street. "Hey," he said. "How you?"

"Okay. How you?"

"Cool."

He didn't look cool, trickling sweat and smelling like an unwashed keg. Let it pass. Get to the point.

"Napoleon," I began, "Mr. Dickens wants you off his property."

"He can go shit in his hat. I got a contract."

"He'll call the cops. He'll dynamite your smokehouse or whatever it is."

"Now wait a minute—" Napoleon's sweaty face readjusted itself in an attempt to register sweet reasonableness. Immediately he decided to abandon the attempt. "Fuck him," he shrugged. "You get me another place, right?"

"I don't think I can."

"Sure you can. Fucking A, man, I slip you something from the business." He winked broadly.

"I don't even know what business you're in."

"Well, shit, man, come on in."

He kicked open the gate, leading the way up the cracked concrete path, stabbing at the door lock with a key until it creaked open.

The house was full of rattles and faint sucking noises, as if it were built on stilts in a swamp. On the floor was a threadbare carpet of an indeterminable color. On the rug was a stained mattress, and on the mattress was half a gray hamburger in a bun green with mold.

Napoleon lumbered across a beam of sunlight. He sank onto the mattress, crossing his tree-trunk legs, and pulled them close to his torso as if they were oars. He belched with the effort and, like a sleazy Buddha, grinned at me.

"Let's have a drink," he said, "just to ward off the chill. You got to take a leak?"

What a weird non sequitur, I thought. "Not particularly."

"You been waiting for me long?"

"Couple of hours."

"You better repark your car. There's an hour limit and the fuzz give out tickets if you're five minutes over."

"Too late now. Damage's done."

"Wanna see the backyard?" He frowned, and it dawned on me, preposterously, that Napoleon, in his obtuse way, was trying to remove me from this dreary room, if only for the duration of a good piss.

"Come to think of it," I said, "where's the can?"

He was delighted with the tractability of my bladder. He pointed. I followed his finger, slamming the bathroom door with a reverberating bang that echoed through the empty house. I stood over the toilet bowl, watching two soggy brown cigarette butts floating in urine. I glanced into the cracked mirror, explored the limited contents of the medicine chest behind it: a jar of Vaseline and a carton of condoms. I flushed the toilet. I turned on the lavatory spigot, which clanked and sputtered like an overheated engine. I returned to the front room.

Napoleon was on the mattress where I had left him, picking tinfoil from the neck of a virgin pinch bottle. He held it up for my inspection, the little pig-eyes oily with anticipation.

"Twelve fucking years old," he said, uncorking the Haig & Haig. "Now that ain't panther piss."

"You must be loaded."

"The gift of a friend," he said proudly, and then, "Shit!" He looked around with a scowl. "I had two Dixie cups around here somewheres."

"Behind you."

He twisted his thick frame without moving his ass to snare a couple of misshapen paper cups at the edge of the mattress. With a reverential gesture he poured them full of booze, cocking a pinky.

"Salud," he said, handing one over.

The cup was filthy, the rim smeared with lipstick. I brought it to my mouth slowly, hesitated. Napoleon drank; one huge guzzle and the cup was dry. What the hell. I took a deep breath and...

Napoleon's eyes went wide, his mouth sucked air. He stiffened, his body thrashing convulsively. He threw back his oxey head. A hoarse cry rose from his throat. The paper cup in his hand crumpled, the pinch bottle thunked to the rug, trickling a tawny springlet of liquor. The scent of bitter almonds pervaded the room. He clutched at his throat, his chest. The veins in his neck went blue and ropey. A whitish froth flecked his blue lips. He lurched to his knees and sprawled forward on his face. The spastic body continued to twitch, but the heart had stopped.

I thought my heart had stopped too. Certainly I had trouble breathing, there in that filtered light with the rest of the room deep in shadow. It was like moving underwater.

My first impulse was of course to crash out of there, away from the corpse and the treacly sour stench of almonds. Almonds. I took a handkerchief from my pocket, wrapped it loosely around the bottle, and smelled the booze that sloshed around the bottom. Bitter almonds. Cyanide. Someone had scragged Napoleon.

I picked up the cork and examined it in the slanted sunlight. A microscopic hole had penetrated the plug where the hypodermic needle had been inserted.

Napoleon had tried to get rid of me before he produced the bottle; it had been hidden somewhere in the unfurnished room. Certainly his brain was insufficiently stunted to think that I would sneak back in his absence and steal his precious booze. What else was hidden with it? What else that he didn't want me to discover?

I studied the room for a small, unquiet eternity: Napoleon lumped on the mattress, the mattress on the rug. I gripped the hem of the rug and pulled it and its fixtures toward me in a corner. Down on all fours, I examined the splintery floor. Almost in the center of the room three floorboards, each about four inches wide and a foot and a half long, had been removed, neatly replaced, and sealed along the edges with brown soap. With a car key I pried the first one loose, then lifted the others. And there, cached in a hollowed recess cut into the substructure, and under a scaly patina of mildew, were Jerry's cowboy boots.

And a few other items—seventy-two identical little vials of brown plastic with pop-on caps, the kind pharmacists use to dispense pills. Each cylinder measured about three inches in height, with a diameter of approximately an inch and three-quarters. Fourteen of them were empty. Fifty-eight were packed with Tijuana Gold, each containing about a quarter of an ounce.

Napoleon's pockets yielded a few keys, four one-ounce plastic bags of dope, and a wallet containing eighty-four dollars, a rubber that looked like it had already been used, a forgery of a driver's license with an east San Fernando

Valley address, and a counterfeit green card which listed Mexico City, not Vileza, as his place of birth. Understandably, Napoleon had no desire to be traced back to Vileza and the vengeful attention of Lorenzo's brother.

In a closet in the empty bedroom hung two sleazo sport shirts, a pair of jeans, and a scuzzy ice-cream suit. In a pocket of the suit were two more rubbers. The rest of his wardrobe held not even a sand flea.

Strictly on automatic, I zombied around the room. Those red boots of Jerry's—Gayle had reported their loss when Jerry had been launched to a better world on a pair of grungy substitute Wellingtons. Laudermilk had been impressed at the time by the oddity of the exchange. And here they were.

Something had to be done about them; once a connection was established between Jerry and Napoleon, the theory of the random killer would collapse like a house of cards. Other catastrophes would swiftly follow unless those damn shitkickers were kept secret.

Without their discovery Napoleon would go to his grave unheeded, unheralded, unknelled—just another dirtbag blown away in a mini-skirmish of the weed wars. His death wouldn't even make a paragraph in the Santa Monica *Outlook*, and Jerry's case history, asleep in the deep files of the Beverly Hills Police, would not be disturbed. But if discovered, the boots could walk Laudermilk between both dead bodies—all three, even. And yours truly.

I tore a square yard of mattress cover away from the fleablown mass and wrapped the boots in it, then changed my mind; the package was too conspicuous. Kicking off my loafers, I pulled on the boots, hooked a couple of fingers in the loafers, and with a free-floating sense of doom, walked out into the sunlight.

TWENTY-FIVE

A shabby sedan was parked across the street from my place when I pulled up. The man at the wheel was waiting for me. He looked familiar, a ginger-colored dullard. He slid out of the driver's seat and came toward me and I like to shit a brick. It was Detective Sergeant Joseph Laudermilk, BHPD.

I began to sweat. It was a stakeout, and I was the mark. In the past hour I had been witness to an unreported homicide, and I had removed the evidence of another, earlier murder. Evidence which I was now wearing.

I shuffled my feet with the kind of inefficiency that can only scream for attention—how do you hide a pair of dead man's boots when your feet are in them?—then jammed those scarlet gunboats as far forward as possible, up under the dashboard. Laudermilk, in his inexorable progress, was still crossing the street. Jesus, I think, maybe he'll get hit by a car. I flash to the gore, the crumpled body, the incoming sirens shrieking death, to no avail. He is upon me.

"Mr. Hopkins."

Oh Christ here it comes. I found myself saying, "I don't have a house for you yet."

"That's not why I'm here."

Had he been following me? Did he already know that Napoleon had been offed?

"You've been impersonating a police officer," he said almost casually. "Namely, me."

"What?" I asked, affecting total incomprehension, stalling for time.

Laudermilk slipped a dirty envelope from his pocket and passed it to me. I read:

Dear Sgt. Laudermilk,
I know something I got to tell you about D. I'll be in L.A. July 18.
Meet you at 4 p.m. where we last met.
Respectfully,
R

I returned the letter. "Why do you think this has anything to do with me?"

"I been checking out all the people I gave my card to the last three-four weeks..."

"I don't know any 'R,' and no 'D' either."

He frowned. His jowls darkened, his eyes shifted focus to the door handle of the car and back to my bland and open face.

"If you're so concerned about 'R'—whoever the hell he is—why don't you put a tail on everybody you gave a card to? See where they go July 18?"

For a long moment, he chewed over my suggestion while I prayed that the nonsensicality of it would escape him. Never mind that none of those potential impersonators had seen the damn note, Laudermilk. Then, "The hell with it," he decided. "You don't expect me to remember, for Christ sakes, all the assholes I gave cards to. Besides, I ask for a hundred tails to take a whole day hound-dogging a hundred bush-league turkeys, I'd be a laughing stock. You keep looking for my house, okay?" He turned abruptly and walked away.

The road crossed the San Fernando Valley, one of nature's rudest eyesores. Only the few vacant lots, scattered here and there between apartment houses, pizza joints, and gas stations, testified to its desert origins—gritty sand blowing and baking under the yellow sun.

Beyond the scorching village of Reseda, beyond the pale of paranoia, I found a graveyard for the exoskeletons of old, eviscerated cars. The wrinkled, rusty hulls were stacked in a metal pyramid, a fitting mausoleum for Jerry's boots.

It was late when I got home. I felt battle-weary and older than dirt. Gayle was waiting for me. Dinner was set, candles were lighted, napkins like snow flowers bunching beside each plate.

Something warm and peaceful clung about the table, on the chandelier. It threw a soft enchantment over the room and drove splinters of light into the silver and crystal on the darkly burnished wood. It was like a commercial for contentment.

She slipped into a fluffy, diaphanous negligee and nothing else, demonstrating the aesthetic adage on the eloquence of simplicity that less, indeed, is more. My feelings of age and exhaustion gave way to a hot flush low in the stomach. I took her hand and led her to the bedroom. Dinner could wait.

TWENTY-SIX

July 18. A red-letter day on my calendar of apprehensions.

I climbed down the narrow path to that fungoid clearing. Cold vapors rose from the trees, and somewhere nearby was Ralph. Was he watching my shaky ascent from the cover of some uncaring rock? Was he waiting to bushwhack me again?

There was the sound of footsteps approaching—the crack of twigs, the swish of branches behind the foliage. Ralph appeared, alert, eyes darting.

I said, "Hi, Ralph."

He swung around to face me, vigilant, as distrustful of me as I was of him.

"What's on your mind?" I asked.

He hesitated, and then he plunged: "I... it was the last day I saw you. The day she died. As I left the house that morning..."

"*Before* she was killed?"

"Yeah. I..." The hinges of his jaw snapped shut. His eyes flamed. "You think I killed her?" he asked disbelievingly. "And then wrote you a letter to get you on my case? You think I'm *that* crazy?"

"You tried to kill me in this damned canyon."

"I had no such intention," he said loftily. "I was only trying to scare you off, that's all she wanted, but..."

"Why'd you write the letter?"

"Because that morning I pulled out of the driveway, hung a right, got about fifty yards, and the hearse died on me—it was cold.

"I tried to get it started, but the engine wouldn't turn over. So I sat there for a minute when a car pulled off the road and parked. This man got out, crossed the highway, and went into Darlene's."

"What'd he look like?"

"He was old. He was dressed like he was an undertaker, and kind of walked like he had a pack on his back. I guess I should have followed him back in the house, but I didn't think anything of it at the time."

"Anything else?"

"No," Ralph said. "Only he had some kind of fancy toothpick in his mouth—gold-plated or something."

Pow. So Senior had been at Four Pines Point the day of Darlene's death. My mind was rerunning our recent encounter through its kaleidoscope. All those questions he'd laid on me, not out of ghoulish curiosity, but because he was trying to learn if the police suspected him of murder.

"Ring a bell?" Ralph asked. "Recognize the old guy?"

I shrugged. He turned and trudged up the hill and, I hoped, out of my life forever. Though it seemed to me I'd said that before.

TWENTY-SEVEN

Senior's back was to the door of his office as I walked in. He was facing the window on the far side, his legs crossed on the sill. He was saying, "Okay, Harry, what's the bottom line? Speak up, man, just start batting out fungoes, okay?" He paused, listened, and laughed pitilessly. "You're living in a fool's paradise, kid… Sure I'll give you a break, but face the fack that what you got is a dead duck on your hands and I'm tryna fly it for you… Harry? Hello, Harry?… Well, for Chrissakes just toss it in the well and see what kinda splash it makes… I'm waiting, Harry… Harry, what can I say? You know me, right? I'm willing to follow anything into the high grass and see if it eats, but that's an offer to throw up… I tell you, Harry, I got four people waiting on the line, so think it over and call me back." He hung up. "Cocksucker," he mumbled eloquently.

"Hello, Senior."

He swiveled slowly in his chair. "I swear," he said, shaking his spongy head, "the things I gotta put up with. If they put my life on the TV it would crack the tube. Coffee?"

"No, thanks."

He poured from a carafe on his desk into a mug that said DISNEYLAND, twisting his face until it looked like a lugubrious bludgeon—gnarls for ears and nose, and knots for eyes and mouth. Mournfully he blinked a couple of knots. "You know how up-and-up I always try to be." The voice was plaintive in its solemnity. "Honesty is next to godliness in my book, know what I mean?" He sighed. "So I got to tell you something. Some what I think is not-so-good news."

"How's that, Senior?" I was wary. There was always something cagey and perfidious about his candor.

"Lemme put it this way—I been thinking about Tod Hunt again. He's nobody's asshole. But the thing is, I haven't heard a thing from him since he went south. I called Jaime who's supposed to be at the Mexico office, and he says Tod fired him a week ago. I calm the boy down and get him to go by our place and the locks are changed, the place is dark. It's some kinda shell game, Jack.

"So," he went on, "I tell Jaime to check Hunt out and guess what?"

"What?"

"That fucking guy owns a whole island off the coast of Baja. A place called San Dismaso." To emphasize the revelation he hunched forward across his desk, head and shoulders drawn down as if by a lead necktie. "It doesn't add up. He tells me he's heading down to kickstart our office, and then he shuts the place up? And meanwhile he's got some kinda... archipelago off the coast?"

Senior wasn't done yet, though. He leaned still further across the desk, planting both elbows for equipoise. "The more I think about it, the more I feel like Hunt's been dividing and conquering us all along, you know what I mean? I lost my boy in the middle of all this, Jack. But if we can find our way through it, Fleet and... Fleet and you can come out ahead." He paused. "I didn't stand by Jerry, and... it's time we started sticking together again, is what I'm saying. That's how we pull out the win. You do right by me, I do right by you."

He was giving me a look. There was something else going on here. "How do you mean?" I asked.

He paused again, and wiped one hand across his mouth. "I happen to know," he glowered, "that you were with Darlene Hunt the day she was killed." One of his elbows slipped, brushing against the mug. It spilled, spreading a black stain across the desk pad.

"Is that right?" I said. "Because—"

"The night before," Senior went on, unfaltering, "was the anniversary of Jerry's death—a month to the day. I kept thinking about him and his high standards and all, and what a good boy he really was. And then and there I decided to do what was right, what he had wanted me to do all along. I decided to challenge Hunt about that beach house. But then I figure, I can't trust Hunt, he'll gimme another song and dance and"—he eyed me accusingly—"I can't trust you—I'm all alone. Then it occurs to me there's a simple way to check out the house—drive out there, take a look at it like I'm a prospective buyer. So that's what I did.

"I park on the road. I ring the bell. I listen for footsteps, but what I hear is water in the pipes—you know how beach houses are, even the mansions. She must be taking a shower and can't hear. I drive back down the road to a greasy spoon. I have ham and eggs and hotcakes and a couple cupsa coffee. I read the real-estate listings in the paper. An hour later I drive back. And you know what's parked in front of her house? You bet your ass you know. Your heap."

"What'd you do then?"

"Nemmind that," he said. "We're not talking about what I did."

"I'll tell you what you did—what any sane man would do. You turned around and drove back to town. So it's a stand-off."

"What's that mean?"

"I was out there, yes, but so were you. We both had our reasons."

"I told you mine."

"Mine was, she called me, early that morning, said she wanted to see me."

"What about?"

"I never found out. She didn't answer the bell for me either, so I came back to town. All of which means… you've got nothing on me, other than I was out there the same time you were. Spread that around and the cops will have both of us by the plums."

"Jesus Christ," he said uncomfortably, "who's talking about going to the cops?"

"I am."

"Not me. All's I want is your voluntary cooperation. Christ," he repeated, "it's like I said, Jack—we've gotta stick together here. I know I can't take this bastard on alone, at least. I'm asking you—I'm tryin' to say we gotta be in the same corner. Otherwise it's all this mess for nothing."

I thought about Darlene, and Junior, and Napoleon. Senior was right. I'd been chasing my own tail for a week. It was time to go find Tod.

TWENTY-EIGHT

I stood at the wheel of the boat I had rented from Scrap Iron, eating a can of cold spaghetti. Propelled by a fresh breeze, the boat cut through the sea with a slight rustle. It keeled starboard and port but always righted itself, a miraculous creature of amazing certitude.

A certitude I lacked. Something nagged at me and would not go away, possibly because I was bone-weary, palsied with fatigue. Canvas had to be trimmed constantly. Even on automatic pilot I had to check the compass every two hours or so, alerted to duty by the shrilling of an alarm clock. On I sailed, through the night and into the sullen dawn. Somehow I knew, I just knew, something was going to get all fouled up.

TWENTY-NINE

The island appeared, at first, like a low, curdled cloud. Slowly it took body, settling down to become a solidity of gray sand, a featureless mass on which, suddenly, dwarfed trees sprouted, matured, took sharp definition.

I beached the boat offshore near the ¡NO ENTRAR! sign fading in the sun. No one had come to greet me. From the high ground at the center of the island, Voodoo, certainly, and his vigilantes would have seen my boat spanking toward them.

The place was abandoned. Voodoo's tin hut was open, the door flapping forlornly in the wind that trickled across the compound. The office was bare. Desk, filing cabinet, the two chairs, even the bulb had been removed from the socket that dropped on a cord from the ceiling. In the clearing the door of the barn was slitted open about a foot, unbarred.

Scarcely breathing, I entered the shed. The shadows were thick. I felt I was shoving against them, against a feral stink of animal excrement.

In the murkiness were two long, narrow tables, on each of which were squatting about a dozen chimpanzees. They sat there, hunched forward, their eyes hollow and grave like figures on the vaulted door of a medieval church. They watched me closely. Around each ape was an assortment of inquisitorial gear—plastic face masks, slim rubber hoses, canvas harnesses, chest straps and leg irons, ganglions of wires, brass-studded collars snaffled to short, thick chains. Scattered on the benches and over the earthen floor were medical instruments—blood-pressure cuffs, gauges and dials and monitors for systolic readings of heart and respiratory rates and body temperatures. On the far wall was an eight-day clock, a Tijuana monstrosity inlaid with mother-of-pearl and filled out with a dull brass pendulum. Its heartbeat was strong and steady. What had Voodoo and his orderlies been up to?

The scrawny torsos of the chimps were shaved in places to accommodate catheters and biomedical sensors, all unplugged. The apes were neither wired for readings nor taped with fittings nor chained to rigs nor socketed into sensors, nor strapped into straightjackets nor clamped into face masks. What then were they doing there, left as it were to their own devices? Why didn't they haul ass, instead of sitting around scratching and spitting, their wizened faces like those of old people resigned to a long Sunday with nothing to do?

I stepped closer, the better to unriddle the mystery. Sometimes, particularly after torment, to do nothing is sheer ecstasy. There's much comfort to be derived in this suffering world from just sitting on your tail, scratching and spitting. They greeted me grinning.

It was an anthropomorphic gloss, though, for they were not at all friendly. As I approached they shifted their weight and went cholerically alert, even as they squawked and squittered. One big old son of a bitch, gray in the muzzle, bared his yellow fangs. He snatched up a glass beaker and, with surprising accuracy, drilled it at me. I ducked. It whizzed past and splintered against a tin cabinet.

The crash of the beaker troubled them. Full of little fidgets and fusses they eyed me, yelping accusingly, lurching to their feet, bouncing on crooked legs like cripples testing a springboard. Their little red button eyes flashed, focused not on me, I realized, but on a point somewhere beyond my shoulder.

I turned. There in the open doorway, silhouetted against the backlight, was a familiar, elegantly slim figure.

I called, "What are you doing here?"

Tod raised his right hand and extended it toward me, as though he were pointing. He was; the pistol fired twice. The slugs tore past my ear, twin theatrical thunderclaps. I dove under the table, under the screaming apes. The bench afforded neither cover nor concealment, but you only think of those things later.

Tod lowered himself to a knee, the better to draw another bead. I looked about for a weapon. All I could see were the chimps on the other table, bouncing around, their adrenaline building, stimulated by the crack of the gun and the scorchy smell of cordite. They snorted and wailed, waving their ropey arms like distraught semaphores.

Tod's pistol flashed again. The bullet smacked the clock right in the face, shattering the dirty glass. In panic it began to chime, it seemed forever, and then it gurgled and ground its gears and fell into an aggrieved silence. The growling of the apes rose to a strident pitch.

The fourth bullet glanced off a zinc lavatory and ricocheted through the shed. The monkeys thrashed around in a spasm of apprehension, thumping their chests in a burlesque mea culpa. They screamed like sirens.

Tod's gun blazed again. The round slammed into a leg of the table, which exploded in evil little needles that pierced my cheek. The amputated leg collapsed, spilling the apes down its slope like a hairy cascade. As if their nervous systems were shot, on fire, their boilers bursting, berserk with fear, they surged toward Tod, the sole obstacle between them and freedom. Spearheaded by the old son of a bitch, and joined by the apes on the far table, they swept on like an avalanche, like a ragtag army lacking nothing but clubs and torches.

They swarmed over him. He dropped like a bundle before he could crank off another shot. The pistol hopped out of his hand and he disappeared under their paws, their yellow teeth, their saliva, their weight.

I guess I became a little unglued. Grabbing a chain, I charged into them, flailing. They ignored me; all their wrath was concentrated on Tod. And then they ran over him and out the door.

Tod was panting heavily; so was I. He shook uncontrollably. He was full of holes. Spittle ran down a corner of his mouth, drowned immediately by thick runnels of blood.

I brushed the hair from his forehead. I was sorry I did; an ape had bitten a jagged deep hole in it. Big bluebottle flies were already buzzing in for the feast. I slapped them away and said stupidly, "You okay?" and a flicker of a shrunken ghostly smile kindled his dull eyes. He seemed shrunken all over, lying so still, diminished by his wounds.

"Thing like this happens, you're supposed to be in shock," all this in a foggy whisper, "but not me…" Again the eyes dimmed, as if he were looking internally, cataloguing his injuries. "I hurt," he said.

"Is there anything around here? A first-aid kit, or something?"

"It's in the back of the shed, next to the scintillation counter."

"The what?"

"Just look in the back."

I found it, a cornucopia of Band-Aids, aspirin, alcohol, anti-tetanus toxin, ointments, unguents, powders, and laxatives, before I saw the hypodermic syringe and the Demerol.

I shot it into his upper arm, less than the appropriate dosage, according to directions on the vial. I didn't know what I was doing, but I didn't want to shoot him to death with a needle. For a moment he lay quiet, like the last column of some ruined temple. Then, "Better," he said, "much better. Now all you've got to do"—he looked at me calmly—"just get me back to LA and you can cut your own orders."

I swallowed with difficulty. "Suppose I manage to save your ass?" I said harshly. "What guarantee do I have that you won't try to kill me again?"

"I only did it..."

I could hardly hear him.

"...because I didn't think I could trust you."

"What'd make you change your mind?"

He ran his tongue over his parched and bloody mouth. He reached out a shaking hand and closed it over mine. "I'll tell you the God's truth, Jack. In order to live I'd lie and cheat and kill—but I wouldn't kill you."

"Why not?"

"Think about it for a minute. Any man who saves your life after you try to kill him—that man's got to be trusted."

There was no reason to doubt his insincerity. But, Christ, I didn't want him to die. That in itself was absurd, because there had been a time not too long ago when I wanted to kill him.

"All right," I said. "I'll get you to the mainland."

"No! I don't want the Mexican police nosing around, and..." he choked on a bubble of blood. "And God knows where or when we'd find a doctor, much less a hospital."

Hospital, my ass. What he needed was a morgue. He was two-thirds of a ghost, about to go out on the tide. But I could be wrong. Even in the best of health, everybody looks worse than they are.

"I can't get you to LA on a sailboat. By the time we dock you'd be... you'd be..."

"Hydrofoil," he said. "The way I got here. It'll do a hundred and twenty miles an hour..."

"And rip you apart, bouncing on the waves."

He looked at me reproachfully. "Christ," he said, "you've got to do something, even if it's wrong." His voice was a dry husk. "There must be some way..."

"Do you have a radio-telephone in the speedboat?"

He nodded weakly. "How about another shot of Demerol?" he asked. I loaded up and inserted the needle between the muscles of his arm.

"Thanks," he said. "Who're you calling?"

"A helicopter service. They could be here in twenty minutes. We could be in LA within the hour."

"That's not... expedient. I know, I tried it once. They have to submit a flight plan, and get prior approval for an international run from the Mexican consulate. We'd have to land at a port of entry to clear customs. There'd be forms to fill out, paperwork, searches for contraband."

"All right. There's another way."

"I hope it's better than—"

"Listen, Tod. How much is your life worth? A million dollars?"

He looked at me contemptuously. "Another million?" he asked. "Is that what you want?"

"It's not for me. It's for the helicopter guy."

"He's got it."

"And he'll want to know what's going on down here."

He's got what he considers a police detective's divine right to ask questions and demand answers, I might have added, but I didn't. No use mentioning police at this time.

"It's none of his business."

"Okay. It's your life."

Tiredly he said, "Tell him the truth."

"What's the truth? What's with you and the chimps?"

"Jack..." He wavered in his decision for a moment.

I leaned close to his mangled body, to catch his words.

"Get me a glass of water, please."

"You shouldn't be drinking this water."

"Under the circumstances, let's not be fastidious."

The zinc lavatory yielded a trickle of brownish liquid. I filled a cracked cup and hurried back to Tod. He gulped it down and closed his eyes. I thought he had passed out. "Tod...?"

After what seemed an eternity he said, "I told you once that I found real estate less than captivating. I searched around and I found something, just a bit of a boon to mankind, still a..." The Demerol was taking effect. He felt no pain. He was reverting to the kind of rococo rhetoric, shaded ever so slightly with self-derision, that I had come to expect from him. "What I was trying to do," he went on, "was to develop a non-toxic cigarette, with Voodoo as the biochemist, and the chimps as guinea pigs."

A long time back, it seemed years ago but it wasn't, Jerry Fleet had come up with some oxymoronic notion like this. Maybe they weren't so different after all. In another life, I thought, these two...

I shook off the reverie. "But why here?" I asked him. "Why not in the States?"

"Cheap labor—the same reason American electronics firms set up in Taiwan or Korea. Secondly, Americans are too squeamish. They become out-raged over experiments with animals." He brushed a hand across his face; the flies had regathered. "And thirdly—well, I came for the girls, Jack."

"And the merger? Why go after Fleet and Fleet?"

He looked at me. "I needed someone who could get the job done and then come down here with me. I was after you. That Fleet office in Mexico City—we'd've gotten you installed and out of the cops' eyesight, and turned the place into Hunt and Hopkins. The healthy cigarette."

"You expect me to believe—"

He winced. "I'm telling you, the real-estate talk was a way to get at you. At least it was after I realized Senior didn't have anything else worth my time. To get you aimed at Darlene without any... conspicuous conspiring, or anything like that. The rest of it—well, who knows whether it would've worked out. You went sour. You got all—resentful. And the cigs didn't turn out any better."

"What happened with the cigarettes?"

"It didn't work." He tried to grin. "Or if it did, Voodoo took the recipe with him when he ran off. All the time I was breathing down your neck, and

I get stabbed in the back by a two-bit chemist. Just when I thought I'd found a way out of the real-estate business. I've been down here trying to see what I could salvage. But hell," he went on, "I never intended to die of natural causes anyway. It's a form of resignation. Got any more Demerol?" he asked. "It's like mother's milk."

"You've had enough for a while. According to the label…"

His eyes were dilated now. They seemed to be smarting in their brilliancy. His voice was subdued when he said, "Why don't you call your friend?"

The *Quel Tapage*—WCN 851—rode at anchor in a little cove off the seaward side of the island. I climbed aboard, shedding water from the thirty-yard swim, and switched on the radio-telephone.

I twisted the dial, picking up the marine channel and the operator in San Pedro, gave her the name of the boat and the call sign. She was reporting traffic on the airwaves and put me on hold. I waited, running a damp hand over the sculptured hardwood and the sparkling chrome of the console, counting the steel drums of high-octane gas stacked up in the stern. It seemed like forever before the galvanic voice in Pedro said, against a soundtrack charged with crackles and sibilation, "Come in, *Quel Tapage*."

"Beverly Hills Police," I told her.

She patched me into a direct line. "Detective Sergeant Laudermilk," I said.

Another symphony of discord. What if he's not there? What if he tells me we're a bit out of his jurisdiction?

A flat voice said, "Sergeant Laudermilk." I pressed the mike switch.

"This is Jack Hopkins," I said, "can you hear me? Over." I released the switch.

"Where are you?" he asked.

With ship-shore communication, the state of the art requires, in the interest of clarity, a technical jargon replete with "Over"s and "Out"s and "Roger"s and "Wilco"s and the like, which I'll jettison to preserve my small cargo of pith and get on with it:

HOPKINS: I'm on an island called San Dismaso, off Baja, Mexico. I got a house for you.

LAUDERMILK: In Mexico? Stick it up your ass.

HOPKINS: In Beverly Hills. North of Santa Monica. It's worth at least a million and you can have it for sixty grand.

LAUDERMILK: [*suspicious*] When can I take possession?

HOPKINS: Is a couple of hours soon enough? All you have to do [*deep breath and plunge*]... is get down here with a police helicopter and haul me and a friend back to LA.

LAUDERMILK: To get the helicopter I need a reason, for Chrissakes.

HOPKINS: Tell them it's a hot lead on the murder of Jerry Fleet. And bring a doctor with you.

LAUDERMILK: Jesus, I don't know...

HOPKINS: So don't bring a doctor. Bring a paramedic.

LAUDERMILK: It ain't the doctor that's the problem. It's the helicopter.

HOPKINS: You want that house or don't you?

LAUDERMILK: Not if it gets my nuts in a wringer. I mean, I could lose my job and get tagged for the fuel and wear and tear on the pilot and this and that, which'ud take me a year to pay off.

HOPKINS: My friend'll pick up the tab, and probably get you a medal for saving his life. He's got a lot of clout.

LAUDERMILK: I'll have to clear it with the captain.

HOPKINS: That shouldn't be too tough for a smart guy like you.

LAUDERMILK: Don't be a smart-ass. Speaking of Jerry Fleet, there's an angle I should investigate. Namely you.

HOPKINS: Me?

LAUDERMILK: From the time Hunt's office was broken into, you've been the dildo in the dead center of one royal cock-up.

HOPKINS: How you figure...?

LAUDERMILK: The perp knew his way around the office. It had to be an inside job.

HOPKINS: So what did I...?

LAUDERMILK: That's just for openers. Mr. Fleet says you had a hate on for his son, and then the son gets clipped. And—

HOPKINS: Mr. Fleet's testimony on anything has never been impeccable.

LAUDERMILK: Mr. Fleet further stated you were humping Mr. Hunt's wife, and shortly thereafter she's chucked off a cliff. Moreover—

HOPKINS: What evidence did he supply to prove...?

LAUDERMILK: It appears you've also been humping Mr. Napoleon Ochoa's little sister—

HOPKINS: On what do you base that?

LAUDERMILK: Her response to certain questions indicated that she had a personal relationship with you. Mr. Jerry Fleet—

HOPKINS: What did he know about it?

LAUDERMILK: We located her through an entry in his desk calendar which his father showed us. Miss Ochoa has identified her missing brother as the victim of cyanide poisoning in Santa Monica. Also I got a visit yesterday from a friend of yours. He thought he'd find you here at Beverly Hills Police.

(Sweet Jesus. I didn't need a clairvoyant to tell me who he was talking about.)

HOPKINS: I can explain.

LAUDERMILK: Good. Mr. Farkleberry's explanation was slightly garbled, confused as he was about your identity. Although he was very cooperative.

(I'm sure he was. I could just see old Ralph, sobbing his heart out as Laudermilk played him like a violin.)

HOPKINS: I'll tell you about it when I get back. Are you coming down or not?

LAUDERMILK: I think I better. What do you want a doctor for? Who's this friend with the clout you're down there with?

What could I say? Could I tell him, "Well, I got this friend, none other than the widower of Darlene Hunt, who's been chewed up by some apes...?" Not yet; he'd find out soon enough. I flipped off the switch, listening to my heart pound. I swam ashore and sprinted—stumbled mostly—back through the brain-broiling heat.

THIRTY

"What took you so long?" he asked thickly, a mucous film coating his half-closed eyes.

His sense of time was intact. I had tarried in the cove, in something akin to dread, having been informed by the authority figure in this mess that I was a prime candidate for frying. I'd told myself that when I got back to Tod he'd mercifully try to shoot me again, and if this time he succeeded my troubles would be over. I eased myself down beside him in the roaring light that poured through the doorway.

"Tod." I shook him gently. "Can you hear me?"

He dropped his head and with some effort raised it again in a fractional nod.

"They'll be here with the helicopter. We don't have much time."

"Demerol." His breath was shallow.

"We've got to talk. Then you get the Demerol."

His focus was blurred, yet his glance conveyed pure venom for my depriving him of his tonic.

"I've got to know what happened so we can nail down an alibi. Or they'll be all over us. We'll be sharing a cell in Folsom."

"Demerol." It was all he could do to string three syllables together.

Nevertheless he added, "Who'll be all over us?"

"The helicopter people," I vamped. "They have to file a log, particularly on a pickup outside the country, and then there's the hospital—you'll have to fill out papers when you're admitted. You might be close to a corpse but you're still Tod Hunt, and your wife was murdered. If we don't have a good story, they just might call in the cops."

"You didn't call the cops, did you?"

"Of course not," I lied. "But one thing could lead to another, get out of hand."

"Give me another shot."

"Later. Why did you kill Napoleon?"

His body went taut.

"Tod. I'm trying to save your life and mine."

He didn't seem to care one way or another. Maybe it was pain. He was neither dead nor alive, but somewhere in between. There was no name I knew for where he was. I tried again.

"Why didn't you come to me when Napoleon wanted a place to live?"

His hand clawed the earth, groping for the mug of water beside him. I tilted a few drops down his throat.

"Why did you go to Jerry Fleet?"

"Demerol," he said. Jesus, he was derailed with it and shipwrecked without it. Maybe if I stuck him again it would loosen his lips. I loaded the syringe and speared him. He took the hit greedily; immediately he settled into a kind of wary euphoria.

"About Jerry Fleet?"

He made an effort to engage me with his eyes, muddy as the water in the mug. "Why should I bore you with such trivia?" he asked.

"You went to Jerry because you wanted him and Napoleon to meet..."

"That's all I have to do?" he said derisively. "Run a social club for misfits?" His vinegar had returned, stoked by the lubricant. It wouldn't last long, I knew, but while it did...

"...so he'd recognize Jerry, even on a dark street..."

"Why would I want Jerry dead?" he asked. Somehow our adversarial roles had been reversed; he was asking all the questions. Which was okay, so long as I had the answers.

"Jerry had come to you, to tell you how smart he was."

"He wanted a pat on the head?"

"In a way. And he wanted you to quit fucking him over. To declare the properties you owned, just as he and Senior had declared theirs—quid pro quo. So he told you about Carmen and the house in the hills."

"Why would he tell me that?"

"Quit stalling. Jerry couldn't keep his mouth shut about anything. He came to you, pleased with himself for being so clever, with that shit-eating grin of self-satisfaction on his face—a man so dumb he'd tell you something you didn't want to hear and expect to be congratulated for it. But he must have scared the hell out of you."

Tod tried filling his chest with air. It rattled around in his throat. "Jerry couldn't scare a flea," he said tiredly, "and anyway, he thought she was one of your girls." He sucked in his breath regretfully. It was an admission prompted by the Demerol or the pain gnawing through it; a statement he would have preferred not making.

"You knew it was only a matter of time before Jerry realized Carmen was all yours—a relationship he might view with suspicion once Darlene was put to rest."

"So," a soft croupy chuckle, hardly an expression of mirth. "I not only killed Napoleon, I killed Jerry?"

"Napoleon killed Jerry—you paid him to do it. Then you had to kill him because some day, such was the quality of his mind, you figured he'd reach a point where he couldn't resist using it against you."

A hollow sigh escaped him. The bleb on the side of his mouth burst like a blister and dribbled blood down his chin. He was too weak to wipe it away so I did it for him.

"The police have nothing on me," he said.

"You're probably right. The cops would think his death was dope-connected." Why tell him they somehow connected me with it?

"Dope?" he asked.

"He was peddling weed."

"He was peddling goats. The goats he cleared off the island."

"Dope. Packed in vials small enough to jam down the animals' throats, but too large for them to eliminate. He trucked the goats to LA, split open their bellies..." I thought for a moment. "No," I said, "I guess you're safe there."

"And I'm safe about Jerry. If the police connected me with his death, they'd have pounced weeks ago. They think he was the random target of a nut."

"That leaves Darlene. What about her?"

"She's your responsibility." He stared up at the cobwebbed rafters with the fixed vacancy of a blind man. "Although for a long while I thought you'd never get around to it."

"Turned out you were right, didn't it?"

He looked at me strangely.

I said, "The night before she died, the night I was chasing around to find Carmen for you, and when I finally did, you said—remember what you said?—sleep late in the morning, we can set back the agenda. And that morning you went out to Four Pines Point..."

"How did you possibly reach that conclusion?"

I wasn't going to argue with him; there was no satisfaction to be derived from his admission of guilt. The issue was irrelevant, we were straying from the point, and there wasn't much time. "The point is," I began...

"I saw you... I saw you with her," he said. "Weeks ago. Before we met that first time. Fucking my wife in my own house."

My heart froze.

"I'd already started in on steamrolling the Fleets—and then I go to get a suit from Malibu and find out those chumps have a philandering thug in their employ. I could have shot you right then, right in the nuts. But it seemed... more felicitous to get you to kill her. And you did, Jack. Don't try to tell me otherwise."

A white shaft of a shriek pierced the clearing. Through the door I saw that big old grizzled ape, the leader of the band, squatting in a tree at the edge of the jungle. His muzzle and his chest were smeared with blood; he was licking his paws clean of it. He snarled, screaming defiance at us. Son of a bitch, hadn't he had enough? I threw a rock at him and turned back to Tod. I wasn't ready to work out the implications of what he'd said—whether he'd dragged me into all this just for cuckolding him, whether he really hadn't been the one who'd killed his wife. I needed to focus on the next few hours.

"The point is," I insisted, "we still need an alibi."

"I've got an alibi. I was at work."

"Who'd be willing to say so?"

"Ms. Velasquez."

"She won't wilt under pressure?"

"She is a cool and steadfast soldier whose devotion to me transcends worship."

"How would she feel about me?"

"Any way I tell her to." He sighed and with a consuming effort brushed the blood from his face. He stared at the smear on his hand. He blinked his eyes as if it took great effort.

So we waited in silence for a sign to come out of the sky. His body lay still and disjointed, then at times it would bow as though bent by a taut string, and his head would grind back against the earth, as if compensating for some intense, internal stress. I sat beside him, brushing the matted hair from his punctured forehead, brushing the flies away. Somehow he endured as the sun yellowed in the late afternoon, sleeping fitfully. Once he woke up and said, "I'm cold." I covered him with my shirt and he closed his eyes and dozed off again.

I heard the helicopter only a split second before I saw it. Tod heard it too, and stirred. It swooped out of the sky like a sudden storm, flashing its rotors, all squall and quake and clatter, a monster of a bird pounding its chest. It hovered over the compound and docked down in the clearing, churning up a cyclone. The overhead prop continued to swing, but lazily, and the dust subsided, revealing the word POLICE, white on blue, on the skin of the cabin. The door swung open.

Tod watched me as I headed toward the two men debarking, Laudermilk followed by a man in a dark suit carrying a black medical bag. "Come on," I told the doctor. He had a gray face and gray hair cut like a Prussian general's. I led them toward the shed, through the shives of light that fell under the trees.

A shot rang out, exploding dust at my feet. And then another, louder, carrying in its wake a flat, leaden dissonance as it veered off the bole of a tree. The three of us hit the earth so fast it seemed to rise up and meet us. Laudermilk yelled, "Police! Drop your weapon!" drawing his pistol.

Everything went excessively bright. The shadows lost their murk, the dust its nebulosity, the doctor his grayness, flat on his face, still gripping his bag. *What the Christ was Hunt trying to do?*

A third shot. I could for a split second track the slug's trajectory, or so

I thought. It whanged into the tail of the helicopter behind us.

And then I knew. He had seen the minatory fist of a word POLICE on the side of the copter and concluded that I had tricked him, trapped him, bullied a confession out of him and brought the authorities down on his bloody head. Laudermilk pointed his pistol at Tod, holding it in both hands, arms extended.

"Don't shoot!" I screamed at him, chopping his hands aside. "He's not after you, he's after me!" As if that made any sense. But Laudermilk took menacing courage from my words. He dashed to the side of the barn, disappearing behind it. I heard the crash of a window breaking, then the firing of his piece. With each shot Tod's shoulders bunched, jerking violently as if they had a life of their own.

I ran to him, knowing it was too late. I held him in my arms and he opened his eyes and said clearly, scornfully, "You bastard."

The doctor pronounced him dead, a formality which required little medical skill—one look and anybody could have reached the same conclusion. Laudermilk, that miserable dildo, came up to me sheathing his pistol. His colorless eyes locked into mine with arrogance and complacency, stupidity and avarice—all stewed together in his piddling little brain.

"What about my house?" he asked.

I said, "You just shot it to death."

He stared at me. "So," he said, "what are you crying about?"

THIRTY-ONE

Sing of the open road.

Tooling up the coast, Highway 101, all systems go. The car purrs like a tickled pussycat, as if a great burden has been lifted from its rusty loins. It is happy at its work, lugging the three of us and an alp of cargo in a utility trailer the size of a small caboose. There was cargo in the car, too, piled up beside me in the front seat. Moving we were, from gaudy, overblown LA to the sweet clean countryside of cowflop and well water. To cultivate our garden.

Gayle sat in back. She had never looked more relaxed, more assured, prettier. Next to her was Carmen, a fragile ornament giving off a musky perfume which drifted out of a little silken bag of rose petals, herbs, and spices she wore on a silver string at her throat.

Everything so lovely. Sing of the open goddamned road.

After Tod died I went into a tailspin. It began before we left San Dismaso, as they slipped him into a body bag and loaded it aboard the helicopter. Then we were airborne.

Laudermilk leaned toward me. "A few formalities," he said above the trob-clatter.

"What?"

"I need your deposition."

His questions were surprisingly few, and my answers unsurprisingly sanitized, highly selective in depicting the part I played as Tod's lieutenant. When necessary I modified the truth in shall we say a manner Laudermilk could not disprove.

I told him about Napoleon, hired by Tod to kill Jerry, smuggling dope from Mexico in the goat-bellies, and, finally, baited by Tod's cyanide. About Tod's killing Darlene, his surprising me on San Dismaso, where I had been sent by my employer, and of Tod's attempt to kill me.

"Why'd he want to kill you?"

"Because he was getting increasingly paranoid. He thought I knew he was a killer, just as he thought Jerry knew what he was up to."

"So what was he up to? He tell you?"

I looked out at the water. "No," I said.

Finally, late that night, I found my way to bed. Gayle sat in the rocker beside me. She held my hand. I slept for thirty-two hours and woke in a state of fog. All the fire had gone out of my body. I tried to think, but only one thought persisted, a nagging, ragged reminder that I was back to making my way too slowly in the world. Strangely, I didn't care. Despite my long sleep I was still tired, tired of the struggle, of the hectic monotony and dull consistencies of a job designed for the demented. Then I remembered I no longer had a job. The night I returned from San Dismaso I'd quit Fleet Realty.

I had gone from the copter pad to Senior's apartment. He had opened the door for me in a nightshirt and a velveteen bathrobe, the nap wormy with age and stained with the droppings of egg yolk. A pair of slippers flapped on his gnarly feet, and blue varicose veins meandered down his matchstick legs like rivers on a map. The room's only illumination fell from a lamp goosenecked over the armchair where he had been sitting. On the long table beside it was an open photograph album. Quickly he closed it, as if it were a dirty book and he ashamed of being caught with his nose in it, a sign of weakness.

"Listen," he blurted, "I had to tell the cops what I knew. Now don't get sore."

"You didn't know anything, Senior. But it's okay, so forget it."

Without the slightest pause, "What'd you find out?" he asked.

I told him.

For a long while he said nothing; then, "He killed Jerry?"

I nodded. "He had him killed."

"The cops don't know about me being out there the day she died?"

"They don't know about either of us being out there."

"We'll keep it that way, right?" He swallowed audibly. "So he killed Jerry."

He blew his nose hard. He probed a hairy nostril with a finger. Fingers were made before handkerchiefs.

"So he killed Jerry…" He couldn't seem to get it through his head. "It's like a shock. We'll talk about it at the office in the morning. In depth."

"I'm quitting, Senior."

"Why?"

"I'm tired."

"Shit, we're all tired. But don't leave me."

"I've had enough of the real-estate business."

"Chrissakes, Jack. You're all I got left." He tried to sound angry, but his voice cracked. "Know what I'm gonna do?" he asked, sniffling. "I'm gonna sue that son of a bitch for every cent he's got. He might have been a rich man in LA, but he's gonna be a pauper in Hell."

As it turned out, he didn't have to. Tod hadn't had the time to cut the old man out; the merger had left the legendary extravaganza of Hunt Realty's property in Senior's wrinkled hands. San Dismaso was on its way to retiree resorthood, with my old employer sitting on top of the pile, and no doubt a few nicotine-addicted chimpanzees scavenging for butts by the pool. Would that Jerry had lived to see it, he probably could have made friends with a few of them.

I spent a lot of time in bed, all mired down. I knew I couldn't go on forever without a job, but my thoughts about employment were unspecific. I would flounder into a vague, visceral restlessness, my mind such as it was drifting down some faraway road. Heading where? To the Big Rock Candy Mountain of the old hobo song, "where they hung the jerk who invented work"? Alluring, but I wasn't even sure of that. I didn't know what I wanted. I was convinced that in the great game (*game?*) of life I wasn't going to get a draw. That sort of attitude can lead to catatonia.

Thing was, I had a perilous disinterest in doing anything—eating, brushing my teeth, thinking. I wasn't even up to casual brooding. If I had any ambition, it was to slip unmolested into oblivion. I would have, had it not been for Gayle. She saw my need for a breakthrough, a change of soil and climate to produce a new crop—a goal, a destination, something.

"Let's get out of LA," she suggested. "Where do you want to go?"

The idea had its appeal, but running away from the scene of the crimes required more energy than I could muster. "Where do you want to go?" I countered.

She wanted to go where the trees grew tall and the wild figs were ripe, in some halcyon clime of hot tubs and heightened consciousness, with a two-day trek to the nearest freeway.

I wasn't enthusiastic, having no particular desire to have my conscious-ness heightened, or even to regain it. Lying in bed, I could hear in the other room the subdued voices of Gayle and Carmen discussing my case.

Carmen had phoned from time to time, then had taken to dropping in on us. I was, I suppose, the frayed rope that first bound them together, but they soon found in each other a brimming congeniality, a rapport that had little to do with me. They became fast friends, best friends, each providing for the other that intimate, indefinable harmony neither had previously experienced.

I had gone to see Carmen directly after leaving Senior, to provide a little comfort after the bizarre and tragic news Laudermilk had broken to her. I expected her to panic over the loss of her brother, to wring her hands, to choke up and gush hot consanguineous tears. I should have known better.

She sat calmly at the kitchen table with her black coffee. "Whenever in the past my brother disappeared," she said, unamazed, "I always expected something like this. Now it has happened."

"Carmen." I got to my feet, a bit wobbly. "There are other subjects we must discuss…"

"Whatever is your wish."

"…but not now." I savored sleep. I wanted to drown in it.

We had our talk late one afternoon, over coffee at my kitchen table.

"What are you going to do?" I asked her.

"About what?"

"Are you staying here? You want to go back to Mexico?"

"I have the house."

"Only until you get kicked out by Tod's executor."

"I have a little money, from the stipend he sent me each week."

"What will you do when it's gone?"

She shrugged. "I shall think on it."

"What about the money Napoleon left with you?"

She looked at me with something like surprise. "You knew—?"

"I guessed. He was pulling in quite a bit, toward the end. And he didn't seem like the type to open a savings account. But he knew enough not to keep it under his own mattress, didn't he?"

She nodded. "I shall send it to my mama and my papa."

"Send half. Keep half. You never can tell..."

"It is blood money. There is the smell of death upon it."

"Money is money."

"If you think it best, then I shall keep half."

The click of the front door key interrupted us. Gayle came in with a twinkle and the sort of gummy smile that visitors reserve for an excursion to the hospital. She waved a letter in my face.

"For you," she said brightly, as if its existence proved that I was on the mend. I dropped it beside my coffee and there it remained until the following evening, when Gayle said, "Maybe you ought to take a look before it dissolves into dust."

The envelope was addressed to the Fleet office and forwarded to me. It was from Mr. Dickens. *"Thought you might get a kick out of this,"* the body of the letter read in its entirety. Enclosed was a clipping from the Oxnard *News*, a one-column cut of my correspondent above a feature story celebrating his ninety-first birthday. He had signed it with a few calligraphic flourishes and added a postscript: *"My offer still holds."*

"What offer?" Gayle wanted to know.

I told her.

"Is the place pretty?"

"I guess so."

"Why don't we give it a whirl? Mind if I take a look?"

"What for? He wants five grand."

"That's a steal."

"Only if you've got five grand."

* * *

She drove up the following Sunday, taking Carmen along for company, and came back in a frenzy of enthusiasm. She had discovered Eden and God was in it. She absolutely adored Mr. Dickens.

"We still don't have five big ones."

"What about... why don't we ask Carmen to come with us? I mean, it would be a big help to me, having her around."

—When I'm wallowing in the clanks, I supposed she meant.

"She knows all about growing things," she continued, "and cooking and all."

"She likes the place?"

"Adores it. And she adored Mr. Dickens. She'll lend us the money or become our partner, or whatever you want."

"Christ, Gayle, she's a kid."

"She's a kid," Gayle said irrefutably, "with five thousand dollars."

Next morning I bounced out of bed at the crack of dawn, alert, relaxed, energized, eager to be up and doing and, as I was prone to say in the real-estate dodge, to concretize the deal. A veritable firestorm was I, no longer cut off from the world of men.

So here we were, the three of us, hell bent for rustication at sixty miles per hour. I glanced at them through the tarnished rearview mirror—two solitary children, yet how beautifully each of them seemed to enhance and fulfill the other. Their heads were together. Their lilting laughter sang a heavenly duet, bridging their soft, serious dialogue.

Gayle had been teaching Carmen to speak English. Today's lesson was anatomy.

"Eye," she said, pointing, and the pupil would repeat after her. "Ear. Nose. Throat."

Carmen patted her cheeks abstractedly with the back of her hairbrush as if it helped her concentrate. Her eyes caught mine fleetingly. I remained aware of their impact after she turned away.

With difficulty I tore my lingering gaze from all I could see of her face in the mirror—the darkly burning eyes, the moist red lips, the tilt of her head as she applauded a lustrous cheek with the brush, the slim repose of her fingers holding it like a flower—by redirecting my attention to my new career. It worked like a cold shower.

I knew nothing about tree farming other than what I would learn from Mr. Dickens. Calluses and heavy lifting lay ahead, wresting a precarious living from the hardscrabble soil. I didn't have a dollar in my kick, nor would I until all debts were paid, the trees harvested, and a few coins trickling in.

But, hell, you can murder any endeavor by dissecting it too closely, and the calluses would be not on my ass but on my hands, where they belonged. What I liked was the concept of growing things. There was something both adventurous and soothing about it.

I saw myself through the years as the proud paterfamilias of thousands of leafy offspring, a man of some potential for doing at long last a bit of good in the world—planting seeds, growing saplings, getting on with my neighbors. Certainly it was an improvement on my failed exertions with Tod Hunt.

When I was wallowing in the sack, Gayle had attempted to awaken my interest in the outside world by stacking the LA *Times* and assorted magazines around the bed until I seemed to be lying in state on a paper catafalque. I wasn't the least inquisitive, even when they dealt with Hunt, who had garnered a few paragraphs here and there, which Gayle circled with a felt-tipped pen. Then one evening she insisted on reading aloud a report on his will, filed for probate. It did not in the least encourage my recovery.

Two million dollars (after taxes) went to Constancia Maria Delores Velasquez. Bulk of the estate—many millions—was bequeathed to Princeton University, which had graduated him, and to the Johns Hopkins Medical School, which had kicked him out. That's *Johns* Hopkins; as for John Hopkins, *nada*.

The pair in the back seat were tumulting it up again. The subject was botany, a kind of pidgin botany with kindergarten overtones. "Tree," said Gayle, "Flower. Weed. Tin can."

"Me Tarzan," I said, "you Jane," joining in the fun. They ignored me.

Problem was, there were two Janes. How could I handle it, them? Was I heading for saturnalia? Debacle? How would it all end? We'll see, I told myself calmly, unperturbed by the prospect, we'll see as we go on, from hour to hour...

"Damn!" Gayle said, "I forgot. We should have a gift for Mr. Dickens."

"What can we get him out here?"

"Maybe I can pick up like a fancy tin of horehound drops at the Malibu shopping center. Maybe I could have it gift-wrapped."

I found a parking space in front of the supermarket. She jumped out before I cut the engine, and Carmen and I were alone. We sat in silence; I wondered if she were as attuned to my proximity as I was lubriciously consumed by hers. I didn't wonder long.

In a low voice she asked, "What are we going to do?"

I twisted around in the front seat, the better to see her without the intervention of the mirror. She sat there, cocking her head slightly, questioningly, just enough for the light to catch it.

"When you're a little older," I said, "maybe."

She shook her head. Leaning forward, she touched my hand that rested on the frayed velour crown of the front seat. She lowered her eyes and I lowered mine to peer inside the neckline of her blouse, past the small silken bag on the silver thread. And then my eyeballs—I couldn't believe them—damned near snapped out of their sockets. She pulled back, but it was too late.

"Where'd you get that?"

"Get what?" she asked guilelessly.

I clawed her shoulder, raking her toward me. A little cry of pain escaped her. I plunged my hand into her blouse, snaring the bit of fluff that smelled of roses. Dangling from it was the sparkle of a pigeon's blood ruby in a band of gold—the other of Darlene's "daytime diamonds."

"Tell me, goddamit!" I dangled the jewel like a pendulum in front of her.

"The ring?" She rearranged her face into a blank uncertain mask.

"What the hell else are we talking about? Where'd you get it?"

Her mouth hung open. I ripped the ring from her neck, handling it like it was radioactive, thrusting it into my jacket.

She said, "Are you mad? The Señor Hunt gave it to me. A token of his regard."

Hunt? He would never have acted so stupidly. He didn't want that ring floating around, certainly not from Carmen's slim neck.

"That's a lie," I said.

She bristled. "I thought you were a man of most delicate sensibilities. A man of honor." She gave me a quick wounded glance. "Where honor should be, there is in you an emptiness."

"Cut out the shit," I told her. "Why did you do it?"

"I see no wisdom," she said haughtily, "in your encouraging me to dwell on—"

"Why'd you kill her? Not for a fucking ring...?"

"It does not deserve the muchness you make of it."

"Tell me!" I shouted. "For your own damn good. Or I'm kicking your ass out of the car!"

"All right," she said. "I will share with you, although you have no right to force my confidence." Her eyes burned dully. "She tried to kill me."

"Why would she do that?"

"I would not say I was her husband's whore. Let go of me."

I hadn't realized I had grabbed her again. "Start from the beginning," I said.

"Not now. Gayle will be back..."

"Now."

She stared at me with cool assurance. "Well," she said, crossing those elegant legs, "early that day she calls. With difficulty she asks that I visit her at the beach. It is a matter of immediacy and grave importance."

"Why with difficulty?"

"Difficulty with the language. Her Spanish is an abomination—house-keeper Spanish. She says she will pay the taxi fare. She makes the apology for expulsing me from her employ, but I know it is insincere."

"Still, you went."

"She promises me vast monies, far beyond the reimbursement for the taxi. Of course I went." She raised her eyebrows with the air of a teacher whose logic is lost on the class. "She greets me with a profusion of warmth. She serves me tea with mint and ice and tasteless cookies on the veranda overlooking the sea. But then she says, 'Would you like two thousand dollars?' 'For what?' I say. 'If you would make the oath in the court that you are the inamorata of the Señor Hunt.' The tight bitch." She frowned. "Are you certain you want to hear all this? There is about your eyes a vacancy."

Not a vacancy, exactly. But an image of Darlene conniving to do it all herself, with the modest expenditure of two thousand dollars. "Go on," I told Carmen.

She shrugged. "Then the Señora Hunt increases the offer. Three. Four. Each time she adds a thousand it seems her temperature rises a point. She says, 'Five and that's final.' I say, 'Fold it gently and wedge it up your slot' and the glass and the ice fly past my ear..."

I remembered another glass fired by the Señora Hunt that flew past my own ear not too long ago.

"...and she rises up and strikes me and gouges at my eyes and chokes my throat. I am not easily turned into savagery, but something must be done. I reach inside my boot for the knife my papa bought me for the rapist, I..." She looked off. "Here comes Gayle," she said, uncrossing her legs, sitting primly erect.

Gayle wrestled with the faulty latch of the car door. "They don't carry horehound drops," she announced querulously. "We've got to stop in Oxnard."

"There's a confectionary on the other side of the road..."

She was gone again, obsessed with horehound drops. I turned back to Carmen. "The knife," I prompted.

"The knife. I stuck her with it until she lets me go." A sulleness hung over her red mouth, her lips compressed. "And now," she went on, "I must admit my fury matches hers. I have spent all but ten dollars on the taxi. How will I get it back? I tear that house apart, but there is nothing. Maybe, I think, the bitch has money in her pocket. There is none. And then..." A righteous, self-congratulatory smile sugared her lips. "...then I see the rings on her fingers. But I am no pig. I take just one. I figure it must be worth at least forty dollars. Right? Then I drag her off the cliff."

We sat in silence. Finally, "How'd you get home?" I asked.

"The bus." She made a wry face. "Another four dollars."

"The taxi driver—after the murder he never reported taking you there?"

"Don't use a word like that! Of course he would not say anything. He was a good and loyal man."

"Why loyal to you?"

"He was a compatriot, from Guanajuato, not ten kilometers from my village."

"Jesus," I mumbled.

She put her hand gently on my bowed head. "You are showing a disproportionate response," she whispered.

"Don't you feel anything?"

"Feel?" she repeated. "I cannot say that what had to be done is likely to weigh on my conscience."

I stared at her disbelievingly, and a terrible thought drilled into my skull: How long until, for God knows what reason, she'd stick *me* with her papa's knife?

Gayle reappeared, holding up a festive tin like a trophy. "Got it," she said smugly, turning to Carmen. "You were talking about conscience? You said conscience?"

"Yes," Carmen said unhurriedly, "I was just saying that I am alone in the world, trying to conform to the dictates of my conscience."

"You're a darling," Gayle said, "so don't fret." She squeezed Carmen's hand. "We'll take care of you."

I started the car and we drove on up the coast.

Two Janes. I tried not to think about them. I tried to concentrate on a notion that was born out of my bedridden days. I would write a screenplay (could I still do it, consumed as I was soon to be with long days of labor among the saplings?). Anyway, I had already written the first couple of shots—written in my mind, that is. Something like:

FADE IN:
EXT. ROSE GARDEN — DAY

An acre of dying roses, bowing and rattling in the wild wind. CAMERA MOVES across the sered field to the edge of a cliff. In b.g. the mad tumultuous ocean.

CAMERA TILTS downward over the wet wedge-shaped rocks to HOLD on:

CLOSE SHOT — A WOMAN and a MAN

She is dead. Blood still on her and her blood on the rocks but only for an intermittent moment until the next merciless sea curls over her like an avalanche, scraping everything clean. The MAN stands above her, just beyond the fierce fingers of the waves.

AFTERWORD

My father died before the edits came through for this book, so the final calls fell to me. His death, lousy in all other respects, delivered a not unwelcome sense of déjà vu: Although it was the first time Millard had died, it was not the first time I had edited this book.

The task initially fell to me when I was fresh out of college, earning less than minimum wage from a textbook publisher who worked the gifted-and-talented racket. I operated the freight elevator, and the boss called me Cheetah.

One day, Cheetah was summoned to a musty corner of the warehouse. Here, the boss informed me he was looking to expand his literary offerings beyond brain teasers and math problemoids, and did I have any ideas? I mentioned that my father had just finished a novel.

Millard had been writing novels ever since he became permanently pissed off at Hollywood for the treatment his friends and fellow citizens had received during the blacklist, and thus was born the exit strategy that would bear fruit half a century later, when he published *Bowl of Cherries* and became America's most famous ninety-year-old boy novelist.

Back in my elevator-operator days, Millard was an unpublished novelist of sixty-six. Which was when I first became his editor.

It was fabulous, an Oedipal fantasy realized, a reversal befitting the search-and-destroy mission for a father at the center of the book in question. After all those years of him telling me how to write, the tables had turned.

We disputed our way through his prose. On the west coast, among his cronies gathered around the table of the Hamburger Hamlet, Millard must have made light of such redaction by his son, and I imagine he was not entirely displeased when six months down the line the boss once again summoned Cheetah to his bunker to say that all novelistic ambitions for the company had gone kaput. *Misadventure* would have to wait another quarter century to see the light of day. By not being published, the old man had won another round.

This time, the edit was easy, and not because the author wasn't around to argue. Except for a spot here and there where the talented Jordan Bass asked for a clarification, I didn't touch a word.

A week before he died Millard was too weak to talk but somehow, despite the needles and exhaustion, he would whisper a word or two for me to take down. For his next novel, he told me. Collaboration and irony to the very end, and beyond.

—Frederick Kaufman, January 2010